D1498869

THE COURTSHIP

OF JOANNA

THE COURTSHIP OF JOANNA

CATHERINE GOURLEY

GRAYWOLF PRESS

SAINT PAUL, MINNESOTA

1988

Library of Congress Cataloging-in-Publication Data
Gourley, Catherine, 1950–
The Courtship of Joanna
I. Title
PS3557.O915C68   1988   813'.54   88-81021
ISBN 1-55597-113-x

Publication of this book is made possible in part by grants
from the Jerome Foundation, the National Endowment for the
Arts, the Minnesota State Arts Board, and the many
corporate, foundation and individual contributors to
Graywolf Press. Graywolf Press is a member organization of
United Arts, Saint Paul.

Published by Graywolf Press, Post Office Box 75006,
Saint Paul, Minnesota 55175. All rights reserved.

9   8   7   6   5   4   3   2
First printing, 1988

To my mother,
RUTH HANNON MCCORMICK,
who showed me the strength of family love,
and to my father,
ROBERT MCCORMICK,
who showed me the humor in everyday living.

THE COURTSHIP

OF JOANNA

October, 1883

Behind the Mountain View, where more than three dozen irregular graves had been dug over the past two years, a small group of mourners had gathered. The old woman sat in the rocking chair they had carried for her, gazing sadly into her cupped, ungloved hands. Her eyes were dry, though it was her husband they were burying. Her son stood beside her, his face lifted to the wind. He cried silently, without shame or anger. As the priest from Butler murmured his Latin prayers, the old woman said without lifting her eyes, "I knew it. Even before they told me, I knew what had happened."

The young man, her son, placed his hand on her shoulder.

"He was calling to me. Annie," she whispered. "Annie."

As the priest kneeled and took a handful of coal-black dirt, the colliery whistle sounded the noon hour from the far end of the road. For a moment, the priest's lips were still as he listened. The others who had come, mostly women and old men, stirred at the sound that echoed through the thin patch of oak trees beyond the small graveyard. It was October, cold already, and the mourners shifted their feet to keep warm. The priest stood and tossed the dirt onto the pine box.

When the women and old men and the priest had gone, the son helped his mother to stand and together they stepped through a tangle of wild roses and scarlet sumac to where two more white crosses had been planted just four months earlier.

After saying her prayer over these graves, the old woman sighed. "Only the two of us now. Sure, and I won't be long for this world either."

Despite himself, the young man smiled and patted her cold hand.

On the ridge above them, the dried, brown oak leaves still clung to the branches though all the other trees were now bare.

(i)

"You aren't afraid?" her father said.

"No, sir." The girl sat straight with shoulders squared underneath her shawl, and in quick glances took in the coal-mining town: the road black with culm, the fat woman with sleeves rolled up and laughing as the water splashed into her pail, the line of flannel underwear that hung lifeless in the side yards. From a bench in front of the company store, two elderly men nodded as the wagon passed though they could not have known who these visitors were. The women, too, who had come to the pump to fill their buckets, turned and stared. Because she was tall and had her father's broad shoulders, Joanna appeared older than sixteen. Her blonde hair was in a braid down her back. The girl swallowed hard.

The priest from Butler who went from the mining patches in the Pennsylvania hills to the farms along the river in the valley had told her family of Mrs. Flynn and her widowed son, Timothy. The old woman who was nearly crippled with arthritis needed a young girl to keep house until spring when relatives would arrive from Ireland. Joanna had just finished her schooling, the oldest girl in the family. The silver dollar each week would help her father purchase the acreage near the river, and so, Joanna had agreed.

When she and her father left the farm at dawn, Joanna had been filled with questions of the coal town, of the old woman, and of the wife and child who had died during the birthing. What were these Irish people like? she wondered for she was German as were all the other farming families she knew. For nearly two hours, she and her father rode, leaving behind the valley still warm with October colors and following the river north into the hills where the trees were already bare. The patch was in a mountain pocket, a colorless place stripped of its trees, which were used for timbering in the mine shafts and tunnels underground. Here, surrounded by the squat houses and ashen banks, Joanna thought only of the bed she shared with Margaret. There was not one night that Joanna fell asleep without her sister's thin legs over her own. She turned in her seat and asked, "I won't have to sleep with the old woman, will I?"

The company houses were crowded one after the other, their plank walks like sprung keys on a piano. Beyond the grey picket fences, beyond the row of privies and animal pens, were the slate banks. They rose above the rooftops and encircled the village. At the far end of the road, the colliery building loomed, its breaker leg boring deep into the earth. Her father stopped before a double dwelling, unpainted like the others. The girl held onto her seat and stared. "There aren't any trees."

Her father lifted the small trunk from the wagon, then reached for her. She followed him through the gate and along the side of the house to the porch stoop where a tin washtub leaned against the banister and where a small mirror was nailed to the post. Frost like lace coated the glass. The door was unlatched, and there in the dark kitchen, in a rocking chair near the coalstove, was Mrs. Flynn.

"The attic room is hers," the old woman spoke in a throaty brogue. On the table before her were two mugs and a teapot, and as Joanna's father carried the trunk up-stairs, Mrs. Flynn reached out with red and twisted fingers to pour two cups. She said, "The tea is still warm. Helen was in just a while ago to see to it." The old woman's hands spilled some of the tea as she poured. Joanna looked away. The kitchen, too, was washed in shadows, clean but as colorless as the town.

"My girl's a hard worker," her father said, having come down from the attic.

"It was my boy's idea to hire help. Not mine."

Joanna cupped the warm mug and stared down at the dark liquid.

Too soon her father pushed back his chair and stood. Joanna stood, too, not wanting to be left behind, but too proud to tell him so. The acreage along the river was rich land, he had told her just that morning. He turned to her now in the dark kitchen. "It'll be quiet at home without you," he said.

Joanna stared at him. Mother was home and Margaret and her brothers.

He kissed her forehead, then turned away. Through the curtainless windows, she watched him go along the side walk to the wagon.

"Well now." The old woman sighed, and Joanna turned to face her again. "Have you eaten?"

"I'm not very hungry," she said, though it had been hours since she had taken the bowl of oatmeal her mother made. On the wall behind the old woman was a crucifix, and Joanna was reminded again of the recent deaths in this house. In June, Timothy's wife and child had died, and then just two weeks ago, Mr. Flynn had been killed in a blasting accident underground.

The old woman was watching her, her swollen hands folded over her lap. Wisps of grey hair framed her face. Joanna moved away from the cold window to the oak chair nearest the woman. She held onto the back of it, and after a moment, reached for her cup. The tea was cold now. Under Mrs. Flynn's steady gaze, Joanna felt too tall, too big for the room. You won't do at all, she thought the old woman might say. The girl bowed her head forward. You won't do at all and you'll have to go back.

"We'll be needing some water," Mrs. Flynn said and nodded to the buckets beside the coal stove. "Lots of it. For cleaning. For cooking. You saw the pump as you rode in."

Joanna nodded and set her cup down, then reached for the buckets, but the old woman called to her at the door.

"You don't want to be wearing that fine shawl of yours to be lugging water." She raised her hand and pointed to the peg beside the door. "Go on. Take that old wrap there. It was Rosie's."

Obediently, Joanna reached for the sweater and slipped her arms through it. It felt coarse and smelled of smoke. She took the buckets and went outside where the soft rumble of the coal breakers at the end of the road sounded like distant thunder.

(ii)

When Timothy Flynn returned from the mines that evening, he noticed little changes: a pie cooling on the porch rail, brown-eyed Susans bowing in a jar, and on the stove, a boiling bucket of water for his bath. He washed on the porch, removing his shirt and pushing up the sleeves of his undershirt. He leaned over the bucket and poured the steaming water on his head. Then he combed his hair in the mirror, took the pie, and went inside.

They ate in silence, and from under downcast eyes, Joanna watched as Mrs. Flynn picked at her stew. Timothy, though, pushed his empty bowl away and sighed. He picked up his knife at once and cut a wedge of pie, licking its syrup from his finger.

"How did you know, Joanna, I was longing for a fine

bit of apple pie?" He smiled at her with eyes that seemed a summer blue, the same color as Mrs. Flynn's perhaps, but more accepting. After a moment, the girl looked away.

"They're the green apples from our farm."

"Is that so? And you picked them just for us?"

"Well, of course, she didn't," Mrs. Flynn said. "The apples were already harvested. It's nearly time for snow."

"And the flowers," Timothy said. "Are they from the farm, too?"

"I found them out back. Near the privy."

His laughter startled her. She had expected him to be older and terribly sad. "Flowers from the outhouse? That's grand." He leaned forward to sniff them. "Well, they don't smell any the worse."

The brown-eyed Susans were the only bit of color Joanna could find. Even so, she was embarrassed now. She stared at her bowl. Like the old woman, she had only taken a few mouthfuls.

"The house looks just fine, Joanna." Timothy took a large bite of pie and smiled at her again.

"You make it sound as if the place was no better than a sty before this morning. I think our Helen was doing a fine job, what with taking care of her brother and her own house and ours as well."

"You know I didn't mean that, Ma. I'm just making our young housekeeper feel welcome. It can't be easy for her to come here."

"And was it any easier for me and Rosie and your poor father to leave our homes and come here?"

Timothy reached across the table and covered his mother's hand with his own. Joanna closed her eyes. Her bowl was full, but she felt as if she could not swallow another bite.

Minutes later, when Mrs. Flynn complained of the pain in her knees, Joanna looked up. "On the farm," the girl said, "my brothers always rub a hot liniment on our mule's hind legs and it seems to give them some comfort.

Maybe I could bring some for your knees and ankles."

The old woman was insulted. "Sure and next they'll be putting a muzzle on me. I'm no bloody mule!"

"Oh, but I didn't mean that, Mrs. Flynn. I didn't mean any offense at all."

"She knows it." Again Timothy's laughter brought warmth and color to the room. He patted her hand once more. "But you're just as stubborn, Ma. And ornery."

"Horse liniment," she muttered. "Burn the skin right off of me, that's what it'd do."

"Not if you cut it with water," Joanna said. "Or mineral oil."

From the other side of the double dwelling a door slammed. Footsteps paced back and forth, then stopped as someone began to cough. Joanna looked at Timothy, but he was concentrating on lighting his pipe. Mrs. Flynn, too, seemed not to hear the sounds next door. She had lifted herself up and inched along the table edge to sit in her rocking chair again. The coughing eased and the pacing began once more.

"Tell us something of the farm," Timothy said.

"The farm?" Joanna smiled. "It's not so large really." At that moment, though, the farm along the river in the valley seemed quite large and open and fresh, not smelling of coal smoke like the Flynn kitchen.

"Oh, the land my father owned," Mrs. Flynn said and began to rock. "The bay at our door. Heaven on earth. Such a green land."

"We have a little orchard," Joanna ventured then. "And in spring the blossoms cover the grass, like snow." She looked up. Mrs. Flynn's eyes were closed. The old woman wasn't listening, but Timothy was watching her.

"Go on," he said.

Again the coughing came from the house next door. "Who lives there?"

"Just Nat and Mary."

"Is he ill?"

Timothy looked at the wall separating their homes. "Nat? I don't think so."

"It's just the mines," Mrs. Flynn said, rocking. "The men bring it home with them. Inside of them. It's just the cough."

"You've never been to a coal patch before?" Timothy asked her.

Joanna shook her head.

"There's good and bad about every place, I suppose," he said and stood.

Joanna stood also and reached for the dishes. If he had asked, she would not have been able to name one thing bad or ugly or dirty about the farm. But Timothy did not ask.

While she was washing the dishes, Mrs. Flynn whispered, but not so softly that Joanna couldn't hear, "She seems fine enough, but it's me own daughter-in-law I'm missing. It's Rosie who should be here with us."

Joanna was still wearing the old sweater, the sleeves pushed up past her elbows as she reached for another plate in the soapy water. She had not thought of what Timothy might think seeing her in it, and now she wondered if she shouldn't remove it.

"We're both missing Rosie, Ma. We can't help that."

Joanna looked at the door, longing to be outside, away from them.

"You'll feel better once the family comes in May."

Joanna closed her eyes. In May, the river near her farm was so cold it cramped her feet and calves. The grass along the shaded bank was knee high and soft like fringe.

"I still look for her," the old woman said. "I hear Helen on the porch and think it's Rosie. Many's the time I can feel them both here watching over us, Rosie and your poor father. Sure and they're with us still." The old woman began to murmur then in Gaelic, words that Joanna did not understand.

"It takes time, Ma," Timothy said, speaking now in

Gaelic, too. "There's nothing to be done. It just takes time." And although Joanna did not understand what they were saying, she could hear how tired his voice was, how the laughter was gone now.

Joanna stirred the pan of soapy water, felt the steam from it on her face. She tried to imagine herself and Margaret dropping from a tree branch into the cold river below, swimming with the current away from her brothers to the small island where they could be alone to talk about Tommy Craig or play some made-up game or just lie on their backs watching clouds.

"I'll take that for you now, if you're done," Timothy said, standing beside her, and his voice—so clear, so close—startled her. He lifted the pan of dirty water and carried it outside to dump behind the porch stoop. He did not come in right away, but stood against the post, his back to the window.

"A pot of tea would warm my poor fingers," the old woman said.

Joanna felt the kettle on the back of the stove. Mrs. Flynn liked her water to steam. She had told her that first thing. Joanna scooped the loose tea into the muslin bag and when the water boiled, poured it over the bag into the pot. The sweet smell of dried mint rose in a cloud, and with it, more thoughts of spring.

That night the three of them sat around the kitchen table. Mrs. Flynn rocked and hummed. Timothy read a week-old paper from Butler. The city was a few hours ride by wagon over the mountain and into the Shawnee Valley. After a bit, Timothy folded the paper, relit his pipe, and asked Joanna again about her family.

"I'm the oldest," she said. "That's why I'm here." At once she wished she could take the words back.

"You haven't met Helen yet, have you?" he said.

"No."

"Well, things won't be so sorry once you meet Helen. She's a young girl like you."

"I'm sixteen," Joanna said.

"That seems like a long time ago to me," he said.

The old woman had fallen asleep in the chair and was breathing deeply, her mouth open.

"Why did you come here?" Joanna asked him.

"To America?"

"To this place."

"There was work."

Joanna was silent. After a moment, she said, "Should I wake her and help her to bed?"

Slowly Timothy nodded. "I'll walk her in. Go on up now, Joanna, if you're tired."

The girl stood, thankful to be dismissed.

Upstairs in the attic room, she lay curled on her side. The room had two windows, one facing the road and the long row of company houses and the other looking down on the privy in the side yard. These windows, too, were curtainless and the glass at night was like dark ice. On the farm, a walnut tree was outside her bedroom window and on October mornings—this morning—its yellow leaves were reflected in her bureau mirror. This attic room, however, had no bureau or mirror. There was just the bed and the trunk her father had carried from the wagon. What had he thought when he saw the coal patch, when he saw the old woman so small in the rocking chair, when he saw this tight little room with two small windows like black eyes? Was he sorry he had brought her here?

Joanna slid her legs down to where the bed was still cool. Margaret would be lying in bed alone now, too. Joanna closed her eyes and thought of spring, of herself and Margaret dropping from a tree branch into the cold river below and swimming away.

(iii)

"It's written right here." Joe Sweeney raised the soiled newspaper close to his eyes and read, "... for the better regulation and ventilation of mines and for the protection of the lives of the miners in the County of Schuylkill." He hit the folded journal with his blackened fist. "Well, it can't be any plainer than that."

"I don't doubt it's written down," Timothy said. He and Joe Sweeney and Charlie Boy Duffy were working the face of a breast near the gangway. With a long iron pole, Timothy was prying at a large clod of dirt and rock along the chamber ceiling. "It isn't coming free," he said and dropped his arms. Water that fell from the chiseled roof dripped off his helmet. "You'll have to blast it," he told Charlie Boy.

"It ain't right," Joe Sweeney said.

Timothy nodded to the paper Joe was holding, a copy of *The Mining Journal* published in Shenandoah, a larger mining community downriver. It was the first time he had seen the publication. "Where did you get it?"

"What does it matter? I just got it, that's all. It's a law, Tim. Mine inspectors are supposed to be hired at each location. It's our right."

"But it's not our money, is it?" Charlie Boy Duffy said. "Or our mine."

Through the dust in the tunnel they heard, rather than saw, the mine foreman Welshie in the gangway reprimanding the mule boy for being slow and dumb.

"Ask him," Charlie Boy Duffy said, then grinned, his teeth showing white in his black face.

Timothy smiled, too. "Go on, Joe. Ask Welshie to hire us a mine inspector and see what he says."

"And while you're at it, you can tell him Ma wants a real church, not services held in the back room of the Mountain View."

"And a school," Timothy said. "Don't you think we need a schoolroom, Charlie?"

"Well now, if not a room, then at least a teacher. But a young one," Charlie said. "Not one of them old farts.

Why, maybe Welshie's woman-friend from Butler could teach us a few things."

The two men's laughter echoed in the dark, timbered room cut from the side of the mountain.

Joe looked from Charlie Boy to Timothy and after a moment, dropped the paper to the wet dirt floor. "Here," he said, reaching for the iron rod. "Let me bar that clod down. I'll show you how it's done."

After a few minutes, though, he gave it up, too. Charlie Boy Duffy prepared the blast and set the dynamite. As the lighted fuse burned its way to the cap, the three men crouched in the safety of a manhole. The cap flashed, followed by an explosion and a shower of dust and bits of rock and coal. When the air had settled again, the three men slowly made their way back into the chamber.

Timothy reached for the journal. The pages were damp. He said, "I never knew you could read, Joe."

"He can't," Charlie Boy said.

Joe shrugged. "It was Helen who read it to me last night."

Charlie Boy laughed. "I knew it. I knew those words were too big for your eyes to read."

"Helen?"

Joe hesitated, looking over his shoulder towards the gangway, but the orange flame from Welshie's helmet had followed the mule boy into another chamber. "I thought you'd want to see it. You know, on account of your Pa's accident a few weeks ago."

Timothy shook his head. "No, Joe."

"I got to thinking. . . "

"You mean Helen got to thinking," Charlie Boy said.

Joe took Timothy's arm. "If what Helen read to me is true, then maybe your Pa's accident could have been prevented. Well, isn't that what an inspector is supposed to do? Sniff out the gas and the soft pockets and the weak timbers?"

"Here." Timothy handed the folded journal to him. "Pa took the same risk as any one of us."

Joe stared hard at Timothy. "Maybe they can reduce the risk. A few more cards in our favor. Did you ever think of that?"

"The company's not about to spend money on mine inspections."

The oil lamp on Timothy's cap shadowed his eyes, illuminating only the tip of his nose, but Joe Sweeney didn't need to see his face to know that he would not take a stand on the matter. Joe shrugged. "Maybe. Maybe not." He tucked the folded journal inside his shirt, then patted his stomach. "But I think I'll just hang onto this a while."

(i v)

Each morning Joanna woke to the colliery whistle, sharp and lonely as a jay. From her attic window, she watched as one by one the miners stepped from their row houses into the dirt road and walked, with caps pushed back and lunch tins under their arms, toward the breaker. The culm banks that circled the patch were blue as ink against the yellow sky. She dressed in the cold, then went down to the warmth of the coal stove where Mrs. Flynn was dozing in her rocking chair. For most of the day she sat there, crocheting when her fingers did not ache too much. Often she sang, staring dreamily past the open door of the stove at the blue coals. She had learned the melody, she said, as a girl, and though it was a sad sound, the woman's soft eyes remembered that time and place, and Joanna, too, longed for the comforting sounds and colors of her own farm.

Rosie's old sweater hung on the peg by the door and Joanna wore it whenever she went out for water or hung laundry on the icy clotheslines. While Mrs. Flynn tended the fire from her place by the stove, Joanna swept the floors, rubbed lye soap into Timothy's shirts until her own fingers were red and sore. She baked bread and the windows were steamed until evening. When he came home after dark, Timothy winked and swore he could smell the bread as far up as the mule barn.

"Well, of course you can," the old woman muttered. "Every house from here to the barn is baking bread."

After supper, the three sat around the table. Always Mrs. Flynn had a story about her home in Ireland. The names of the brothers and cousins became familiar to Joanna. Pat and Joseph Hannon, Kathleen and Marty Boyle were like shadows cast through the old woman's stories onto the white-washed kitchen walls.

On Saturdays, Timothy came home with his pay and gave it to his mother. The old woman counted the coins twice before they disappeared into the folds of the apron she always wore even though she did none of the cooking, except to mash the potatoes with a fork or to scoop the seeds from an acorn squash. After three weeks, Joanna's father came late on a Saturday afternoon to take her home for a visit, her first since coming to the patch in October. Mrs. Flynn fished her rosary and three silver dollars from her apron pocket and gave the money to him.

Once more Joanna was in her father's wagon, riding past the row houses, the water pump, and the company store, out of the shadow of the culm banks, leaving the trailing yellow smoke from the colliery behind. The superintendent's home was at the end of the road, as far away as possible from the dirt and noise of the breaker. It was three stories high and, unlike the company houses, painted yellow and white. The windows were long and shuttered and the front porch faced the stream and the covered bridge. Although his house was much larger, it reminded Joanna of her own on the farm, where even now her mother and Margaret were no doubt peeking through the window to catch sight of the wagon. In the superintendent's home, however, no one pushed aside the lacy curtains to wonder who was leaving the patch on a cold Saturday afternoon.

They crossed the bridge and on the other side the road circled a field. The sun was setting behind the mountain ridge and Joanna tilted her head back and breathed deeply. There was no coal smoke here, just a cold wetness.

Her father's farmhouse faced the river. In the time since she had left, the rows of corn stalks between the house and the water had been cut and turned under. As the wagon pulled up to the porch steps, Joanna heard her brothers' voices in the dark as they ran from the riverbank towards her. Margaret and her mother were waiting on the porch in the warm yellow light shining from the open kitchen door. Her father's house had two doors, she realized proudly, and a front parlor, though none of the children were allowed into that room except on very special occasions. No one slept downstairs here. The house was theirs totally. No doors slamming, no footsteps, no harsh coughing from the other side of the wall. As her sister squeezed her hands, welcoming her home, Joanna wondered bitterly why her father needed the silver dollars at all.

"It should be the other way around," she told her sister that night as they lay in bed together. "We have so much more than they do. It's very sad."

After listening to all Joanna had told her, Margaret, who was two years younger, said strongly, "I will never leave home. And I will never marry a miner."

Joanna turned to her. "Why would you say that? I'm not going to stay there forever and I'm certainly not going to marry a coal miner."

Timothy Flynn owned no wagon or mule and whenever he had errands in Butler, it was Joe Sweeney's wagon he used. It was a two-hour ride from the farm to the coal patch in the mountains. Her father had told her that he would not come for her again until Christmas, and then not again until after the Flynn cousins arrived from Ireland sometime in May. Joanna had gone to the patch with some reluctance but thinking of it as an adventure. Now she resented the fact that she had to return while Margaret could stay.

"I saw Tommy Craig twice," her sister whispered in her ear. "After church. Alone." Margaret giggled softly.

"I'm needed there," Joanna said. "The old woman needs me. She relies on me for everything."

Margaret said nothing.

"I have to go back," Joanna said, her voice firm and proud. "It's a very important thing that I am doing."

"Are there any cute boys?" Margaret asked.

Boys? Joanna wondered. There were men, some broad and tall like Timothy; some short and a little hunched over like Joe Sweeney. But they were men, not boys. Even the children, those who sat all day in the breaker sorting coal, were dressed in the same heavy coats and boots, their faces and hands black with their work. Joanna didn't answer. She rolled onto her side, her back to her sister, and closed her eyes.

She woke Sunday morning to the smell of smoked sausages and fresh bread. The morning light from her window was intersected by the branches of the large walnut tree. She had slept hard and it was late. Margaret was gone and the bed was empty. For a moment she pretended that she had never left and everything was as it had been. But she couldn't hold onto it. The smoked meat was so different a smell to her now. Although Mrs. Flynn spoke of spiced beef at Christmas time, tied with ribbon and decorated with holly, they ate little beef in the patch. She spoke of coddle stew made with bacon, pork sausages, and leeks, served hot with a glass of dark stout. But more often they ate plain foods, stews made of vegetable stock and tough meat.

Still, Joanna enjoyed lying in her bed, listening to the
sounds in the kitchen downstairs, knowing she was not
needed to shake the fire or carry water back from the
pump.

On Sunday afternoon, while preparing the veal cutlets
for supper, her mother asked, "Is the old woman in much
pain?"

Her concern for Mrs. Flynn rather than for her own
daughter hurt Joanna. She dipped the piece of veal into the
beaten egg and then pressed it into the bread crumbs. "In
the mornings, yes," she answered reluctantly. "By noon,
she seems alright."

Her mother shook her head.

"I do all the work."

"They treat you well?"

Again reluctantly, Joanna nodded.

In the yard, her youngest brother was shouting. A
wagon had pulled off the country road towards their
house. "That must be Father Jordan," her mother said,
wiping her hands.

"Why is he coming here?" Joanna asked.

"For Sunday dinner. It's a special day having you here."
She touched Joanna's cheek, then turned for the door.

She had so little time before she had to go back. Joanna
did not want to share her family with anyone, and especially not the priest who had first told them of the Irish
woman and her son in the coal patch. Her mother left the
kitchen and went out onto the porch. Joanna stood over
the stove. She poked at the breaded veal cutlets browning
in the pan. She had little appetite for the wiener schnitzel,
though it had once been her favorite dish. She knew her
mother had prepared it for her.

As they ate their Sunday dinner, Joanna's brothers
argued and kicked each other beneath the table. Margaret
chatted about school. Joanna said very little.

"Father Jordan has offered to ride you back, Joanna,"
her mother said.

Joanna looked at her father, who was sitting across from her. He had given up his place at the head of table to the priest. "Father Jordan is returning to Butler this afternoon and he doesn't mind riding into the patch along the way."

"Not at all," the priest said. "I don't mind at all."

"It'll save me a long cold ride in the dark back here," her father said.

After he had finished his meal, the priest leaned back in his chair. "So, tell us, Joanna, how is poor Mrs. Flynn?"

"Fine," she said quietly.

"It's a terrible thing," he said, "to lose those you love. Three deaths in such a short time is almost too much to bear. But her faith is strong."

Joanna thought she understood what he meant for she felt now as if she had lost her family, too. After dinner she excused herself and wandered alone down to the river where the water moved dark and fast and deep. The coal patch was in the mountain above, not far really, but it might as well have been on the other side of the world, so different it was from this open place of yellow fields and clear, clean water. The river and the fields, at least, were unchanged. She let the cold water run between her fingers. It was a Christian thing she was doing, the priest had said during dinner. But Joanna knew that wasn't so. Her heart wasn't in it. She resented them—the old woman whispering in Gaelic, Margaret kissing Tommy Craig in the dark, and her father not taking her back to the patch himself.

"Joanna!" she heard her mother call from the porch. It was time.

When she returned to the house, the priest was waiting in the yard.

"I've a few jars of apple butter for Mrs. Flynn," her mother said, setting the jars in the wagon behind the seat.

The apple trees were not so many as to call an orchard, Joanna realized now, looking out at them. Still, when they were harvested, her family and the family of the farms nearby, including Tommy Craig, would spend a whole day working together, peeling and coring, making apple butter and cider. This year, however, only Margaret had been there for the apple snitzen party.

On a shelf near the barn door was the sticky bottle of rubbing liniment, and impulsively, Joanna turned to the barn to get it. Then she climbed into the wagon, though Father Jordan was not quite ready, and waited. When she looked up, she saw that the branches of the walnut tree outside her bedroom window were bare now, too, and grey.

(i)

Mrs. Flynn stretched her thick white legs in front of the stove and Joanna knelt before her to rub the oily liniment over the woman's swollen knees and feet. From the steaming pot on the stove, she lifted flannel rags and let them air cool a moment before wrapping them tightly around Mrs. Flynn's legs. As each rag cooled, Joanna replaced it with a warmer one. The liniment burned and during the first few treatments, the old woman had cried out. Joanna's hands stung.

"It's just one pain taking the place of another," the old woman said crossly. Despite her apparent irritability, she enjoyed the treatments each afternoon. "You should be a nurse, Joanna," she mumbled. "Soon you'll be free of my burden. I know. I know I am a burden. Being old is a curse." Her fingers went under her shawl and took a letter from her apron pocket. "When Kathleen and Marty come, you won't have to care for this old lady anymore. Read it to me once more," she asked. "Rosie was always reading to me and such a sweet voice she had."

The sheet of paper was soiled and limp now. Joanna had read the letter so many times that she could recite it by heart. Still, she wiped her hands on her apron and took the envelope that had come from County Mayo, dated August, 1883. It was addressed to Aunt Annie Flynn and every time Joanna saw the name, she smiled. Annie was a young girl's name and it did not fit this cranky old woman in the rocking chair. She read slowly. With each reading, her curiosity about these people grew. Kathleen's penmanship was fat and slow, as if she had taken a long time to form the words. Last year's crop was only fair; Jaimie Hannon was ill with pneumonia; the family had had a mass read for Rosie and Mr. Flynn. The letter had been written after the deaths of Timothy's wife and father, yet seeing Rosie's name written there seemed to conjure her spirit just as the old woolen sweater hanging from the peg by the door seemed to say that Rosie was still at home. Although she thought of Rosie often, Joanna could not picture the woman. She was faceless. But the girl was not brave enough yet to ask the old woman about her.

When she came to the part in the letter where young Marty Boyle and two other lads had stolen guns from the landlord and were questioned by the police, Joanna stopped reading to ask the old woman, "I thought you owned the land in Ireland. Who is the landlord?"

Mrs. Flynn waved her hand impatiently as if chasing a fly from under her nose. "They took it from us. Sure they paid my brother a little bit of money for it, but not what it was worth."

"Who?"

"The gentry, that's who. An Englishman. We were never land barons, if that's what you were thinking. My poor father had no time for riding horses all afternoon just for the fun of it." The old woman leaned forward. "The boy is only stealing back a little bit of what was once ours." It was clear from her voice that she was neither surprised nor worried by Marty Boyle's troubles with the landlord or the police.

Joanna continued to read. The old woman closed her

eyes. In a few moments, her white head bobbed to the side and she dozed. The girl covered her bare legs with the quilt, then set the letter on the table where Mrs. Flynn could reach it when she awoke. She went to the window. Each new snowfall softened the angles of the company houses. The snow swirled from the roofs, drifted against the stockade fences, and for a time, buried the coal dirt. But soon it, too, was dusted with the soot from the colliery smokestacks. She remembered how at the farm the snow lay unbroken, stretching from the porch across the fallow fields all the way to the river. Here in the coal patch, Joanna was lost, forgotten like the stubbles of corn beneath the snow. If she should never go back, if her family should somehow lose the farm as Mrs. Flynn had lost her home. . . . The girl shook her head to chase the thought.

Helen Sweeney was coming through the side yard just then, and waved for Joanna to come outside. The girl glanced over her shoulder at Mrs. Flynn, snoring softly now, then reached for the sweater, but hesitated. She took instead her heavy shawl, wrapped it about her shoulders, and opened the door.

On the slate banks behind the houses, children were sledding. She and Helen hurried past the row of privies and climbed to the top of the bank. There were only a few sleds and the children had tripled up, squeezed one behind the other or sandwiched on their bellies. Older boys sat in the cupped bowl of a coal shovel, the wooden handle between their legs, and spun as they slid down the banks. The cloudy blue-green water in the stripping hole was frozen and there, too, children were running and sliding, chased by a barking dog.

"Go down with me," Helen urged. Joanna gathered her long skirt about her legs and sat with her arms around Helen's waist. From behind someone pushed them forward.

"Oh Lord!" Joanna cried. "We're going to hit the out-house!" She ducked her head behind Helen. The girls fell sideways and the sled bounced away from them, hitting the stockade fence below. With legs and skirts entangled, they lay in the snow, laughing. From the top of the hill came shouts to hurry back with the sled.

"Look at you!"

"Tim!" Helen cried, delighted.

He stood on the other side of the fence. His face was black and he still wore his miner's cap. Joanna stood at once and brushed the snow from her skirt.

"Mr. Flynn," she said, embarrassed. "Is there something wrong?" It could not be past four o'clock and most nights he did not come home until seven. She apologized. "I only stepped out for a moment. Mrs. Flynn was a-sleep."

"There's nothing wrong except that I came early. Gas in one of the tunnels."

"Is Joe coming, too?" Helen asked.

"He and Charlie Boy are fighting their thirst at the Mountain View."

Joanna looked in the direction of the saloon, where during the day the old men sat quietly on the long front porch. Even on snowy days they sat out, as if having been underground for so many years they now savored the fresh air. A smaller back room of the Mountain View served as their church on Sundays. It was here, too, that the Widow Dickerson taught school in the mornings. The room had its own back door so the children could enter without going through the barroom. Soon after Joanna had arrived in the patch, Helen had pointed out the schoolteacher. Like Mrs. Flynn, she was a widow, too, but much younger, younger than even Joanna's mother it seemed. "A miner's wife," Helen had explained with a grimace. Like Margaret, Helen had made it clear that she would never marry a miner just to become a widow. "When her husband died," Helen said, "she started teach-

ing school to pay her rent on the company house. They
would have forced her out otherwise."

"The company would throw her out?"

"Everyone has to pay his rent, Joanna. Nothing is ever
free."

Joanna had thought about it only a moment before saying, "I would have just left."

"And go where?" Helen had asked. "She had no
money." But then Helen had surprised her by saying,
"My mother left, you know. One morning she was there
and in the afternoon she was gone. Just like that. She left
us behind and just ran away."

"To where?"

"I'm sure I don't know. And I don't care, either." Then
Helen reconsidered. "She might have gone traveling with
some man. Maybe they went out west to the Ohio. It was
a long time ago. I'm not even sure I can remember what
she looks like."

"Joanna?"

The girl looked up.

Helen was pulling her arm. From the top of the bank,
the children were shouting for their sled. "Joanna? Are
you coming or not?"

Joanna looked to Timothy. "I should go back to fix supper."

He surprised both girls then by setting his lunch tin in
the snow and hopping the fence. "Supper can wait. It's not
always I can get a chance to slide in the snow myself." He
took the sled's rope from Helen. "Well? Com'on then," he
said and turned for the bank.

The two girls smiled and followed him to the top.

"Now," he said, sitting with legs spread and arms wide,
"who will take a ride with a dirty old miner?"

"What do I care about a bit of coal dirt?" Helen laughed.
She sat on the sled in front of him, her knees tight against
her chest, and made room for Joanna behind her.

"Jo?" he asked.

The girl held back.

"Sit in front of me. I'll do the steering and we won't fall off this time."

His legs were much too long as he squatted there. The only other grown man she knew was her father and he would never do such a playful thing. Timothy Flynn was smiling up at her, the coal dirt creased in the wrinkles around his eyes. She liked the way he smiled. She stepped over the sled and sat down. Her legs were tight against Helen's back. Although Timothy Flynn did not hold her about the waist, but rather gripped the sides of the sled, Joanna could feel his breath warm on the back of her head.

The sled bounced forward. It glided faster this time. "Lean," she heard him whisper as he pressed his arm against hers to steer the sled. It curved neatly and came to a stop alongside the stockade fence. Helen took the rope and headed up a third time.

"Stay if you want, Jo," he said.

The girl looked back over her shoulder at the children playing. "No. I better go back with you. She'll be missing me by now." And together they walked through the narrow yard to the house.

After supper that evening Mrs. Flynn reprimanded him. "I'll be reminding you, Tim, that you are recently widowed, and it isn't fitting for a man in your position to be sledding with children."

Joanna stared at her hands in her lap. She did not consider herself a child.

"Life goes on, Ma."

"A big man like you rolling in the snow."

He laughed. "We weren't rolling in the snow, were we, Joanna?"

He was looking at her with that wide smile, but the old woman was watching her, too, and Mrs. Flynn's eyes were hard and as cold as the dark attic windows. It was clear to Joanna that Mrs. Flynn thought it wrong for Timothy to have been with her. She had a sudden image of herself and Timothy lying in the snow together and laughing, just as she and Helen had been. Embarrassed, she stood up and said defensively, "Of course we weren't rolling in the snow." She went to the stove and felt the kettle.

"And what are you doing now, girl?"

"I thought I'd make us some fresh tea."

"More tea," the old woman muttered.

"You always like tea after supper," Joanna said without looking at her.

"If you keep feeding me tea that old bedpan will overflow tonight for sure."

Timothy laughed outloud again, then asked, "Do you go sledding at home?"

The truth was she did, but Joanna tossed her head. "I used to. Not any more, though."

Mrs. Flynn laughed softly to herself and Joanna glanced over her shoulder.

"I'm usually too busy with chores and school and helping my mother take care of my brothers," she said in a voice slightly on edge. But that wasn't really the truth, either. Her brothers needed little supervision now and everyone did their share of the work about the farm.

"When I was a girl," the old woman said then, "I would walk along the bay near our house and just kneel on the rocks where the waves were lapping and wouldn't the fish just hop right into my apron?"

"I don't believe that," Joanna said.

Mrs. Flynn raised an eyebrow in mild surprise.

Outside, Joe Sweeney knocked on the window, startling them. He came into the kitchen carrying a box wrapped in newspaper. "Look here at what I got today," he said and set the box on the table, pushing away the newspapers. It was a bird cage and inside was a bird with three yellow marks the length of its back and on both wings.

"It's a filthy bird," Mrs. Flynn said, "and I don't want it on my table."

Helen had come in behind him.

"It's a special bird." He waved for Joanna and Timothy to come closer. "I bought it just this afternoon at the Mountain View."

Mrs. Flynn rolled her eyes. "Why in all of heaven would you buy a bird, Joe Sweeney, when there are plenty outside of your window each morning?"

Joe was short and stout, with a heavy beard that aged him. He appeared elfish and was forever squinting, as if he had just come up from the gangway and the light hurt his eyes. Now he peered inside the cage. "It's a singing bird," he said. "A canary."

Mrs. Flynn sat back. "That's no singing bird."

Joanna stuck her finger through the pegged side of the cage to touch the bird's back. It fluttered away from her hand. "It looks painted."

"Bring it here," Mrs. Flynn said.

As Joanna handed the wooden cage to her, she said, "It looks like a sparrow that's been painted."

The old woman peered into the cage. Slowly then, she began to smile. "You are a bloody fool, Joe Sweeney. Someone takes an ordinary tree bird and paints it yellow and you buy it for a canary!" Then she laughed. "A singing canary!"

Joe ran his hand over his chin, smiling, now, too.

The old woman hugged the wooden cage to her stomach, leaned way back in the rocker, and laughed loudly. After a few minutes, she wiped her eyes and said, "And who sold you this article, Joe? Was it Welshie?"

Joe pulled his knit cap from his head and sat at the table. "I wouldn't buy a plug of tobacco from the likes of him."

The foreman of the mines lived alone in a company house set apart from the others near the railroad tracks and the silt dam. He lived with a woman, though they were not married. Joanna had seen her at the company store and at the water pump, but the other women in the patch did not associate very often with her. "There's a long rope strung from one end of the kitchen to the other and blankets are hung over it to make a wall," Helen had told Joanna. Everything she knew about the people in the patch she had heard first from Helen. In her innocence, Joanna had leaned forward to ask, "Wouldn't the coal company give her a house of her own?" Helen laughed at her. "She's a whore, Joanna. Don't you know what that is? There's a bed on the other side of the curtain and the men pay to sleep with her. Why even Joe's done it a few times himself."

Mrs. Flynn was still laughing. "Well, Joe, if it wasn't Welshie, then who was it this time who tricked you?"

"Charlie Boy," said Helen.

Mrs. Flynn handed the bird cage to Helen. "You ought to just let it fly free now."

"Not in here," Joe Sweeney said, "or it'll do a job on our heads."

"How much did you pay for it?" Timothy asked.

"I sort of have it on credit," Joe said.

"Go on, Helen," the old woman said. "Put it outside."

"Where's that fiddle of yours, Tim?" Joe said. "I'll make this birdie sing."

Timothy thought a moment, then turned for his room. He came back with a scratched violin case. Joe opened it and took the bow, tightening it until it bent. Then he lifted the fiddle.

"Dirty things," Mrs. Flynn said as she leaned forward to look into the cage again. But still she was smiling.

Joe pulled the bow across the strings, turned the pegs a little, then sawed across the strings again. He stamped both feet as if marching as he played. Joanna looked at the common wall separating their house from Nat and Mary's and wondered what in the world they would think of this commotion.

The bird fluttered at the wooden pegs of its cage. "You're doing nothing but frightening the poor thing," Timothy said. He took the violin from him then, and holding it with his chin and shoulder, he loosened the bow and tuned the strings. He began to tap his foot lightly and after a moment, started to play a scratching reel. Helen and Joanna clapped their hands and Mrs. Flynn's head nodded in rhythm. As Timothy bowed faster, his black hair fell over his eyes.

Joe sat with his legs crossed like a woman, swinging his foot. His white skin showed above his socks. Suddenly, he stood and began to dance by himself, hopping on one foot and then the other, looking all the more like an elf and Joanna laughed at him.

"When I was a girl," Mrs. Flynn said once the song was over, "many a man was interested in my ankles." As she lifted her skirt to show them, Joanna covered her mouth in mild surprise. Never would her mother do such a frivolous thing as showing her bare legs to company, even if it were only Helen and Joe. Mrs. Flynn's legs were thick and white, her boots loosely laced. After a moment, she smoothed her skirt down and began to rock again. Her smile was gone.

Now Timothy played a soft melody and Joanna recognized it at once as the song the old woman sometimes hummed during the day. Joanna leaned against the wall near the stove and watched him. His eyes were closed. His fingers, still blackened though he had washed, moved slowly over the thin neck of the violin. He is thinking of her, the girl thought sadly. The old sweater hung on the peg by the door.

And then the rocker stopped. The old woman waved her hand. "That's enough," she said. She struggled to sit up and Joanna went to her, helping her to stand. Heavy on Joanna's arm, the old woman moved towards the dark hallway and her bedroom door. "That's enough for tonight," she said quietly, as if reprimanding herself now. "I won't be having music in this house. Not again for a long, long time."

When Joanna came back to the kitchen, having helped

Mrs. Flynn to bed, Joe and Helen were gone. The table was cleared and the violin was packed inside its worn case once more.

Timothy took his pipe and knocked the bowl of it against the stove, then opened the grate to shake down the ashes. As Joanna watched him, crouched in front of the stove and poking at the blue flame, she wondered if he, too, were sorry the music had stopped and Joe and Helen had left.

"They took the bird?" she asked.

He laughed quietly. "Yes."

After a moment, she said, "I could fix some tea."

"Please, Jo. No more tea." He looked up at her.

"I didn't know you could play music."

"A little."

"It was very good."

He closed the stove door and stood. "I haven't played for a long while."

The room was still. Joanna moved to the attic door. Timothy was filling his pipe again. "Well, good night," she said at last.

"Yes," he said. "Good night."

But she did not at once go up. She stood with her hand on the door and waited. Perhaps he and Rosie used to sit by the fire at night to talk after Mrs. Flynn had gone to her bed. Had they been happy in this company house? Why, if they had been married for six years as Helen had told her, were there no other children?

Timothy turned in his chair. "What is it, Jo?"

No one, not even her father or Margaret had ever called her Jo. She liked hearing him say it for he made her feel as if she were a friend, someone special to him. She shook her head. "I was just thinking." She paused. "How long have you lived here?"

"The four of us came just three years ago," he said. He set down his pipe and looked at her more directly. "There are times though when it does seem longer."

She had been in the coal patch just two months, but for her, too, it seemed a long time since that first day when she had found the brown-eyed Susans in the yard and put them on his supper table. "Why here?" she asked. "The agent who came to our village in County Mayo offered us work with this company and our passage. We're obligated."

"But must you stay here? Why not go farther down into the valley along the river where there is farmland?"

He turned back to the stove. "I'm no farmer, Jo. I guess I found that out years ago. I couldn't make it work." He gave his attention now to lighting his pipe again. "If you want," he said, "you could leave the door open so more heat will go upstairs."

The smoke from his pipe hung like dust above the oil lamp. Joanna pushed the door open wider and went up to her room. But even there with the door open she could smell his pipe. With her flannel gown over her knees and feet, she sat on the attic floor near the window. The snow was still falling. It lay on the roof of the kitchen just below her window and the smoke from the stovepipe rose to meet it. A single bird was hunched near the pipe for warmth.

(ii)

More than a year ago Welshie had brought a woman back from Butler to live in his house and to service the miners on pay day. Had there been a hotel, he might have put her there. But the coal patch had only the Mountain View, a saloon with a large meeting room in the rear where during the day children read their lessons and where, on those Sundays when he could make it over the mountain, Father Jordan said Mass. In the evening the miners, mostly Welsh and Irish but a few Italians and Poles, drank at the bar, played dominoes at a corner table, and argued among themselves.

The Irish and the Welsh generally were sympathetic to each others' grievances towards the English. The Irish wanted home rule; the Welsh were religious dissenters. And so the animosity Joe Sweeney felt towards Welshie was not so much an ethnic prejudice as it was a labor issue. The mine foreman had set himself apart from the others voluntarily. He represented the company. While Joe and Timothy and Charlie Boy lay on their backs working at a seam of anthracite—using the pick, digging with their fingers, blasting and propping—Welshie wandered through the maze of tunnels overseeing the operation, pushing them deeper into the mountain, encouraging them to rob the pillars for an extra quarter ton of coal. It had not surprised Timothy a few weeks ago when Joe had stuffed the mining journal into his shirt for safekeeping. Joe's griping was just so many words. Like the others, he did his job and stayed out of Welshie's way, cursing him now and again but never confronting him. And like the others, too, he had often stepped across the road at night to the house near the silt dam where Welshie's woman led him to the narrow bed behind the blanket that hung across the kitchen.

"I can't much stomach the man," Joe said as the foreman walked into the Mountain View this night. "But his woman's not too sour."

Timothy looked at Welshie across the room. His concern was for his family, not only his mother now but also Kathleen and Marty who were coming in the spring. Timothy took his mug of beer and left Joe and Charlie Boy to their game of dominoes. He approached Welshie at the bar.

"What makes you think I'll be hiring come spring?" said the foreman, who was well over six feet.

"I don't know it. I'm asking you to give the boy a chance."

"I don't buy a bill of goods before I see them."

"Marty's scrappy. And strong. He'll do alright below."

"And what does he know of mining?"

"I can train him."

Welshie shook his head. "No, I don't make promises to anyone. And I can't take chances on inexperienced workers."

"Now you know that isn't true. You've recently hired the Italians."

Welshie looked across the room. "The Dagos come cheap."

"All I'm asking you, Welshie, is to give the boy a chance."

Welshie wiped the beer from his mouth with the back of his leathery hand. "You and your Pa already cost me plenty. Bad judgment cost him his life and me a week's work cleaning out the cave-in."

Timothy Flynn was not a political man. The heated discussions about home rule did not interest him now nor did the soiled pages of the mining journal Joe Sweeney had salvaged. But he turned to Welshie and said, "No. That's not how it happened and you know it. Pa set the blast right. The room wasn't marked for gas."

"You bring that boy here and he'll have to find his own way," he said.

"I'm thinking you might change your mind once the cold comes and the demand's up. You'll need a strong back then."

"And a thick head." Welshie smiled. "You Irish got that much anyway." He took his drink and moved to a place farther down along the bar.

Joe came across the room then with his empty mug. He placed his hand on Timothy's shoulder. "What was that about?"

Timothy shook his head. "Not to worry." He slid his glass and Joe's to the edge of the bar. "Here," he called to Mike. "Give us another."

(iii)

In the display case of the company store were rows of buttons—black, white, green—shiny like rock candy. On the shelf above were twines of satiny ribbon and embroidery floss. Joanna pointed to the dark blue ribbon, deciding at last. "A yard of that, please."

She signed for the blueing and the sack of flour, the cost of which would be deducted from Timothy's wages at the end of the month, but she paid for the ribbon herself with money her father had given her the day he brought her to the patch. It was the first thing she ever bought for herself in a store. In the attic were the Christmas gifts for her family. There was an embroidered pillow case for her mother and sassafras sticks for her brothers and Margaret. After supper tomorrow, Christmas Eve, Joanna's father was coming for her. Unlike the Flynns, who were still in mourning, her family would have a pine tree and hot apple cider with cinnamon sticks. The other farming families in the valley would gather at the church and there would be singing and unwrappings. Joanna had no gifts for the Flynns, but as she walked home from the company store, she decided to bake a sponge cake.

That afternoon when the other chores were completed and Mrs. Flynn was napping in her room, Joanna began the batter. But the old woman was not cheered as she shuffled into the kitchen, using the wall for support. Her deep voice rose above the girl's singing. "And what is it you're doing now?"

Joanna took her by the arm and helped her to the chair. "It's Christmas, Mrs. Flynn, as if you didn't know. And I'm baking you and Mr. Flynn a wonderful cake to celebrate."

"A cake is it?" The old woman looked away as if she had been insulted. "I'll have none of it."

But Mrs. Flynn liked sweet things and Joanna began again to whip the batter and to sing softly to herself.

"I say there will be no celebrating in this house, not this

Christmas!" The rocking chair creaked as the woman leaned forward to point one long finger at the girl. "It's time you listened to me, Joanna Kluger. This house is in mourning for me poor old husband and for Rosie Flynn, God rest their souls, and mourning must continue for one full year."

Joanna set the wooden spoon down. Although Mrs. Flynn never said it outright, Joanna knew that everything she did—the cleaning and the cooking and the caring—was compared to how Rosie had done it and so often Joanna's efforts were second best. After a moment, the girl answered. "I don't mean any disrespect, Mrs. Flynn, but since the batter is started and there's a healthy amount of sugar to it, not to mention the eggs, what harm can there be in baking it?"

The old woman sat back, muttering.

Joanna's spirits could not be dampened that day, however, and as soon as Mrs. Flynn had gone back to her room, the girl walked through the snow in the side yard, went beyond the privy and climbed the culm bank to a patch of woods not far from where she and Helen had gone sledding. Here there were fir trees, and Joanna ripped away a few snow-covered branches.

That evening she arranged the Christmas greens on the table around a burning candle. The crusty sponge cake sat on the cupboard. She sang while setting the table. When she heard Timothy's steps along the house and on the porch, she turned and faced the door, waiting anxiously.

He stamped the snow from his boots, then came inside. "What a fine thing it is to come home to a woman singing after a long day of picks and blasts and crying mules."

"You heard me?" Joanna smiled.

He removed his miner's cap and set it and his lunch tin on the floor. "What's this?" He crossed to the cupboard to sniff the cake.

Joanna's eyes were bright for she had known he would notice right away and be pleased. "Merry Christmas, Mr.

Flynn!" She leaned over his shoulder to look at her cake, too. "I thought you might like something sweet tomorrow for the holiday. I just couldn't go away and not leave you something. But you've got to promise not to touch it until Christmas Eve."

He put his arm around her shoulder and squeezed. "It'll be hard waiting 'til then."

"Dear Saints!" Mrs. Flynn cried. "Now it's me holy candle she's burning!" The old woman wavered in the doorway. She looked from the candle to where Timothy and Joanna were standing.

Joanna moved away from him. "I found it in the cupboard," she said.

"I'll not have the likes of her in my house no longer," the old woman shouted at Timothy. "Her being frivolous and singing all day long just to torment me. And enticing you, she is, with cakes."

Joanna caught her breath and covered her mouth with her hand.

Timothy went to his mother and put his arm around her. "Sit down, Ma. It's just a cake."

"Do you hear what I am telling you? Enticing you from the very beginning what with bringing flowers for the table and Rosie not dead but six months." The old woman cried out and clutched her chest as if struck, then she levelled her shaking fingers at Joanna again. "I'll just not put up with you any longer."

Joanna ran. She slipped off the porch step into the snow, but hearing Timothy call after her, she got up and ran through the yard for the outhouse they shared with Nat and Mary. Inside, she huddled on the floor with her face turned against the wall, and cried.

She heard his footsteps over the crusted snow. He went past, to the fence, and then came back. When he opened the privy door, she looked up. "Jo," he said softly. "Come out of there."

She pressed her face into the corner again. The space be-

tween the boards was wide enough that she could have
peeked through to see him coming down the yard after
her.

Timothy opened the door wider and put one foot inside.
"Jo, please."

Her shoulders were shaking. Her braid, curled over her
back, just brushed the plank floor. The word enticing
pounded inside her head and all she could think of was
Welshie's woman and the blankets strung across the
kitchen.

"Ma's not meaning what she says tonight. You have got
to try and understand." He waited while her sobs quieted.
"Ma's just thinking about last year when we were all together. Rosie sang, too, and baked cakes. So you see, Jo,
it's nothing you've done. You're only reminding her."

Joanna lifted her head. "She doesn't like me."

He smiled. "She likes you very much, but she's not one
to show it. It's just a hard life we're living."

"No," she said more forcefully. "She doesn't like me.
And she doesn't want me here at all." She stared hard at
him. Even in the dark she could see that once again his hair
had fallen over his eyes. "She wants Rosie, not me. I'm
not Rosie. I don't want to be like her."

He stooped beside her and put his hand alongside her
head. "No one expects you to be like Rosie."

"She talks about her all the time," Joanna said then.
"How Rosie used to read to her, how Rosie had such a
sweet voice, how Rosie folded your shirts this way and
that."

"Stop crying, now. No one is mad at you."

He had not washed and his face was still dirty from the
mines. He took her hand and helped her to her feet,
then led her outside. The outhouse door banged behind
them, and seemed to echo through the cold. A small
square of light from the kitchen window shone over the
porch steps. He did not let her hand go, but turned to her
and squeezed it.

"Listen to me. Rosie was a fine woman. And you're a fine person, too. It just hasn't been easy for Ma leaving her home to come here, knowing she could never go back. We were a family when we came here. Rosie and Pa were all she had then and now they're both gone."

In the road they heard Charlie Boy Duffy and Joe Sweeney laughing as they came home from the Mountain View. Joanna wiped her eyes. "I'm sorry," she said.

He put his hand on her hair again and she turned into it so that his hand moved across her cheek. "You understand now, don't you?"

She looked up at him. "What was she like? Rosie?"

He dropped his hand and shook his head as if he could not remember. "She was... I don't know. Pretty." He looked up at the sky, then out to the road, though Joe and Charlie Boy were gone and it was quiet again. "She played the piano and was proud of owning such a fine thing. We had to leave it behind when we came over." He sighed. "She was pretty," he said again as if the memory had grown clearer. "If the boy had lived, for sure he would have had the same red hair."

No one had ever mentioned the dead child before. Tenderly, Joanna brushed the hair from Timothy's eyes. "How awful," she whispered. "Oh, Tim. I'm so sorry for you."

At once, she realized the intimacy of her gesture and worse, how painful her question must be. She became flustered and turned away. Timothy, too, stepped back. "It's a hard life," he repeated.

"I should never have asked." She stared at the snow cupped about her legs. Her skirt was wet. Mrs. Flynn had been right, after all, she thought. Her walk that afternoon for the Christmas greens had been only for Timothy. Without looking up at him, she said, "Maybe you should find a new housekeeper."

"There's no need. You did nothing wrong, Jo."

"I don't want to stay here anymore."

"Is that really how you feel?"

She did not answer. She knew only that the old woman had hurt her, and that just moments ago she had embarrassed herself by reaching out to touch him.

"There's nothing wrong with giving a little comfort to one who needs it," he said then as if reading her mind. "Don't be ashamed of that, Jo, not ever."

From somewhere deep in the woods came the faint cry of a wolf. It was not the first time she had heard the night sounds of animals, here or at the farm. Still, both she and Timothy looked back at the dark culm banks. The cry came again, moved farther into the night. Joanna thought she might cry again—for Timothy, for the baby boy that had died, and for herself.

Timothy took her arm. "Come back with me now, and say no more of leaving. I don't want you to go."

She looked at him hopefully. When had she begun to wish that the Flynn cousins would never come from Ireland?

"Ma can't get on without you, Jo."

At once the girl's hopes vanished into the night like the cry of the wolf. Of course, Timothy thought of her only as a child, someone who ran and slid in the snow, or worse, just someone who washed and cleaned his clothes and tended to his old mother. The image of Welshie's woman suddenly loomed before her again. Loud and garish, Joanna had seen her on the porch of the Mountain View, teasing the old men who sat out, who laughed and coughed simultaneously as the woman twisted her shoulders and leaned forward to pat their ashen cheeks.

"I meant no harm by baking the cake," she said, "but Mrs. Flynn is right. I did it for you."

He put his hand under her chin. "I think it is a fine Christmas gift, Joanna." After a moment, he stepped aside. "Go on into the house now. It's cold. I'll be in after I wash up."

In the kitchen, the candle had been snuffed and a small

corner of the cake was cut and eaten. Mrs. Flynn, however, was in her room once more. Timothy spied the cake and he smiled at Joanna. "You see, she can't be too angry with us."

Joanna turned away for the stove and filled a bowl with soup. As she started towards the hall and his mother's room, Timothy crossed to her and reached for the hot bowl. "I'll take it in for you." Gratefully she gave it to him.

Joanna and Timothy ate in silence that night. Scattered on the table between them were the Christmas greens. Timothy fingered a soft branch. "They smell fine," he said, but for Joanna the sweetness was gone.

In the bedroom, they heard the old woman moving about, reminding them both that they were not alone.

(i)

An early March thaw had brought the mud already. Joanna spread ashes along the side of the house, then took the flour sack from under the porch and walked back beyond the fence to where the culm banks began. The snow was gone; the sleds useless. Joanna joined another woman and her child who were scavenging the banks for bits of coal to be burned in the kitchen stoves. Using the toe of her boot, Joanna pushed aside the rocks. She examined the coal as Helen had shown her months ago and dropped into the flour sack only what could be burned.

The little girl, who was wearing a bright scarf too large for her so that it covered her eyes from view, had crawled quite high. She held a fistful of sticks. The mother called to her from below in a language Joanna guessed was Italian for she had heard it spoken at times in the company store. As the child turned, the culm gave way and she fell forward, sliding face down over the rocks. Joanna dropped her flour sack, and being closer, picked the child up and pushed the scarf back so she could see the little girl's face. Her lip was bleeding, but only when Joanna tried to wipe the dirt from her cheek and mouth did the child begin to cry.

The mother took her, smiling shyly, and Joanna was surprised to see that she was not much older than herself. She remembered then what Helen had once told her about the young Mrs. Dickerson who taught school, that she had married a miner to become a widow. But this young mother with her dark eyes and olive skin was not a widow, yet. Joanna had seen her only a few times before and yet she felt something vaguely in common with her. Perhaps it was that they were both different—new to the patch. As the mother sat her child on top of the wheelbarrow, which she had filled with lumps of coal, Joanna thought, I shall never get used to living here.

The sun was bright on the windows of the colliery building below, but the air was still cold and tight in Joanna's cheeks. She was happy for the sun and the chance to be outside. As she filled her flour sack with coal, she climbed around the bank. When the bag was filled, she did not go home at once, but went farther up, into the woods that had become her private place. It was here that she had picked her Christmas greens, and here that she came whenever the sun was bright and her chores were done. The mountain laurels were waist high and in the shadows of the hemlocks there were still icy patches of snow. This was the one place where Joanna could be alone, for even in the attic room there were the disturbing sounds of Nat and Mary next door.

From this spot, she could see all of the mining patch and yet feel free from it: the grey colliery, the stream near it running fast now with melting snow, the row of company houses. Farther down was the company store and across from it, the Mountain View. More often lately Timothy went there after supper and when he did, Joanna sat with Mrs. Flynn. Often Helen joined them and the three played gin rummy. The old woman had not mentioned the sponge cake or the holy candle again and she and Joanna carried on as before.

"What's this?" Helen had asked one evening, picking up

Mrs. Flynn's empty tea cup. With both hands, she held the cup close and stared into it. "Oh, dear." Helen's eyes widened. "Look at this."

"It's nothing but a bit of dried mint," Mrs. Flynn said.

"No, there's a message for you."

"Ever since you went to see that gypsy circus in Butler last May you have been acting queer, Helen Sweeney."

Helen raised her eyebrows. "I can see your future. Just as clear as anything."

"And I'm thinking the little people have got hold of you and your brother both, what with him buying that painted bird and you seeing things in a dirty cup." Still, the old woman rubbed her chin. "Well, go on, girl. What is it? What does it say?"

"A change. A big change for you."

Mrs. Flynn sat back, amused. "Oh, well now. That must be Kathleen and Marty, my own brother's children coming to live with us."

Helen grinned. "I don't think so. It's even bigger than that. Your whole life is about to change for the better."

"Then it must be money," Joanna said.

"And where would I be getting a sack of money?"

Helen shrugged. "Maybe it isn't money at all, but a man, Mrs. Flynn. A gentleman caller for you."

"God save me!" the old woman gasped, putting her hand to her breast and sitting back. "Helen Sweeney, you'll go rinse out that dirty cup right now and stop talking this foolishness. And my man dead but seven months." She turned to Joanna then. "And why are you laughing?"

The girl covered her mouth with her hand.

"Sure and next that fool Helen Sweeney will tell me to go to the dance at the Mountain View."

The thought of old Mrs. Flynn dancing made Joanna laugh out loud. In the valley, the farming families often held socials and the children as well as the elderly danced together. Still, all winter Mrs. Flynn had not ventured outside of the house, not even to attend Mass. On those Sunday afternoons when Father Jordan could make it over the snowy mountain roads to the patch, he visited Mrs. Flynn personally in the kitchen and heard her confession. Every time Joanna left them alone she wondered what sins the old woman could have committed since the last time he had come.

Sometimes at those dances in the valley her partner was her father and he held her rigidly, almost proudly, at arm's length. When Margaret was her partner, they raced about the floor and laughed. More often lately, though, her partner had been Tommy Craig, a tall and lanky farm boy with curly blond hair, and he always held her close.

"Did you let him kiss you?" Helen asked. Mrs. Flynn was leering at her, waiting for her answer, too.

"A few times," she admitted quietly.

"The only man I've kissed was Charlie Boy Duffy."

Mrs. Flynn clapped her hands. "And there's a waste of time and talent."

"Mrs. Flynn!" Joanna said, surprised.

"Everybody knows Charlie Boy will be living with his Ma and Pa until they die."

"Just because I let him kiss me doesn't mean I want him to move in," Helen said. "What do you know anyway?"

"Well, now." Mrs. Flynn smoothed her grey hair from her face. "I may not look like much to you now, but I have brushed cheeks with more than one man."

That morning, alone in the woods above the mining patch, Joanna dropped her sack and pretended that Tommy Craig had asked her to dance again. She spread her skirt and curtsied, then took hold of the branch of a fir tree and began to dance with her skirt lifted. She spun, then waltzed into the tree and felt its branch arms around her. Still embraced, she locked her arms around the tree trunk and smiled up at her imagined partner. But she had no interest in Tommy Craig now, nor he in her. During the Christmas social in the valley he had danced only with her sister Margaret. Instead, Joanna pictured Timothy as her partner. Taller than she, he was standing with his hands on her shoulders, looking at her just as he had that night in the snow before Christmas Eve. She stepped back, out of the tangle of fir branches. It was wrong. Timothy would never dance with her—not next Saturday at the Mountain View or ever.

Mrs. Flynn had joked about brushing cheeks with more than one man and she had teased Helen about Charlie Boy Duffy moving in with her. Yet at the same time she referred to Welsh's woman as "that article," as if she were a worn piece of clothing. It all confused Joanna. On the night she had baked the Christmas cake, the old woman had made Joanna feel like she was the "article." Even here, alone in the woods and wondering what it would feel like to be held by Timothy, Joanna felt guilty.

She had just picked up her sack of coal to return to the house when she heard Helen calling for her. Joanna stepped out from behind the mountain laurels. Helen was climbing the bank towards her.

"She said I'd find you here."

"Mrs. Flynn?" Joanna looked down at the Flynn house. There was a window in back, but that was Timothy's room. Even so, the old woman couldn't see her way up here. "How does she know I come here?"

"There's been an accident," Helen said. She sat down on a rock, her elbows on her knees, her face cupped in her hands. "A cave-in."

Joanna looked towards the colliery. The yellow smoke rose steadily from the stacks. Two mules were in the fenced yard at the barn and a man was crossing the stripping road to the superintendent's building. There was no sign of panic.

"Down river," Helen said irritably. "At Shenandoah. They mined too close to the riverbed and the water just crashed right through. At least twenty men are still trapped below, but they'll never dig them out in time."

She kicked at the dirt. "Oh, Joanna. I tell you, you're lucky to be leaving this place soon."

"Are they dead?" She tucked her skirt around her legs and sat on the cold ground beside Helen.

"Some." Helen threw her head back and groaned at the blue sky. "I was born in this patch and I shall die here, too."

The two girls sat in the dappled sun that promised spring. The wind played at their muddied skirts.

"My father was killed in a rock fall six years ago." Joanna looked towards the breaker and the colliery. Timothy was underground.

"Miners," Helen said bitterly. "We're all miners. When you live with them and cook their meals and wash their clothes and care, then you become a miner, too. It's like you go underground with them, and when someone is crushed or poisoned by the air down below, it isn't surprising. It just happens all the time. You can go mad thinking about it. But at least you're getting out, Joanna."

Already it was March. Already Kathleen and Marty Boyle were on board ship. "I'll only be a few hours away," she said quietly. "We can visit."

"Don't you understand? You'll be out of this blackness!" Helen turned to her. "You've made no secret of the fact that you don't like it here. Well, do you think I do?"

Joanna just stared at her. Helen had never complained like this before. Her friend lived alone with her brother, seeing to his needs for six years, and before that, to those of her father as well. "You can go away from here," Joanna said at last. "You can leave, too."

"Run away?" Helen smiled sadly. "Like my mother?" After a moment she said, "The thing is, I never knew if she ran away because of what the man offered her or because of what was here. I mean, there are always stray men who wander into the patch, stay a while, and leave. Was she so desperate that she just latched on to anybody? Or did she really love him?"

"Of course, she loved him," Joanna said, though she could not have known. But Helen wasn't listening.

"I do know one thing, though. Nothing is free. Sure, you can sign your name at the company store for flour and bolts of muslin, but they own a good part of you." Helen sighed. "You've either got to have money to get away or a man."

In the mule yard by the company barn, a boy was shoveling manure. At the opposite end of the town, lost behind the rooftops and trees, was the covered bridge and the only road out of the patch. At that moment Joanna felt that she would never leave here, that her father would never come for her, that her farm, like Mrs. Flynn's land, was already lost to her.

"I was eight when she left," Helen said, following Joanna's gaze down the road past the superintendent's home. "My father died three years later. Now only Joe and I are left." Then she squeezed Joanna's arm and said, more eagerly, "I have never told anyone this, Joanna, not even my brother."

"What?"

Helen smiled. "I have always thought that I would like to be a teacher."

Joanna smiled, too. "Like Mrs. Dickerson?"

Helen shook her head. "No, not like her. Not here. Not in the back room of a saloon but in a real schoolhouse with a bell. In Butler, maybe. I'd have my own desk and books. That would be a meaningful, wonderful life, wouldn't it? Working with children." She let go of her friend's arm. The dream had brightened her spirits a little. "What do you want, Joanna? It is almost time for you to decide. You'll be gone before summer."

She did not answer immediately. Below, a few geese had wandered into the soupy road, their clatter like foolish laughter carried on the wind. Joanna watched them moving about without apparent direction and thought, "That's me, not knowing what to do or what is right or wrong." She wanted both to leave the patch and to stay. "I don't know," she said at last. She could not picture herself alone, apart from other people. She saw herself at home with her mother in the kitchen, or in the fields with her father and brothers, but she also saw herself here with Timothy and old Mrs. Flynn. "I just don't know what will happen to me."

Late that afternoon, Joanna carried clean covers to Timothy's room. She smoothed them over the pallet and shook his pillows, but once this chore was done, she did not leave his room. She looked at the dresser tops where his books were stacked one on top of the other. Worn a little along the bindings and with thin, yellowed pages, they were carried from Ireland. She fingered them, opened the cover. He had written some comments along the margin of the first page. She next opened his drawer, wondering if he kept a picture of Rosie there. But all she found were the long underwear and socks she had folded and placed there two days ago. The violin case was in the corner and on the small table near the bed was a pearly-handled knife. Some evenings he carved tiny animals from the scraps of wood on the floor near the stove, only to toss them onto the coals before going to bed.

Joanna stared at his bed and wondered for the hundredth time what sort of person Rosie was. Often she imagined them, Rosie and Timothy, moving quietly about this room, whispering so softly that Mrs. Flynn in the next room could not hear. That afternoon again an image came to Joanna: Rosie and Timothy lying together in bed, the quilt covering them. Her red hair was undone and spread over her shoulders; she lay with her head on Timothy's bare chest.

"Joanna." Mrs. Flynn called from the kitchen and instantly Rosie vanished. The bed was empty and smooth. "Joanna, the soup!"

The girl hurried into the kitchen.

"I'd move it myself if I could."

"I'll get it, I'll get it," the girl said sharply. With a towel over the handle, she slid the boiling pot to the side, away from the heat.

Mrs. Flynn lifted her head. "And what's the matter with you today?"

"Nothing." Joanna wiped what little had spilled over, then gave the old woman a vague smile. "I'm sorry."

"There's got to be a better life than this," Timothy said that evening, unaccustomed bitterness in his voice as he spoke about the mining accident. "I have a notion of going out west to the Ohio or to Illinois. What do you say to that, Ma?"

Joanna looked up.

"Sure and it's been four hard years here," the old woman said.

"I could do it, too. In two months' time when Marty and Kathleen come."

Joanna stared at him, her spoon poised over her bowl.

"And how do you feel about going west, Jo?" he asked.

She looked first at Mrs. Flynn, then down at her bowl. "Why, I have no opinion about it whatsoever, Mr. Flynn. I have never been west, or even to Butler for that matter."

"I suppose you'll be glad to go home to that river of yours come May," he said. And again like Helen, he seemed resentful.

"I am looking forward to it."

"Can there be a boy waiting for you there?"

It angered Joanna that he would tease her, that he would use the word "boy" and not "man." She thought of Tommy Craig, but he was not waiting on her at all. Still, she answered sharply, "Why yes, there certainly could be, Mr. Flynn."

"Oh?"

Tommy Craig was only a farmer's son. She thought a moment, then said arrogantly, "A teacher friend."

Timothy smiled. "A teacher, is he?"

Joanna pressed her lips together and cocked her chin.

"Yes, Mr. Flynn, a teacher. There are other people in this world besides coal miners. Teaching is a wonderful, meaningful life."

"Is that so now? It seems a bit of a bore to me. Woman's work, I'd say."

"Well, it's a sight better than spending your life in a black hole with dumb mules doing the same thing day in and day out without any hope at all for something better!"

Mrs. Flynn set her spoon on her plate and looked curiously at her son and then at Joanna. "Be still now, both of you."

"I never knew you felt that way, Jo. I'm sorry to hear it." He ate another mouthful, then shoved his bowl aside. He stood. "I guess we all do what we're suited for." He took his cap from the peg by the door. "I'll be at the Mountain View." He walked out. His plate was half full.

Joanna lowered her head, not wanting to look at Mrs. Flynn. She mumbled an apology.

But the old woman's voice was soft when she spoke, not scolding. "It's just the cave, Joanna. A cave rattles them. Gets to us all." She sighed and began to eat again. "He'll have an ale with Joe and be fine and dandy come morning, not to worry."

Still, why he had questioned her about a boyfriend at all confused Joanna for days afterward.

(ii)

Joanna undid her long braid and brushed her thick blonde hair over her shoulders. The weight of it down her back made her feel pretty, though there was no mirror in the attic to tell for certain. From her trunk, she took the blue satin ribbon she had bought for herself at Christmas and had saved for a special time. She tied it around her throat. Once more she smoothed the skirt of her gingham dress, then turned to the stairs, ready to face them.

Mrs. Flynn stared as Joanna served the cabbage and potatoes. Timothy nodded shyly as if Joanna were no more than a stranger to whom he was being polite. Just someone to wash his clothes and cook his meals, she thought angrily. When Mrs. Flynn innocently commented that her Rosie never did wear her hair down, Joanna banged the pot on the stove. While eating, whenever Joanna looked up, Timothy looked down. She set her knife and fork on the table then and looked directly at him. "What is it, Mr. Flynn? You are looking at me as if I had two heads."

"Not two heads exactly," he said and smiled. "I guess I just never realized you had that much hair." Then he laughed to himself.

Annoyed, Joanna stood and began to clear the table.

"I'm not quite finished yet, Joanna," the old woman said.

With a sigh, the girl sat down again to wait.

"If you have to get on to that party at the Mountain View," Timothy said, "I suppose I could wash the dishes for you tonight."

It was as if he wanted her to go. She said pointedly, "Oh, no, Mr. Flynn. That would be woman's work."

Then he sighed, too, and once more Mrs. Flynn looked from Joanna to Timothy and shook her head.

When Helen called for her, Joanna took her heavy shawl from the peg and covered her shoulders. Suddenly she was reluctant to go. It was different at home. She knew everyone. She had grown up with Tommy Craig and the others. Now she wasn't sure she wanted to go into the back room of the Mountain View and dance in front of a line of strange coal miners.

Mrs. Flynn said, "I'll send Timothy later to walk you girls home."

"There's no need," Helen said. "Joe and Charlie Boy will see us home."

Timothy was sitting on the porch stoop and he stood as the girls came outside. Joanna had wanted to look at herself in the mirror hanging on the porch post, but with Timothy watching, she did not. She stepped past him and followed Helen over the ash walk to the gate.

On the sloping porch of the Mountain View were two separate groups of women and young men. From inside came the sounds of an accordion and a scratchy fiddle. Red bunting was draped over the rough walls of the back room. The windows were opened, though it was not yet April, and couples danced to a reel. Old men and women, in line with the young, strutted around each other, weaving with the music.

Helen watched the dancing until she could no longer stand still. "Be my partner, Joanna," she said, taking her hands. "I'll be the man if you want."

"I'm taller," Joanna said. "I'll be the man."

The two girls got in line.

The neighbors Nat and Mary were dancing, though not looking at each other as they trotted about the room. Welshie's woman, too, had come to dance. She wore a bright scarf tied about her small waist. In line, too, was the young, dark-skinned mother Joanna had seen last week picking coal on the culm bank. Her husband balanced the child on his shoulder as he danced.

When the music was over, Mary sat down to fan herself. Beads of perspiration covered her forehead. The sleeves of her blouse were rolled up past her elbows revealing her fat arms. She nodded now to Welshie's woman who was talking to Charlie Boy Duffy. "So Mrs. Barton has come out to show herself tonight. And it looks, Helen, like she's taken a shine to your Charlie Boy."

"He's not my boy at all," Helen said. Still, she watched them from across the room. Even though the music had stopped, Welshie's woman swayed back and forth.

Mrs. Barton claimed to be a widow and that she was

renting the room from Welshie and glad to have it. She had begun to take in wash to earn her keep, and most mornings there were clothes on the lines on the hill behind Welshie's house. "There's more than clothes being rubbed in that place," Mary said.

Joanna had shied away towards the barroom door. She peered inside the smoky room and saw Joe Sweeney playing cards at a table with other men. She recognized Welshie at the bar. But Timothy was not with them. Most evenings he went to the Mountain View with Joe and Charlie Boy. Why had he not come tonight? When the music began again, Helen found her out and pulled her into line once more.

Throughout the evening, Joanna looked for him, expecting to see him standing along the wall with the other men. And she looked for him again on the porch of the Mountain View when she and Helen stepped out for cool air.

"You aren't having fun, are you?" Helen said.

"Sure I am.

"Helen reached for her friend's hand and turned it palm up. "Shall I read your fortune?"

Joanna smiled. "I don't believe in it."

"Believe in what? Fate or love?"

"It is just a game you make up because there is nothing else to do."

"Maybe." Helen's finger tickled Joanna's palm. "That line is very deep, Joanna. Why won't you tell me about him?"

Joanna pulled her hand free. "There's no one to tell you about."

"He cares for you, too."

"Please, Helen. Don't tease me."

Helen leaned her arms on the porch banister. "What does it feel like to be in love?"

"I'm sure I don't know."

From the Mountain View came the whining voices of the accordion and the fiddle. Someone was singing. Helen shook her head. "Sounds like Charlie Boy."

Laughter now spilled from the open windows.

"That's Welshie's house over there," Helen said. "I wonder who will walk Mrs. Barton home tonight?" She looked sideways at Joanna.

"Not Charlie Boy."

Helen smiled. "No, I think not." After a moment, she said very quietly, "My mother. Sometimes I wonder if she was like Mrs. Barton." And then she shrugged, laughed it off. "You do like him, don't you?"

Joanna closed her eyes. It was wrong. The year of mourning was not yet up. He was older than she by ten years. Rosie's sweater still hung by the door.

When the dancing was over and Timothy still had not come as Mrs. Flynn said he might, Joanna walked home along the muddy road with Helen and Charlie Boy. They left her at the gate.

"Joanna?"

Timothy was standing in the shadows on the porch. His hands were in his pockets. She wondered how long he had been there, for it was just how he was standing earlier when she had left. He came down the ash walk then to open the gate for her.

"We heard the music all the way down here. Was it a fun time for you?"

She nodded.

"You were late in coming. I was about to go for you." He followed her to the porch. "It's past ten."

"Yes, well, we stayed until the end."

"Joanna."

She turned on the porch. Timothy was below her and in the soft light from the kitchen window, he seemed sad. He always seemed sad, as if he, too, were lost in the coal-patch town. It occurred to her then that her feelings for him were not love at all but pity.

"Will you sit and talk awhile?"

Yes, she wanted to say. Yes, I will sit all night long listening to you, watching you. But she lowered her head and her long, blonde hair fell forward. "It's late, Mr. Flynn."

"You talk to me as if I were only your employer. Once you called me Tim. Won't you call me that now?"

She said nothing.

"We've known each other a while. We're friends, isn't that so?"

She sighed. "Yes. Friends."

"The cousins come in three weeks, Joanna. Maybe four."

They were just friends. She turned that over, wondering what it meant and wondering what one friend says to another at ten o'clock at night, outside alone. "Mrs. Flynn will be happy when they come." She closed her eyes. She felt foolish. She did not want to talk about Kathleen or Marty Boyle.

"You have made a difference, Jo."

"Have I?" She lifted her head and smiled at him, but she did not believe it. What she did believe, however, was that she had changed somehow. She was no longer the same girl who rode into town on her father's wagon, who lay curled in the cold attic bed, afraid of the voices from Nat and Mary's side of the house.

"Before you came, Ma was lost."

"Oh."

After a moment, he said, "I guess we both were. You've made a difference for both of us."

He was only being nice to her. "It's late," she repeated.

"That it is," he said, turning away now, too. "And I suppose I shouldn't be keeping you out here in the damp." He sat on the porch stoop again, his back to her.

She thought that maybe she should sit on the step beside him. Maybe she could lean her head on his arm and then he wouldn't seem so lonely. She glanced sideways into the small, cracked mirror that hung on the porch post, but it was too dark to see her reflection. He's thinking of her, she thought. Not me. She reached for the door.

"Will you come in?" she asked.

"Soon," he answered.

(iii)

Before the colliery whistle blew at dawn on Monday, a thunderstorm woke Joanna and drew her to the window. In the quick flashes of lightning she saw Nat splash through the drenched backyard to the privy. Joanna shivered as she dressed. The rain fell hard and straight all morning. Then suddenly, just after eleven, the colliery whistle sounded again, ten short blasts that cut through the grey sheets of rain and shook the windows like gusts of hail against the glass.

"Dear Saints," Mrs. Flynn cried and blessed herself.

"What is it?"

Again the whistle sounded ten short blasts.

"Bring me the holy candle."

"Why?" Joanna asked. "What's happening?"

"Light it, girl. Light it."

"Mrs. Flynn?"

The old woman's head bowed as she murmured in Gaelic.

She could not see through the condensation on the window and so Joanna grabbed her shawl, and draping it over her head, went out onto the porch stoop. The rain streamed from the angled roof into a pool of water at the step bottom. Ten more times the colliery whistle cried. The door of Helen's house across the way was open. Women hurried through the mud towards the breaker building at the end of the road.

Joanna stepped down into the flooded yard. From one of the company buildings at the end of the road black and yellow smoke billowed. She unlatched the gate and stood in the middle of the road. "Is it a cave?" she cried to the boy that ran past.

Flames licked the corner of the colliery building, tasting the breaker leg, now biting into it. Buckets of water passed quickly from one hand to another, but in minutes the shaft was a fiery snake, hissing and crackling, flushing the rain-wet faces of the women and children. And then the buckets stopped. Trancelike, the men and the women and the breaker boys who had fled from the building watched as the fire climbed diagonally across the sky to the colliery roof.

One car came up and the miners spilled out of it. Then a second and third car surfaced, but each helmeted, broad-shouldered figure was like the other and Joanna could not tell if Timothy was freed or if he was still trapped below.

She turned away, holding her stomach, and struggled through the thick mud back to the house. Her shawl had fallen to her shoulders and her hair and clothes were drenched.

As the girl came to the door, Mrs. Flynn looked up, but seeing Joanna's white face, she lowered her head and began to mumble again her Gaelic prayers. "There's been an explosion," she said. Joanna went to her and put her arms around her. She whispered, "They're getting the men up. Maybe two dozen or more already." But both she and the old woman knew that there were nearly one hundred men below.

"I've lost my man," Mrs. Flynn said. "I lost Rosie and then my man. I can't lose Tim. Dear God, I can't lose him."

Joanna helped the old woman through the hallway to her bed. She covered her with the quilt, then sat on the bed beside her to wait. With each flash of lightning, the girl tensed.

Once when Joanna had been tending a calf in the field at the farm, she heard her father call to her in a voice that revealed no pain or urgency but when she reached him, slumped against the stone wall, his face was pale. He reached for her, leaned on her, and tried to walk, but his leg gave way and he fell against the wall again.

"Pa?" She pulled free of him. "Pa?"

Then she saw the sickle in the grass and the wet on his pant leg just below the knee. There was blood over his boot and on his hands. Where he had grabbed her arm was a bloody print on her blouse.

"Come here," he said, his voice still calm. When she hesitated, he said more angrily, "Come here, Joanna, it's only blood."

"I'll go for help," she said, but he got hold of her skirt, pulling her towards him. He lifted it and ripped her petticoat, tying the strip of material above his knee.

"Get a stick," he told her and the girl obeyed. Following his directions, she slipped it through the bandage and twisted it tighter for a tourniquet. He put his weight on her shoulder and stood. "Help me to the house." With his arm heavy on her shoulder, he was able to climb the slope from the river to the barn.

Joanna felt the same heaviness now on her shoulders and neck as she waited. The rain fell steadily against the windows. I shall never, never come back to this place, the girl thought desperately. When the Flynn cousins arrived, she would gladly go home and forget this family and this awful, black place.

"Joanna?" Mrs. Flynn, too, had not moved. She lay on her back, staring at the ceiling. "Give me your hand, Joanna."

The girl slipped her hand under the quilt and Mrs. Flynn's warm fingers circled hers.

"You're cold."

"Yes, Ma'am."

"Come here, Joanna, and lie beside me."

After a moment, the girl stood and went around to the other side of the bed and lay there under the quilt.

"The day my man died," Mrs. Flynn began in a quiet voice, calmer now than before, "I knew it."

"Please," the girl said. "Don't talk about it."

"Even before it happened, I just had this feeling. Even before they brought him back to me here, I knew he was gone."

The windows were fogged and the room, damp. The old woman reached for Joanna's hand again. "I heard him call my name. Annie, he said. Annie. And I thought, what is this? Joe has come home early? But no one was there."

Joanna bit her lip. "He's not dead," she whispered. "Timothy isn't dead."

"Annie. I heard it just as clear as anything. I made my way to the window, but nothing. Then minutes later, we all heard the whistle. There had been an accident." The old woman closed her eyes. "Gas. That's what they told me. Methane gas or something coming out of the earth. I don't remember. He was already dead and gone, crushed by the rocks. But he had called to me from below or wherever it is God had sent him. Like he was trying to tell me."

Joanna's fingers burned, the old woman was squeezing them so tightly.

"The lantern had a hole, just a little hole, in it. That's what they said."

"Please, Mrs. Flynn."

"His voice wasn't so sad or painful when he called to me. I take comfort in that. Yes, I can take comfort in that."

Joanna felt helpless. She stared at the ceiling. She could hear the rain drumming on the roof far above.

"Sure and I felt it. Even before it happened. But the thing is, he knew about such things as gas. He never would have taken a cracked lantern into that dark place. No."

She wasn't certain how much time had passed when she

heard the kitchen door. Perhaps it was an hour or more. Joanna glanced at Mrs. Flynn, but the old woman's eyes were closed. She had not heard the door. Joanna freed her hand and raised her head to listen more closely. Then she slipped out of the bed and went into the hallway. "Tim?"

He was there near the stove, his back to her, and when he turned, she cried out, then covered her mouth with both hands. His head was bare and wet. His face was dark from the mines. "Jo," he said and smiled. He went to her then and touched her cheek.

"We thought you were dead," she whispered.

"You haven't lost me yet, Jo, so don't be crying now as if you had."

She pushed against him, pressing her cheek to his hand, smelling the smoke and the rain in his clothes.

At once his arms pressed her closer. "God save me," he said. He kissed her hair, still damp, and kissed her forehead and brow. "God save me," he repeated. "You're just a girl."

"No." She looked up at him and shook her head. "No. Not anymore. Maybe when I came, but not now, Tim." She reached her arms up around his neck and kissed him.

"I'm ten years older, Jo," he said, his mouth against her hair. "But what shall I do with you? I want to keep you here and never let you go back to that farm."

"I don't want to go back. I don't want to leave you."

He looked down at her. "This is the only life I know. Can you stay then, Jo, knowing that? This is my life, Jo. I'm not good for anything else."

She had no fondness for this dingy town. The sharp-angled shanties smelled of cabbage and pork, and each dawn she cringed in bed hearing the colliery whistle. Yet she took his hand and squeezed it, as hard as Mrs. Flynn had pressed hers in bed. "I want to make you happy again. I can do that, Tim. I can make you happy."

"You make me happy, Jo. You certainly make me

happy." He winced as he raised his right arm to stroke her hair.

"You're hurt."

"It isn't much, I think."

Boiled water and some soap was all he wanted for it, but he caught her arm as Joanna reached for the bucket. "I care for you deeply, Jo. You know that, don't you?"

After a moment, she nodded. "Yes, I think I did know it."

"And you for me? I wasn't sure of that."

She did not look away shyly now. She reached for him, pushing the black hair out of his eyes as she had that night in the snow before Christmas Eve. "From the very first night I knew you were special for me. It's true, I swear it."

As they parted—he for the bedroom and his mother, and she to heat water for his shoulder—both silently vowed a better life for the other.

(i)

There were no wild flowers to pick from the woods in late April, and she had no wedding veil, but Joanna stole apple blossoms from the trees on her father's farm and wore them in her hair. Her dress was a simple cotton without eyelet or lace. She stood beside Timothy in the parlor of the farmhouse and was married by the same priest who had buried Timothy's wife and father and who had first told Joanna's parents of the family in the mining patch who needed a girl to keep house.

Timothy was uncomfortable in his tweed suit for it was too warm for the spring day. It had been four weeks since the explosion and fire in the mine, but still his arm was in a sling. As he came beside Joanna, he smiled and took for himself an apple blossom from her hair to tuck in his lapel.

Mrs. Flynn sat in an arm chair, with Helen on one side and Joe Sweeney on the other. She was uneasy. It was a bad omen, she thought, for Timothy to marry before his year of mourning had ended. It was not his bride, but the suddenness of the vows that worried her.

During the three weeks before the wedding, Joanna had fluttered about the kitchen. She sang while sweeping and sang while cracking walnuts for bread. She boasted of the garden she would plant that summer and of the sauerkraut she could make to last all winter. She sang and talked until Mrs. Flynn begged for a moment's peace.

She no longer braided her hair, but pinned it up to appear older. And she had made little changes in the house, as well. She sewed blue-gingham curtains for the kitchen window and the door. She had begun to twine a bright rag runner to go the length of the kitchen. From the company store she purchased a can of sky-blue paint and double-coated the floorboards of the attic room she would share with Timothy. The thought of sleeping in Rosie's bed gave Joanna a queer feeling and she argued that Marty Boyle would be more comfortable in that corner room off the kitchen. A few days before the wedding she had carried Timothy's things upstairs. She lined his books in a row on the floor under the window. She set his pearly-handled carving knife on top of the little bedtable she had also brought up.

"Someday we'll live on a paved street," she told Mrs. Flynn. "And there will be red maple trees like a canopy over the porch. And we'll have shutters for the windows and an iron fence all around."

The old woman's voice was tired. "Timothy is a fine man, Joanna. I don't doubt you know that by now. And he might have his dreams of leaving this patch and the coal behind, but he'll not be going far. Hear me now, Joanna," the old woman warned. "I know about him."

The girl ignored her seriousness. "Wouldn't it be fine to have a weeping willow tree in the backyard? A real backyard, Mrs. Flynn, without these awful slate banks all around making you feel like you've fallen into a hole? You could sit out under the willow and listen to the birds."

"I'll be long dead and buried beside my man right here in this place before I'll be seeing such a thing."

Now, in the parlor of the farmhouse, the priest closed

his book and nodded. It was done. Timothy leaned closer to kiss Joanna's cheek. Her brothers fidgeted, impatient to eat the food set out on the sideboard. Joanna turned to her father first. Just as when he danced with her, he held his oldest daughter at arm's length and leaned forward to kiss her cheek. She went then to her mother and Margaret, accepting their kisses, and then she knelt before Mrs. Flynn, just as she had so many times in the drafty kitchen when she rubbed the burning liniment on the old woman's legs. "I love him," she whispered, though she had not yet said it to Timothy.

Mrs. Flynn patted the girl's hair. "It takes more than love, Joanna." The old woman smiled. "And the courting must continue long after the wedding night."

Joe Sweeney put his hand under Joanna's arm to lift her. "I want to dance with the bride," he said. "Timothy's brought his violin."

"Should the groom be playing on his wedding day?" she asked.

"Well now, I'd play for you, but I don't think anyone would stay to listen."

Outside, a wagon carrying friends from the neighboring farm had stopped at the door. Amid the laughter of these wedding guests, Tommy Craig among them, the old woman was left alone. As she listened to the music and watched the party, she tapped her hand on the arm of the chair. She was fond of Joanna, but afraid for her, too, anticipating the time when the singing would stop and the colliery whistle would once more blast ten times in the middle of the morning.

(ii)

"It's a shame they couldn't have waited for Kathleen and Marty to come," Mrs. Flynn told Joanna's mother. "It can only be another week now. But your Joanna is stubborn.

Once she gets a thing in her head, be it baking cakes or painting the floorboards, nothing can keep her from doing it."

"Would you like more cider, Mrs. Flynn?" the girl's mother asked.

"That I would," the old woman said. "And you can pour a bit of that good whiskey in it. I'll take no objection to that."

Helen, who was sitting beside the old woman again, sighed happily. "Did you dance at your wedding?"

The old woman looked at her. "My wedding?" she said as if she had forgotten she was ever married. "Well now, if I didn't, I should have." Joanna and Margaret had taken their father's hands and pulled him to the center of the room. He soon tired of their dance, however, and joined Joe Sweeney and the other men outside on the porch. "Headstrong, she is," Mrs. Flynn said. "Like her refusing to take the front room. It's bigger than that attic and cooler sleeping come summer, too, but she'll have none of it."

"Mrs. Flynn," Helen laughed. "She just wants some privacy."

The old woman grunted. "And what does she think I'd be doing, putting my ear to the wall?"

When Joanna's mother returned with the cup of cider, she said, "This is a happy day for us, though it was quite a surprise."

"I wasn't a bit surprised," said Mrs. Flynn.

"Here we thought she would be coming home to us, and now she is leaving us for good. She seems very happy, though."

"She is," Helen said at once.

Mrs. Flynn, however, looked again at the bride, who was dancing now with a neighbor boy. "A happy day, yes. And we do well to remember them." She drank more of the cider, smacked her lips from the whiskey's added tartness, then said, "You know, of course, I wanted them to wait a while longer before getting married."

"Yes, until your relatives came," Joanna's mother said in a conciliatory tone, reminding her that they had already discussed this.

"Yes," the old woman said. "We do well to remember the good times."

Later that afternoon when most of the wedding guests had gone, Joanna found Timothy with Joe Sweeney outside on the porch. She hesitated in approaching them, but Timothy saw her and held out his good arm. "Come here, Jo. We've been watching your river and the birds."

She smiled then and took his hand. "There's a spot upriver, not too far, where wild turkeys roost on the cliffs."

"It's a beautiful farm," he said. "I can understand why you would be so homesick."

She slipped her arm around his waist and smiled. "I'm not sorry to leave it now."

It was Joe who turned away then, leaving them alone. When the screen door banged, a flock of red-winged blackbirds started up from the corn stubble in the field. The birds circled, and sensing no danger, settled down again to feed.

(iii)

In the fading afternoon light, they left the party at the farm and rode in Joe's wagon back to the mining patch. Mrs. Flynn yawned and said such a long ride twice in one day was too much for an old woman. It was the first time she had been out of the patch since Rosie's death. When they arrived home, it was already dark. The old woman sat nearer the stove and Joanna brought the quilt from the bed to cover the woman's legs, so chilled she said she was.

"We get old even before we know it," Mrs. Flynn sighed under Joanna's attention. "We can't even do the simple things for ourselves. That's the sadness of it."

Timothy sat at his place at the table. As she had every

night for seven months, Joanna warmed their supper. She worked with her back to him, but the smoke from his pipe drifted over her shoulder and she turned back to look at him. The old woman was dozing already, though she had not yet eaten. Joanna turned back to the pot on the stove. Tonight they would be alone, just she and Timothy sitting by the fire.

"Each time I look up at that window with your fancy curtains now, I think there's someone peeking in at us."

Joanna helped the old woman to stand. "Who would want to peek in at us? There must be more interesting houses to look in on."

"Welshie's?" The old woman laughed.

Joanna set the stew before her.

"There was a time when my fingers did what I told them to and I could sew," Mrs. Flynn said. "Sure and my tatting was admired by all the women. To think I didn't even bring one doily with me when I left the old country. Ah well, we leave some things behind and find new."

Mrs. Flynn leaned forward and sniffed the steaming bowl. The long ride and the cool air had given her an appetite. Joanna, however, ate very little. "Kathleen is a fine cook," she said. "We Irish all are. We had to be for the times when there wasn't much to throw in the pot." The old woman patted Joanna's hand. Rosie's thin band now circled Joanna's middle finger. "But not to worry. We take the good times with the bad."

Joanna put her other hand over Mrs. Flynn's and pressed. "Let's have only good times from now on." From across the table she felt Timothy watching her.

"Kathleen will be a help to you, Joanna, when she comes." And then Mrs. Flynn gave a little laugh. "But what will we do with Marty?"

"Welshie says they aren't hiring at all until the breaker is rebuilt," Timothy said. He added, "He may not hire Marty even then."

"He's a fine boy, our Marty. But not one to put his shoulder to the pick, I'm afraid."

"He's a thief," Timothy said. "As a boy he'd steal chickens and eggs or whatever caught his eye. He pockets things."

"There won't be much for him to be stealing here," Mrs. Flynn said. "We won't need to be worrying about that. Still he'll need a job. Here or in Butler." She put her hands on the table, lifting herself. "Help me to my room, Tim. An old woman like myself needs plenty of rest. And don't my feet feel like I'm the one who's been dancing all afternoon?"

As Joanna cleared the table and set the dishes in the tub of hot water, she heard the old woman talking still to Timothy in the bedroom. Then he came back into the kitchen and sat at the table again.

"I guess you don't care very much for Marty Boyle."

"He was just a boy when I last saw him. It's the work I'm not sure of. The company just isn't hiring. We'll be lucky if they call me back to work before summer."

If Timothy never went down in the mines again, Joanna would not care. Marty could have his job.

"What is it, Jo?"

Before today, she had not seen him in a collar and suit. He seemed almost a stranger. "You look very handsome. Like a businessman. Like the superintendent himself."

Timothy laughed. "I tell you, it's scratching my neck. I'll be glad to take it off." He paused a moment, a little self-conscious. "I mean," he said, smiling, "it's itchy."

He waited until she had wiped the dishes and set them on the shelf. Then he went to her and squeezed her shoulders. Joanna untied her apron and looped it on the peg. Rosie's sweater was gone. She had folded it away in one of Mrs. Flynn's drawers.

"They don't know about me. Do they?"

Timothy ran his thumb over her cheek. "They will like

you very much, Jo. Of that I'm certain." He reached for the oil lamp, then opened the door for the attic stairs.

It was not so late. Joanna looked back at the chairs by the stove. "Do you want to sit a while?"

"Do you?"

"No," she said, "I suppose not."

On the kitchen table was the china bowl her mother had given her as a wedding present. It had belonged to Joanna's grandmother, who brought it to this country from Germany. For as long as Joanna could remember, the dish had set in the cabinet in the farmhouse parlor with the few other fine dishes her mother owned. Carefully Joanna picked it up and admired it again. "Where shall we put it?"

"Upstairs," he said. He still held the door open for her.

"It won't be broken there."

"But no one will see it if it's in the attic."

"We will. Let's take it upstairs."

Once more she looked about the kitchen. Everything was in its place. In the bedroom, Mrs. Flynn was already asleep and breathing deeply. Timothy held out his hand for her.

He had to stoop in the attic doorway so as not to hit his head and Joanna laughed nervously at him. He winced as he eased his arm out of the sling, then seeing Joanna's concern, he said, "It's healing. It's healing. A few more weeks, that's all."

She set her grandmother's bowl on the bureau top. Because Timothy's arm was still sore, Joe Sweeney and Charlie Boy had carried the dresser to the attic just last evening. The added furniture made the room appear smaller, but not as empty now. Timothy needed Joanna's help to undo the stiff collar of his suit. Her fingers against his throat were cold, and he took her hands and kissed them, a gesture that clearly surprised, yet thrilled her.

"Come here, Jo." He drew her to the bed.

She had thought about this night only vaguely, knowing what it was about but not sure how it would happen or what her role should be. She had seen Mrs. Barton teasing the old men on the porch of the Mountain View, leaning close to pinch their arms; she had heard Mrs. Flynn boast of brushing cheeks with more than one man; but she had also seen her own mother lifting her face to accept her husband's kiss without reaching up to hold him. Now as Timothy reached for her, touching the curls that had come loose from the long ride over the mountain, Joanna imitated his movement, touching his black hair and his forehead. He next reached for the hairpin. Joanna's fingers removed the pin and brushed her hair down. As he stroked her hair, following it over her back, she leaned closer to brush her face against his cheek. Joanna closed her eyes. "How does it feel to be in love?" Helen had wondered that night on the porch of the Mountain View. It felt good, the girl thought. It felt right.

For the first time since the afternoon of the mine fire, they held each other. His was different from all the other embraces she had known—her father who held her rigidly, her sister who squeezed, and Tommy Craig who had once huddled shyly on her shoulder. There was strength in Timothy's arms, despite his injury. There was no shyness or uncertainty in the way he pressed her close. There was no hurry. He seemed content to just hold her and touch her hair. Again the girl imitated his behavior, running her fingers now through his thick, coarse hair.

Timothy lifted her chin. "Look at me, Jo."

She seemed to be floating. He kissed her and his fingers now were tight in her hair, holding her against him. He stared at her then and whispered her name. His fingers loosened and Joanna leaned away, but smiled. She stood, folded his suit jacket and shirt, then set them neatly on the trunk. With her back to him, she undid the buttons of her dress and laid it, too, across the trunk.

The bed was against the wall. She slid to the inside of it and pulled the thin quilt over her. As she waited, lying still, staring up at the rafters, she thought of how he had kissed her there in the kitchen the day of the mine fire. He held her face then, too. He had kissed her mouth, her eyes. . . .

He lay down beside her on the narrow bed, found her hand, and squeezed it. And all the sounds of the house— the wind on the windows and in the stovepipe, Mrs. Flynn shifting in her bed below, even the footsteps of Nat and Mary next door—were familiar and more comforting now with Timothy beside her. It felt good. It felt right.

Joanna turned to him.

After, when Timothy had fallen asleep, Joanna lay with her head on his chest as she had once imagined Rosie had done. She stared in the dark at her grandmother's bowl on the bureau. It was hers now and it felt good. It felt right.

(i)

Joanna was taking the clothes off the line that hung low in the yard and was folding them into the basket when she saw the wagon. She did not call to Mrs. Flynn, but stood where she was and watched as Timothy brought the old mule to a stop before the gate. In the seat beside him was Kathleen Boyle and in the back, her brother. Even before the wagon had stopped completely, Marty Boyle jumped down, reached for his bag, and pushed through the gate. Kathleen took Timothy's hand as she stepped down from the wagon onto the uneven boardwalk. She then put her hand to her throat, holding her cape as she surveyed the row houses. From where Joanna stood, she could not tell Kathleen's impression.

"You must be the new wife," Marty Boyle said. He had tossed his bag onto the porch stoop and turned to look at Joanna. "We just found out about you." He came through the yard then to kiss her cheek. "I suppose I'm not the first to kiss the bride." He winked mischievously.

All week she had worried about how Timothy would tell them, but she was unprepared for Marty's boldness. Startled, Joanna stepped back. He was shorter and much more stocky than Timothy. His red hair reminded her at once of Rosie, or at least how Joanna imagined her. Joanna lifted the laundry basket to her hip so that it was between them, then extended her hand and said what she had practiced all week in the attic room alone. "I'm Joanna Flynn. I want to welcome you to our home, Mr. Boyle."

"No, no," he said. "Marty. I'm Marty, not Mr. Boyle. You talk to me as if I were some sort of mine boss. Is that how you cowtail to the mine bosses here?" He took her hand then and shook it. "You're a lot younger than Rosie."

"I'm seventeen." He could not be more than nineteen himself.

Marty turned to take in the row houses, the coal banks, and the breaker, still charred from the fire. "So this is home. Well, it's not much to look at."

"Here's Joanna," Timothy said as he followed Kathleen into the yard.

Her bonnet shaded her face so that again Joanna could not be certain if the woman was pleased or disappointed by what she saw. Just as she had a moment earlier with Marty, Joanna extended her hand and repeated her little speech. "Welcome to our home, Miss Boyle." It sounded so formal, she now realized, and somewhat cold. But Kathleen came forward, put her hands on Joanna's shoulders, and kissed her cheek—but softly.

"We are all family now," she said with a smile. "You must call me Kathleen." She turned to her brother. "Take the basket, Marty." She looped her arm through Joanna's and led her to the porch steps, as if Joanna were the newcomer and not she.

In the kitchen, Kathleen hugged Mrs. Flynn and the old woman cried. "I thought I'd never see this day," she said as she wiped her eyes.

"Nor I," Marty said. "It was a slow boat and not much to do."

"Except gamble at cards," Kathleen said with distaste.

"I've a talent for it," Marty said and winked this time at Mrs. Flynn, who delighted in it.

She waved him closer, and then held his face between her hands and kissed him twice again. "And aren't you a fine looking man." She smoothed his coppery hair.

"What did you expect?"

"A boy. Why just a boy. The very one I remember chasing the landlord's chickens."

"Well, now." He straightened. "I never did stop doing that."

Timothy, too, stood near the old woman's chair. Forgotten for the moment, Joanna waited by the door, feeling once more like the girl hired to keep house.

Later that evening when the dishes had been washed and set on the shelf, they sat at the table and talked of home. Every few moments, the old woman leaned forward to interrupt with her opinion of a person or to ask for a relative. These were names that Joanna had not heard the old woman speak of before. More than once she reached to squeeze Kathleen's hand and say, "Aren't you a sight for my poor eyes."

"When we were growing up, Timothy and I were like sister and brother," Kathleen explained to Joanna.

"You fluttered about him like a mother hen," Mrs. Flynn said.

"We had our little secrets, too," Timothy said and Kathleen nodded.

She was three years older than Timothy, with the same dark hair, which she wore in a knob. She was short like her brother, and although she was plump, her dark eyes and her face were pretty. Joanna wondered at once about the secrets they shared.

"What a shame it is you never married, Kathleen," the old woman said. "But there's hope for you yet. I never married until I was twenty-nine, though I had more than one man following my skirts." It was a boast Joanna had heard so often she no longer paid attention. She watched the old woman squeeze Kathleen's hand again. "There's a few good men in this patch, that is if you can see beneath the coal dirt. Your poor uncle, God have mercy on his soul, could never get his hands clean."

Without meaning to, Joanna looked at Timothy's hands on the table. Although he had not been below in weeks, the coal dirt was still creased in his palms and knuckles. She had not noticed before.

"This mining business has no appeal for me, I don't mind telling you that right off," Marty said. Restless, he moved from his chair to the cupboard, peered out of the window, then sat down again. Timothy had set out the whiskey bottle for this family reunion and now Marty poured himself another shot.

"If it weren't for the mine fire, I might have had a job lined up for you right away. Now, I don't know." Timothy, too, reached for the bottle again. "There are experienced men they haven't called back yet."

"That Welshie was never one to be trusted," Mrs. Flynn said.

"Welshie? Marty asked.

"The foreman," Mrs. Flynn said. "Joe Sweeney and Charlie Boy Duffy were called back last week, but not our Timothy."

Although Timothy had not worn the sling for over a week, Joanna knew how his arm ached in the mornings. He had difficulty raising his arm over his head, but when she offered to give him the hot liniment treatment, he made light of the pain. When he was not called back to work, he blamed it on his bum arm. Mrs. Flynn had other ideas.

"When your uncle died, there was some question." The old woman leaned forward as if about to reveal a secret. "It wasn't marked. The chamber he was working wasn't

marked but they let him go in after the extra bit of coal."
She looked from Kathleen's face to Marty's. "Robbing the
pillars. That's what they want the men to do and they
don't care what may happen to the men should the pillar
collapse."

"Robbing the pillars?" Marty looked to Timothy.
He signed. The old woman had begun the story and
reluctantly he explained. "There are columns of rock that
support the gangways and chambers. But there is coal in
these pillars, too, and in time it's picked away until the pillars themselves are no good. One day a blast in another
room or gangway. . . " He set his pipe down. "It's a risk
we all take."

"It was more than a risk," the old woman said.
"Welshie as good as pushed those rocks down on him.
And then coming here and telling us it was gas and a hole
in the lantern that caused the explosion."

The room was silent. Timothy did not argue with her
now. The chamber his father was working that morning
had already given up its share of anthracite. Its pillars were
weakened so that the blast he'd set had caved in the roof,
trapping him. But there should have been time for him to
clear the area. Unless there was gas in the chamber and the
lantern had exploded first.

"It took them over an hour to dig him out." Mrs. Flynn
stared at her hands on the table. "I got to believe he was
alive for part of that time."

"Don't think about it," Joanna said. Kathleen put her
arm around the old woman to comfort her.

"I heard him calling my name. As clear as a bell. Right
here I was in this kitchen. Where else would I be?"

Joanna closed her eyes. The story brought back all of the
fear and pain of that morning of the fire just two months
ago when she had not known if Timothy were alive or
dead.

The glass of whiskey had held Marty to the table, but

now that it was empty, he stood again and paced. "No, I don't think this mining is for me. Oh, it's not that I'm afraid of going down to rob the pillars," he said hotly.

"Marty, sit down," Kathleen said.

"It's just that I'm thinking, why leave one landlord to work for another?"

Joanna saw Timothy frown.

"The landlords left us precious little, Tim. It's only gotten worse since you left, not better. We don't even have a say in running our own country."

"It's not the same here," Timothy said quietly.

"Why, they're robbed our pillars over there, too. Years and years of stealing this bit of land and that, giving us no more than a penny to warm our pockets." Marty leaned on the table and looked into Timothy's face. "It was our land. They took it."

Timothy bit his pipe stem. "You've got to put it behind you now, Marty. It is no longer your fight. This can be a new start for you here."

But Marty went on, as if Timothy had not spoken at all. "I was too keen for them. I fished the salmon right out of their streams and they never caught me."

"There's nothing wrong with fighting for what is yours," Mrs. Flynn said.

Marty grinned at what he took to be her approval. "At night, I cut the fences and sure, I set a fire or two. And then there was that business of the guns. We broke in and stole them and buried them in a place they still don't know about."

So Marty Boyle was a thief. Joanna stared at this stranger in the house. His arrogance made her uneasy. "What would you want with guns?" she asked.

"When the time is right, we'll dig them up and pass them about to our people and they'll use them."

"Not you, Marty," Kathleen said. "You're out of it now."

He sat on the chair again, rocked back to balance it on two legs. "We'll be a nation again, when the time is right."

"You'll have no need for guns here," Timothy said. "Just a pick and shovel."

Marty grinned. "Don't count on me, Tim. Oh, I'll pay my way, but it may not be picking coal for some mine boss."

Joanna had heard enough. She wanted only to go upstairs, to be alone with her husband. As if sensing her fatigue, Timothy reached across the table to pat her hand. But when he stood, he did not turn for the attic door. He stretched, grimacing a little as he tried to straighten his bad arm. Kathleen reached for the teapot.

"I'll fix the tea," Joanna said, standing now, too.

"I don't mind," Kathleen said. "I want to be of help."

Mrs. Flynn rocked far back in her chair so that the toes of her unlaced boots lifted a bit off the floor. The tongues of the shoes flapped forward as if exhausted. The old woman shook her head and smiled once more. "I never thought I'd see the day when Kathleen and Marty would be right here with us."

Timothy knocked his pipe into the coal grate, then began again to fill the bowl with tobacco. "What of our cousin Michael?" he asked Kathleen. "Is he still well?"

Reluctantly, Joanna sat down again. This night she would not go up alone. She wanted them all to see that she was not just the girl Timothy had hired to keep house. She watched as Kathleen filled the pot and set it on the table before Timothy. They were cousins, yes, but she felt jealous of their shared past.

Marty, too, had tired of the conversation in the kitchen. He pushed his chair back and went to the door. "I'm going to poke around a little and see what goes on in this dirty coal patch."

(i i)

The superintendent did not look at Timothy, but at the papers on his desk. "Yes, we have rehired some men."

"If it's the arm," Timothy said, "it's healing."

Again this morning he had gone without the sling. He stood before the superintendent's desk with his hands in his pockets so as not to call attention to the crook in his arm.

"We're not taking everyone back," the superintendent said. "It's May, and the truth is, Tim, the demand's down. The market prices in New York are low. Come August, it'll pick up again. You know that as well as any man."

"I can't wait until then," he said sharply. "I need to support my family."

Across the room, Welshie turned away from the dirty window through which he had been staring. He slouched in the low-ceilinged office, his head thrust forward. The red moustache that hung over the corners of his mouth gave the impression that he was scowling. "Your family's grown," Welshie said. "It was a mistake for you to bring that boy over here when there was no work for him."

"Marty? Marty has nothing to do with this."

"He's trouble," Welshie said. "A boy who talks big gets himself into trouble no matter where he goes. I turned him down, too. Yesterday."

"Marty asked you for a job?" It clearly surprised Timothy that despite the boy's protestations he had applied for work with the company after all.

"It seems that young cousin of yours has been telling stories," the superintendent said. "Guns and fights and home rule. We don't want that sort of rebellion here."

The day Joe Sweeney had brought that mining journal into the tunnels was, in a very small way, a rebellion. Occasionally in the Mountain View they heard rumors of unionizing efforts in the larger coal towns along the mountain ridge, but no such efforts had been started in the patch. Although miners' wages were not fixed, but determined by the New York and Philadelphia market prices, and although they often worked beyond the mandated eight-hour shifts, Timothy had no desire to rebel or strike against the company. He needed work, anyway he could get it. He looked up. "What of the inspector's job?"

The superintendent and Welshie exchanged looks. Then the superintendent closed his ledger. "We're not hiring a mine inspector now."

"After the Shenandoah accident, an inspector was hired."

"Mining on the southern ridge is not the same as here," the superintendent said. "The tunnels are deeper, there's more pressure, more gas."

"I know about the ruling. I know it's a law."

"The law is always open to interpretation. In a few more years when our operations expand and our tunnels go deeper, then perhaps the profits will allow for inspections."

Timothy smiled. Money he understood. "The fire cost you plenty of money in lost shipments. Isn't that so? If you had an inspector on duty, maybe that fire could have been prevented. And other accidents, as well."

"Like the one that killed your pa?" Welshie said.

"There'd be less accidents if more propping were done," Timothy said. "Or if the pillars weren't picked clean."

"That chamber was safe. I checked it myself. It was his error, not mine. His lantern."

"I've got no grudge against you, Welshie."

"And I've got no use for a mine inspector following me around."

Timothy looked to the superintendent. "I know the operations here as well as any man, Welshie included. I want that inspector job."

The superintendent removed his pince-nez and rubbed his eyes. "I can't use you below, Tim. Not now. Come back in August when your arm is properly healed, when the demand is up. By then the owners will have made their decision on the inspector's position."

"Dangerous work," Welshie said. "Down there alone, sniffing gas, poking the soft pockets in the roofs."

"All mining's dangerous. I guess I know that by now. But a man's got to eat."

Welshie nodded towards the window. "There are nearly twenty men just like you waiting out there and each one's got to eat."

Timothy leaned on the superintendent's desk. Most of those men outside were foreigners who had come from Italy only a few months ago and whose English was still very poor. Timothy said, "I've done more years below in the dark than any one of them. I know the tunnels. I carved out my share of them. I know where the gas is. I'm your best man, and when the demand does go up, you're going to need me."

"You might do to oversee the boys in the breaker," Welshie offered.

Timothy straightened. "I want the inspector's job and I'll be coming again tomorrow to ask you for it and the day after that and the day after that if I have to."

He took his cap from his pocket and pulled it down to shade his eyes. He nodded to both men, then left.

Outside, tacked to the door was a sign that read, "A fair day's wage for a fair day's work."

(iii)

From a patch of woods behind the company store, where the swirled iridescent silt dam choked the white bir-ches, the jeers and oaths of more than two dozen men rose and fell like a stormy wind. The men crowded around a chalked circle, in the center of which a gamecock flapped its bloody feathers, screeched, and reared. On their haun-ches, the men hooted and imitated the bird's cries. Welshie's gamecock was down, out of the rink, but still twitching in the dust. Neither the excited cries nor the heavy wagers could arouse it again, but before the pitter, a miner from downriver, could declare Welshie's bird dead, Marty Boyle scooped his own screaming bird into his arms and strutted about with it above his head. Now a new gust of shouts went up as the men shoved and protested.

With his back to the noise, Joe Sweeney stooped and counted a fistful of money. When he turned to pay the winnings, Welshie called out, "Hold on, Joe. That money is mine now."

"The hell it is!" Marty laughed. "The game is over and I won it."

"You forfeit, Mick."

"Forfeit?" Marty stopped his parading to face the mine foreman. "What are you saying forfeit? Your bird's a goner. Use your eyes. I won it."

"You don't know the rules, Mick, for if you did you'd know I'm right." Welshie grinned. "Ask the pitter. Ask anyone here. You can't remove either bird 'til one's declared dead."

"Well, I can and I did."

"Then you're as dumb as your cock," Welshie laughed and the others laughed with him.

Marty slung his bird aside and as he grabbed for Welshie's shoulder, the other miners backed away, leaving just the two of them in the bloodied circle. "I'll teach you rules," the boy said.

Welshie was taller and broader than Marty and he continued to smile condescendingly at him. "It's plenty of thirsty men here wanting their fair share of the pot," he said. He snapped some bills from Joe Sweeney's hand and fanned them in Marty's face. "Now, I've a queer feeling that they'll be snorting mad if we don't give them what is rightly theirs."

"He's right, Marty boy," Joe Sweeney said and handed

the money to the pitter. "You lost it, boy, though it should've been yours."

Marty looked around at the faces leering at him. Joe slapped him on the back. "Com'on now. We'll go have us a drink."

As they started up the hill towards the train tracks, Welshie called out, "Someone buy the dumb Mick a drink on me."

Marty stopped and spit. "I wouldn't take your black money."

Welshie grinned. "Ah, now. That's a shame, boy, for I've just taken yours."

As the pitter counted out the winnings, Welshie tossed his dying bird into the swamp.

(i v)

In April Joanna had turned over a small square of rocky soil in the yard, but by late May the garden she had bragged about to Mrs. Flynn had spread to the back of the fence. She was planting a circle, green-leafed and lacy, around herself, and each morning she left Kathleen with Mrs. Flynn in the kitchen and went out to weed and water and prune.

Occasionally Timothy was there, but not to help her with the planting. He took the sledge hammer, and swinging it overhead, struck the old tree stump. Each time the blow was hindered somewhat by the arm that had been broken in the mine explosion in March. Because it had not been properly set, the company doctor said Timothy would never regain full use of it. Timothy would not accept that. He lifted the hammer to his shoulder again and brought it down against the tree stump. No matter how many times he swung and struck, it was never with the strength he once had, the strength he needed to be able to pick and load each day the tons of coal by which his wages were computed. Joanna set aside her shovel and went to him, as she had before on other mornings.

"Not again, Tim. Please." She put her hands over the handle.

The front of his shirt was wet from sweating. "It's alright, Jo. You've got to expect a little pain if I am to get it back in shape." He pulled the hammer away. "Step back."

She did not move. "Maybe you should go back to that company doctor."

He wiped the sweat from his forehead. "Jo, move out of my way." His voice was sharp.

"I was thinking, Tim. What if we went west, like you said once. We could do that."

"No."

"But why not? We could leave the house to Marty and Kathleen if they didn't want to come with us."

"It takes money, Jo. More money than I have."

The last two months without work had forced them, as well as other families, into debt at the company store, but the girl knew that Mrs. Flynn had some money of her own, not in the deep apron pockets, but hidden in the ticking of her pillow. There was also her father. All the silver dollars Mrs. Flynn had given him last winter were, in a way, Joanna's.

She said, "I could get some money from my father. Not so much, but maybe enough to go away from here. And we can send it back after you have found work. Let me ask my father, Tim."

This only angered him more. "I'm not asking anyone for a loan."

"But if we went west, there would be the railroad to work for and you'd never have to go down in the mines again. After a while, we could buy a real piece of land to farm."

"I'm no farmer, Jo. I've told you that. And I can't be taking anyone's money, be it a loan or not." He stood up. "I guess I can support my own family."

"It's me, isn't it? You're angry with me."

He sighed impatiently and eased the hammer down again. "It's not you I'm mad at. Why would it be you, Jo?"

She reached up to smooth his hair out of his eyes. "I want us to be happy."

"I need to work, Jo. That's all there is to it."

"You sound just like Marty," she said, angry now herself. "Carrying on about how he doesn't need anybody's help."

Along the back fence the wild violets and johnny-jumpups she had transplanted from the woods were in bloom. The mining patch had no name. She lived in a place that had no name and no importance other than the coal underground. She did not belong here. She was as transplanted as the wildflowers in the garden.

"Do you miss the farm that much, Jo?"

When she didn't answer, he swung the sledge hammer. It hit the tree stump with a dull thud.

She crossed her arms in front of her. Of course, she missed the farm. She missed the color of it, the live sounds of birds and wind. Here there was just the constant rumble of the breakers crushing coal and sending it down the chutes to empty into the railroad cars. At the farm, she was the oldest of the five children and she missed that, too. In the Flynn house she still felt like a girl, not a woman. Her marriage had not changed that at all. Perhaps what she missed most was not being the one to fix Timothy's tea after dinner, or to comb and braid the old woman's hair. Kathleen did those small things now.

A few days ago as they sat in the kitchen talking—as always of Ireland—Mrs. Flynn had said she was longing for the treacle soda bread she had eaten as a girl. Joanna remembered the Fastnachts she and Margaret and her mother had made, warm squares of cake rolled in sugar. But Mrs. Flynn had a taste for treacle. Soda bread was easy enough, Joanna thought, and so the next morning while Kathleen was visiting Nat and Mary, Joanna started the mixture, adding the raisins and black molasses just like the old woman had described. But it failed. The mixture was too stiff and brittle.

"You can't be making treacle here in this place anyway," Mrs. Flynn had scolded her.

"It's just soda bread with molasses." Certainly the German candies her mother made were more difficult, more delicious.

"We've no decent oven here. In Ireland we had turf sod on top so as to give heat all-around. It's the only way to cook treacle."

"Sod? You'd cook with sod?" Joanna voice was a little sharp, remembering clearly the disappointing Christmas cake she had baked to surprise Timothy. Why she had even begun this project now was beyond her. She tossed her dish towel on the table and sat down. Mrs. Flynn and Joanna stared at each other across the table.

"It wouldn't taste right anyway," the old woman said bitterly. "Baked with coal."

At that moment Kathleen had come in. As Joanna watched, she added more milk and melted butter until the mixture was the right consistency. Then with floured hands, she flattened the dough into a circle, placed it on a baking pan, and cut a large cross into the top with the knife.

Even though it had been baked on a bed of glowing anthracite, Mrs. Flynn licked her fingers. Joanna had taken only a small corner. Yes, the Fastnachts were more delicious.

Again Timothy swung the hammer and grunted. Joanna turned away from him. Charlie Boy's goat was wandering freely, as it often did, feeding on the weeds that fringed the culm banks. As she turned, she saw the goat poke its bearded head through a space where a picket was missing in the fence, stretching for the wild violets.

Joanna clapped her hands. "Get out!" she shouted and started for the fence. The goat lifted its head, tearing away the leaves of the plant. Joanna picked up a dirt clod and flung it at the animal. Its hind legs pushed back, but its head was stuck. "Get out," she shouted again and threw a second ball of wet dirt at it.

Timothy freed the goat. There were tears in Joanna's eyes as she knelt over her damaged flowerbed. "Dirty thing," she spoke to herself. "Charlie Boy ought to keep it tied or not keep it at all." She patted the dirt around the plants firmly.

Timothy reached for her. "There's no harm done, Joanna. It's just a few flowers."

"I'm trying to make this place look halfway decent," she said then. "And what have you done all morning except beat an old tree stump?"

He began to laugh.

Joanna glared at him.

"I'm sorry, Jo." He lifted her to her feet. "You really clobbered the old goat."

She looked beyond the fence to where the goat was staring dumbly. A glob of mud was on its nose between its eyes. She smiled. "I guess it was funny."

"You've got a better aim and swing than I do now."

"He'll only come back again," she said. "He always does."

Timothy put his arm over her shoulder and led her up the yard. "I'll mend your fence for you." He leaned over for the sledge hammer again.

"Tim . . ."

"I'm putting it away now."

"Why is it so important that we stay here? That you go back down in the mines?"

He was quiet a moment. "It's what I know."

"You can learn some other way."

He looked at her. "We've both got to learn, I suppose. Don't we?"

Something Mrs. Flynn had said weeks ago came back to her then. She said that Timothy would not be going far from this place, despite his dreams. It suddenly occurred to Joanna that the reason he would not leave the patch had nothing at all to do with money or mining coal. Could it be Rosie and the child, buried in the field behind the Mountain View, who were holding him here?

"Give it time, Jo," he was saying now, but his voice seemed far away. "It'll get better. Once they call me back and I can earn my way, things will be better."

On Decoration Day, Kathleen stayed home with Mrs. Flynn while the others went down the mountain to Butler for the parade and a picnic. Marty Boyle sat in the back of Joe Swanson's wagon and entertained Helen with his interests.

There was a young maid named Cassy
Who thought of herself as classy
She returned to town
Seeking pearls and a gown
But fell on hard times and turned harassy

"Harassy?" Helen twisted a curl of her auburn hair around her forefinger. "And just what do you mean by harassy?"

Marty grinned. "That's just say the poor girl never did get her pearls."

"So what did she get?" Helen raised him; Joanna did not care much for Marty Boyle. She thought him vulgar and proud. Helen, however, had not ceased smiling since he had arrived in the patch two weeks ago. He sat across from the girls with his legs extended and his arms across the back board of the wagon.

(i)

On Decoration Day, Kathleen stayed home with Mrs. Flynn while the others went down the mountain to Butler for the parade and a picnic. Marty Boyle sat in the back of Joe Sweeney's wagon and entertained Helen with his limericks.

> *There was a young maid named Cassy*
> *Who thought of herself as classy*
> *She ventured to town*
> *Seeking pearls and a gown*
> *But fell on hard times and turned brassy.*

"Brassy?" Helen twisted a curl of her auburn hair around her forefinger. "And just what do you mean by brassy?"

Marty grinned. "Let's just say the poor girl never did get her pearls."

"So what did she get?" Helen teased him. Joanna did not care much for Marty Boyle. She thought him vulgar and proud. Helen, however, had not ceased smiling since he had arrived in the patch two weeks ago. He sat across from the girls with his legs extended and his arms across the back board of the wagon.

"Brassy like Mrs. Barton?" Helen said, not letting it go.
"Mrs. Barton?"

From the front of the wagon, Joe gave a hoot. "She has no pearls or gown, boy, that's for sure.

"Joanna was kneeling behind Timothy, holding onto his shoulders as the wagon skirted a pond in a clearing. "She takes in wash," she said over her shoulder.

Helen leaned forward to whisper, "And just about anything else."

The boy said, "So she's fallen on hard times, too, the poor lady, having to take in wash."

"The harder the better," Joe said.

"Joe!" Joanna cried. Timothy was laughing, too. She locked her arms around his neck and whispered, "This will be fun, Tim. I haven't been on a picnic in a whole year. And I've never once seen a city parade."

"When was the last time you two girls of the patch ventured to town?" Marty asked.

"Two years ago for the parade," Helen said. "We were all together then. Remember, Tim?"

Joanna was riding with her face turned to the wind and her eyes closed, enjoying the air. Now she glanced over her shoulder at Helen, who looked up at her apologetically. Two years ago it was Rosie in the wagon, not Joanna. Helen turned to Marty again and said more brightly, "I had my fortune read by a gypsy. I happen to be good at telling prophecies myself. I knew Joanna would marry Tim."

It was no use, Joanna thought. Despite Helen's silly chatter, Rosie had somehow been summoned into the wagon with them. This picnic, too, was something Timothy had done with Rosie first. Joanna sat back on the floor of the wagon. "Helen's real gift is for gossiping," she said.

"Joanna has never been to Butler," Helen said.
"Oh?"

Joanna said, with an air, "I'm not from the patch."

"None of us are from the patch," Helen said. "The question is, which one of us will leave?"

(i i)

Butler was a checkerboard of dark houses and intersecting paved streets. Two- and three-story brick buildings, more than Joanna had ever seen, lined Broad Street and red, white, and blue bunting hung over the roofs of the storefronts. The wagon moved slowly along the crowded street. Joe turned at the brewery, hoping to hitch his mule and buckboard there for free. The man sitting on the barrel in front of the stables eyed them critically. He chewed, then spat in the dust. Already the faint sounds of the parade drums could be heard, and the girls moaned impatiently. Reluctantly Joe pulled the requested twenty-five-cent piece from his breast pocket, squinted at it to be sure, but before he could hand it over, Marty had flipped his own quarter to the stableman. "Save your money, Joe, for a souvenir."

They stood together under the striped awning of a millinery shop on Broad Street to watch the parade. First came the somber Blue and Grey of the Grand Army of the Republic, and then the clergy, the bands, and the bonneted Daughters of the American Revolution. Prancing fire horses pulled the water tank, and last came the thick-hoofed brewery horses. As they passed, Marty Boyle, who had lit up the cigar he had bought at a corner smokeshop, gestured at the rump of one of the slow moving animals as if he meant to prod it with the burning tip. Timothy put a restraining hand on the boy's shoulder, but both he and Joe were smiling. Marty had treated them both to cigars as well, and Joanna wondered where the coins were coming from.

They followed the parade up the hill to the cemetery and

there under the deep shade of maples and elms, school children recited Christian verses while the younger children chased each other around the stone markers. The ladies held onto men's arms, and seeing this, Joanna reached for Timothy.

With the services over, the crowd dispersed. Helen went ahead, stopping Marty and Joe at each storefront to browse over the displays. It was not the shop windows that attracted Joanna, however, but the large, pillared homes along the avenue. As she and Timothy walked slowly, she admired the long shuttered windows, the heavy wooden doors, and the sweeping porches shaded by trellised wisteria. When the front door of one such home opened and a lady in taffeta stepped out, Joanna stopped. The women held a parasol in her gloved hand as she led a little girl down the brick walk to the waiting carriage. The two chestnut horses, more glossy than any in the parade and certainly more handsome than any of the company mules, turned onto Broad Street away from the cemetery and the wandering throngs of people.

"Where do you think they're going?" she asked Timothy.

"To eat, no doubt. I'm hungry, too, Joanna. Let's find Joe and the wagon."

"Who are these people?" she said, more to herself than to Timothy. Wistfully she gazed at the house, holding onto the spoked, iron fence, imagining what it must be like inside, the heavy draperies, the brass and iron beds, the polished wooden floor and stone fireplaces. "Wouldn't you love to peek inside? If Helen were here, I bet she would."

Timothy, too, was staring at the house with its peaked slate roof and wide chimneys, but he was frowning.

"Tim," she said. "What is it?"

"I can't give it to you, Jo. Not now. Maybe never."

"Give me what?"

"Fine things like this. They're the owners, Jo. Of coal mines, and railroads, and breweries. They're the owners and we aren't." He looked at her with a sad smile. "We never will be."

"Don't talk like that."

"It's true what Marty says. It's not much better here. It's under some landlord's thumb we are still. We will always be under someone's thumb."

Again Joanna looked across the trim lawn, but somehow it seemed changed now, as if a cloud had darkened the day. The iron fence was cold and high. She withdrew her bare hand. She had married a poor man, and that was what he had tried to tell her in the garden a few days ago and what he was trying to tell her now. At that moment, she was ashamed of their shanty of a house with its thin gingham curtains and oilcloth and tar-paper roof. For that one moment, she believed that she would live and die in the mining patch just as Rosie had lived and died. She turned away from the house and from Timothy.

"Joanna."

She began to walk faster.

"Joanna."

Fine things, fine things, she thought with each quick step. How did he know what fine things she wanted? She had never asked him for anything.

He took her hand and made her stop. "Joanna."

"You sound as if we don't deserve anything more than what we've already got."

"Oh, for sure you deserve more. It's just that I'm not the one to give it to you." He almost sounded resentful, as if he had made a mistake in marrying her.

"I don't want things," she said. Their own home is what she wanted, a place near hemlocks and mountain laurels, where she could breathe, where they could raise a child. She wanted a place where Kathleen did not hurry to wash each dish or where Mrs. Flynn would not ask where

she was going each time Joanna stepped outside. She
wanted a house that had not been Rosie's first. And she
wondered why he did not want those things, too.

"I didn't mean to hurt your feelings." He raised her bare
fingers to his mouth and kissed them, a gesture that or-
dinarily made her catch her breath. Today, however, she
slipped her hand from his.

"I never said I wanted anything fancy. Not once."

"I know it. I'm sorry."

They began to walk again, more slowly. They passed
the shops in silence, not bothering to look in the windows.
Then he said, more brightly, "Who knows? If the right
opportunity comes, that inspector's job for example, then
maybe we can move to a larger house with enough rooms
for everyone to sit alone when they wanted to. Maybe I
could even build it. I'm not so bad with a hammer."

"Maybe someday you'll be the superintendent." She
had meant it sarcastically but Timothy laughed out loud
and tucked her arm into his.

"And wouldn't that be fine? I'd wear a tweed suit with a
vest pulling at the buttons over my fat belly and little
glasses to pinch my nose."

At this description of the superintendent, Joanna
couldn't help herself. She laughed then, too.

(iii)

They picnicked on a grassy hill above a pond where
people were boating. They sat in the sun and ate hard-
boiled eggs, pickles, and cheese. Across the way were the
railroad tracks and the warehouses and factories of Butler.

"Now there's a place for you," Timothy told Marty and
pointed. "The silk mill. Though it's mostly women and
girls who weave and fill, they might be needing a strong
foreman."

Marty nodded. "It takes a strong man indeed to handle
women."

"A job, Marty," Helen laughed. "A job."

"It's adventure I'm wanting," the boy said. "I don't want to hole up in a coal mine or a factory either."

"Look at what I've got," Joe Sweeney said, climbing the hill towards them. He was wearing a pair of thin, wire-rimmed spectacles. He had carefully placed them on the bridge of his nose. "It's my souvenir," he told Marty and smiled.

Marty said, "You look smart, Joe."

"And how much did you spend on them?" Helen asked.

"A quarter. The very one I was about to give up at the brewery."

"And can you see any better?" Marty asked.

"No," he answered honestly.

"Ask him about the singing canary he bought from Charlie Boy," Helen said to Marty.

"Oh, brother," Joe said, lying back in the grass. He shaded his face with his cap. "I don't need a wife. I've got Helen to nag me."

"How about we take a dip?" Marty asked.

"It's too cold," Helen laughed.

But he was already unlacing his boots. "Give me a hand, Helen," he said and lifted his foot so she would tug off his shoe. He rolled down his cotton socks and rolled up his pant legs, then ran down into the water. "Well?" he shouted, turning to them. "What are you waiting for? Come and wash the winter off your feet."

Helen removed her boots then, too. As she stepped into the lake, she cried out from the cold. She hiked her skirt to her knees and splashed him.

Joanna sat on the hill with her arms about her knees, smiling at the way Marty and Helen were playing. Timothy put his hand on her neck. "You want to go in, don't you?"

"Not without you."

"But I can't swim."

"You can't?" She laughed.

And then Helen screamed. She slipped on the mossy rock bottom. Her arms flailed the air as Marty caught her. She held onto him, laughing at her own clumsiness. And Joanna thought, she did that on purpose.

With Marty's help, Helen stepped back onto the bank. Her feet were red and numb and her skirt, soaked to her knees. She sat in the sun and let Marty squeeze the water from her skirt. Then he rubbed her bare feet to warm them. It was almost an intimate gesture and Joanna looked away.

"I could teach you," Joanna said.

"Teach me what?"

"How to swim."

Timothy smiled. "Where? In the silt dam? No, thank you."

"In the river at the farm, where I learned and where I taught Margaret and every one of my brothers."

"It'd be no easy task teaching me at my age."

"Why do you always think you're so old?"

He shrugged.

Joanna continued. "We could go there one day. Just the two of us. Alone. Borrow Joe's wagon."

He shook his head. "They'll be calling me back to work soon, Jo. I know it."

She put her fingers over his lips. "Just say you'll go there with me one day."

"I guess it's too late for me now to be the superintendent," he said, then nodded to where Joe Sweeney was still splashing in the stream. "Joe's got the glasses."

"And the belly," she said and Timothy laughed again.

In late afternoon, they walked back along the tracks to the brewery stables. The streets of Butler were not so crowded now. As the two girls waited for Joe and Marty to hitch the wagon, Helen whispered, "He's wonderful, isn't he?"

"Who?"

"Really, Joanna, don't you see how different he is? He

has more life in him than any of those mulish men in our town."

Joanna took her friend's hand. "Shall I read your fortune now, Helen Sweeney?"

"You can laugh at me, Joanna, but I do believe in fate. Marty Boyle is the one who will take me away from this place. I can just feel it!" Helen hugged her arms, her face flushed, happy and alive herself.

When the wagon came around, Joanna asked to sit up front.

"But you can sleep in the back," Timothy said. "It's a long ride and it'll be dark before we get back."

She shook her head. "I want to sit with you."

"We're all in the same wagon," Joe said.

Still, Joanna lifted her skirt and stepped up to sit beside Timothy. "I'm not sleepy," she said, smiling as she felt Timothy's shoulder against hers. As they left town, Helen and Marty Boyle were singing in the back of the wagon.

(i v)

During the last week in June, Timothy was given the inspector's job. He came into the house just after noon, beaming with pride. "I've got good news for all the ladies in my life," he announced grandly. With his arm around Joanna's shoulder, he told them the inspector's job was his at last. "It was always mine," he said with a laugh. "They just wouldn't admit it until now."

Joanna went cold right through, although Timothy could not have felt her shiver. She knew then that they would never leave the patch. Their opportunity had passed.

Later, he found her in the garden, on her knees, weeding. He knelt beside her. "Be happy for me, Jo."

The girl did not answer. She dug her fingers into the hard soil and twisted at the root of a weed.

"I was burning up inside, Jo. Mad at myself for not being able to work. This will be good for us, Jo. It'll make all the difference."

She could not look at him for as soon as he had spoken, her eyes had filled with tears. "I thought you liked the farm," she said. "The river and all the birds."

"That will always be a special place for us."

She felt his hand soft on her head, and although her hair was pinned up, he passed his hand down over her shoulder and back the way he often did when they were alone in bed. She did not understand. The girl had thought that she would have made all the difference for him, not some mining job. But this was too difficult for her to express. Instead, she said, "You could have waited to tell me first, alone. Not with them in the room."

He smiled. "Is that it then? I'm sorry, Jo. I didn't know it mattered to you. I wasn't thinking."

But, of course, that wasn't it entirely. After he went, leaving her there in the garden, Joanna began again to attack the weeds. Being a miner was that dark side of him she did not understand, the dark side that she thought would not give up Rosie or the child.

The sun was hot on her head. Joanna sat back once more, feeling exhausted. She wiped the perspiration from her forehead. Timothy would go below again, and all she could do was wait in the light at the top of the shaft.

(i)

Summer nights in the attic were hot and still. Only the
night sounds of a dog barking or a child crying came
through the open windows. Before dawn each morning,
Timothy rose from the narrow bed where Joanna lay, her
cotton gown damp against her back. He watched her a
moment, sometimes touching her blonde hair over the pillow. He dressed in the close darkness, then went
downstairs to breakfast alone on a chunk of bread and a
cold boiled egg.

As he walked towards the mine shaft in the early morning, he passed the double dwellings, each with the same
rectangular porch stoop and tar-papered roofs. Each had
an attic room with windows open. There was a pleasant-
ness in such uniformity, such symmetry. One knew his
place and what was expected of him.

Underground, even on the hottest summer nights, the
gangways were wet and cold. Timothy wandered alone
through them, his headlamp following the tracks from one
dripping cavern to another. He walked through the ankle-
deep water to inspect the timbers and the chutes filled with
bits of coal, shiny like coins under the light from his
lantern. The earth sighed as he probed the walls and

chiseled roofs between the beams. Long roots hung like cobwebs from the roofs. Should the earth pop or whistle, or if the air suddenly soured with sulfur, he scratched three chalk lines outside the room and nailed a yellow card through the bark of a supporting timber.

When Timothy came up, the sky was pale yellow. Miners waited, grey and helmeted, as uniform as the rows of company houses. As Timothy emerged, they sat two by two in the cars and went below.

By the time Timothy had climbed the steps to the superintendent's office to make his report, Joanna was already in the garden. The morning-glories she had planted hung over the fence like a braided lavender rug. She picked a flower to wear behind her ear.

The shovel and spade were stored above the rafters of the outhouse, and on this July morning as Joanna pulled the shovel out, a bird's nest fell from the beams. She picked it up. It was as light as paper and empty now. Pine needles and dry oak leaves were woven into it. She picked a bit of down from inside and blew it from her fingertips. This was last spring's nest. She looked up at the rafters from where it had fallen. A clever place, she thought, protected from the rain and the grackles. Standing on the wooden seat, she wedged the nest between the beam and the ceiling again. As she went outside into the sun, she smiled to herself.

Each morning before the day grew hot, Joanna worked her garden, mounding the potatoes and cutting back the roots of the cabbage to prevent the heads from splitting. Everything Joanna knew about planting she had learned from her mother. On the farm, the soil was loose and rich, the color of deep chocolate, but Joanna's garden in the patch was culm grey and hard. Even so, the stalks of corn were as high as the fence now and there were butternut squash and celeriac. On the farm, Joanna had not enjoyed the work, not as much as now. This garden in the patch was hers alone and she was proud when Marty had said one evening at the table, "If nothing else, we'll not go hungry what with Joanna's vegetables."

Joanna stood and rubbed the small of her back, then went to the rain barrel beside the porch to fill her pail. She stared at her dark reflection and wondered if she looked older now than she had five months ago when no man had yet held or kissed her or slept each night with his arm over her stomach. The image of the Italian woman and her little girl climbing up the culm bank came back to her then. How surprised Joanna had been when she looked into the mother's face and realized that the woman was not much older than she. Joanna touched her stomach. It was hard, firmer. She had told no one what she suspected. She was not ill in the morning as she remembered her mother once was, but there were times in the garden when even the morning heat made her dizzy. She dipped both hands into the barrel of tepid water and wet her face and neck.

"Hello!" Timothy called from the yard. Today he carried the full pail of water for her back to the fence where the morning-glories were thriving.

Joanna reached for his hand. "I've something to show you," she said, and led him to the outhouse door. She pointed to the bird's nest in the rafters. "I knocked it down by accident," she said. "Isn't it a funny place for a nest?"

Timothy looked at her and smiled, then plucked the morning-glory bloom, already folded, from behind her ear.

(ii)

Before supper that evening as Timothy came downstairs, his hair combed and his clothes neat, Marty burst through the door. His crusty boots dropped culm as he crossed to the table and set in the center a wad of loose bills and coins as if they were a bouquet of wildflowers he had picked. He pulled a chair out, sat down, and stated with pride, "Now there's something for you." He wiped his sweaty brow on his shirt sleeve and said he was starving.

No one in the room moved. Mrs. Flynn was already seated at her place at the table, but Joanna and Kathleen were at the stove. Joanna's first thought when he had entered was that she would have to sweep the floor after him once more, but when he set so much money on the table, she could not take her eyes from it.

Timothy said, "Where have you been, Marty?"

"What's the matter, Tim? Haven't you ever seen thirty-four dollars before? Go on, count it."

"Thirty-four dollars?" Joanna repeated. "That's one month's salary."

Marty said, "A fair day's wage for a fair day's work. Isn't that what is written on the superintendent's door, Tim? What they really mean is break your back and we'll throw you a few crumbs." He pointed. "Now there's a fair day's wage."

Mrs. Flynn eyed the youth suspiciously. "And is it stolen?"

Marty laughed. He leaned back in his chair and rocked it on two legs. "I don't have to steal money. I've many a bad habit, but I swear by all that's holy, that money there was earned." He looked to his sister. "What's to eat? I'm starving."

"You'll have to clean up before I'll be serving you," Kathleen said.

Timothy stared at him. "Earned how?"

The boy smirked, clearly enjoying this scene. "I've a talent, Tim, and it isn't swinging a pick."

"Where have you been, Marty?"

"Over one coal field to another. Joe loaned me his mule and wagon."

"So gambling money it is," Timothy said.

"Take it, Tim. It's yours. I owe you more than that."

Timothy shook his head. "You owe me nothing."

"You paid for Kathleen's and my passage. And took us into your home, small that it is." He laughed. "I want no charity, Tim. I will pay my way and Kathleen's, too."

"Charity?" Mrs. Flynn cried. "How can you say such a thing? We're your very own family."

Timothy stared hard at him. "I don't want your gambling money. I won't be taking it nor any other thing you get that way."

Marty sat forward. The front legs of the chair came down with a crack. "Cockfighting is legal."

"That money is as good as stolen."

"What are you talking about? It was a fair match by weight."

Timothy grabbed a fistful of the dollars. A loose coin fell to the table and rolled off onto the floor. "Don't you understand? This is miners' money, their wages. They are people no better off than ourselves. I can't be taking this from them."

"Oh." Marty scratched his head, then stood. "The way I see it we can't be worrying about everybody else. If they're dumb enough to wager the little bit they have, then I'd be a fool not to take my own winnings. And you're the bigger fool for letting your bloody conscience keep your family paupers!"

"Marty!" Kathleen cried.

Joanna saw the anger in Timothy's face. His jaw was set hard just like on those afternoons when he had taken the sledge hammer into the yard and beaten the tree stump. His fist clenched the wrinkled bills. "This is my home," he said quietly. "You'll do as I say."

"And what would you have me do? Return it coin by coin to each man who was there? They'd laugh in my face. And then they'd only blow it away on some other game, and you know it."

Timothy did not answer. In the silence, the heat from the stove made Joanna dizzy and she put her arms around her stomach. At last Timothy lowered his hand and let the money go. He took his chair. When he spoke, his voice was steady and firm. "I don't much care what you do with your money," he said, "but get it off my table."

Marty turned to Mrs. Flynn, as if she were the one who should decide. When she said nothing, Marty grabbed the bills and coins and stuffed them into his pocket. Then he walked out.

"Marty?" Kathleen called after him.

"Let him go," Timothy said.

As Joanna stepped out on the porch for the broom and pan, she saw Marty hop the fence and cross to Helen and Joe's house. He opened the door without knocking and went inside.

"He means well," Kathleen was saying as Joanna came back into the kitchen. "He just gets too hot. It's been like this for the last two years. It was breaking Ma's heart."

"He's not about to change," the old woman said. "It's in his blood. My own father was a fighter, too."

Joanna swept the floor, then stooped to pick up the fallen coin. She turned it over in her palm. Thirty-four dollars was more money than she had ever seen before.

"We were afraid he'd be jailed for sure over those guns," Kathleen continued. "He can't seem to keep still or quiet. If it wasn't a boundary dispute or some trespassing charge he was fighting over, it was religion or cards, whatever foolish thing he thought was important at the time."

"Territorial," Mrs. Flynn said, as if trying the word on for size. "Like a dog marking his corner of the yard." The old woman sighed. "He didn't go to jail, he came here. And we'll just have to put up with him."

"For the time being anyway," Timothy said.

Joanna set the coin in the cup on the cupboard shelf and sat down to her place beside Timothy at the table.

"I thought it would be different here," Kathleen said.

She set her knife and fork across her plate, upset by the angry scene between Marty and Timothy.

"Just forget it," Timothy said. "It's over for now."

Kathleen nodded, but still she did not eat. "On board ship, too, he got into a fight with a man who accused him of cheating. The thing is, I believe he does cheat."

"A bad seed," Mrs. Flynn said as she dipped her crust of bread into the gravy in her bowl. "But he is one of our own, one of us, and we'll take care of him."

The money played on Joanna's mind all during supper and afterwards. She remembered too well what Helen had once said, that only money or a man could help you escape from the patch.

(iii)

Marty stood on the slanted porch of the Mountain View, the dollar bills and coins a small bulge in his pocket. The drone of crickets filled the air. It was not yet dark. From the open doors and windows behind him came shouting voices and laughter but he did not want to go back inside. He had left Helen more than an hour ago and now, having won his hand at cards, he was restless for something more. He was still angry, too, for Timothy's words had stung. He had scolded him as if he were a boy.

Across the street, the clerk was just now locking the door of the company store. Farther down the road, in the side yard above the silt dam, Welshie's woman was taking down laundry and folding it into a basket. Marty looked up and down the dirt road at the children playing. Then he stepped off the porch.

Mrs. Barton was bending over her basket as Marty approached. She was thin and her dull brown hair, streaked with grey, was wrapped in a loose knot at the nape of her neck. She glanced sideways at him, then straightened up and waited. The boy stopped just inside the fence and after a moment when he said nothing, she turned and reached again for her sheet lifting on the clothes line in a sudden but slight breeze.

Marty walked towards her, and reached also for the loose ends of the sheet to help her fold it. He grinned. "Welshie's not here," she said dryly. "I know it. Why should I want to look at him when I can look at you?"

She took the last piece off the line, then bent over again to pat the folded pile deeper into the basket. Then she lifted it. "Not tonight," she said and walked towards the house.

Marty followed her to the open door. "Hey," he called and she turned. Her blouse was unbuttoned at the neck. She was sweating. Marty stared at the dampness on her skin. "I've got money," he said.

Mrs. Barton stared at him, then smiled. "You're not one of them. Your neck is clean. And your hands."

Her blouse was loose on her thin shoulders and wet under her arms. Her thin fingers and wrists held the basket in front of her stomach. Marty stared at her middle. On the slight breeze off the silt dam came the odor of stagnant water and the steady pulse of insects. "I can come back later," he said. "When it's dark."

"Don't come back," she said. "Not tonight. Not tomorrow."

Marty looked up at her then. Her face was drawn and tired. On her upper arm was a brown and yellowing bruise the size of a man's fist. "What's this?" he said and touched her arm. "He hits you?"

Mrs. Barton didn't move. She didn't speak.

Behind her, in the room, he saw the foot of the narrow bed, but the blanket Joe had told him about was down. "I've got money if that's what you need." Marty pulled a handful out of his pocket.

"Such clean hands," she said. "You never saw the inside of a coal mine, that's for sure."

She set the basket just inside the door, then pulled a handkerchief from her skirt and wiped the perspiration from her forehead and the back of her neck. Seeing how Marty still stared, she next put it to her throat and wiped the sweat there, moving it down just inside her blouse. And then she laughed at him. "Save your money, Mick. It's too warm to poke around tonight anyway," she said. "I'll let you know when you can come in, but it's not tonight and it won't be tomorrow."

She turned away and closed the door on him.

(i v)

In the woods beyond the culm banks, Joanna wandered alone. Inside the ash bucket she carried were the wild phlox and wood lilies she had dug up to transplant in her garden. Her search for wildflowers lured her farther into the woods than she had gone before. The constant sounds of the pulleys and the shakers did not reach her there. Instead, she followed the sound of running water, sidestepping down the bank through a mound of rhododendron. There in the gully was a creek, the same stream that circled the mining patch and emptied into the silt dam along the railroad tracks below Welshie's house. Here above the mines, however, the stream ran clear. Joanna set her bucket on the bank, then knelt over the water and cupped her hands to drink.

The coal company had not wounded the land this far up. The ground was brown, not black with gritty culm. Across the stream, the trees were thick and tall, and the summer light fell in dim and dusty beams. Mushrooms, Joanna thought. In the autumn there would be mushrooms growing there, she was almost certain of it. The girl laughed at her good fortune in finding this spot, and could not wait until that evening to tell Timothy about this quiet, beautiful place so close, yet so removed from the patch. As she got to her feet, she noticed what at first glance appeared to be a cave. As she stepped nearer, she realized with a sinking feeling, that it was a mine shaft. The entrance was framed with wooden beams and the opening overgrown with vines that hung like a beaded curtain. The twisted vines stirred a little in the cold draft that was coming from inside. As she stood in front of the opening, Joanna felt the draft against her arms and face. She put her hands out to part the green curtain and peered inside.

There were no rail tracks here as there were leading into the mine shaft in town. The space was wide and high. She stepped in. The sunlight from outside fell short of where she stood and only darkness lay ahead. The draft that rose from this darkness was colder now and smelled of dirt. She walked farther into the tunnel. The walls narrowed and the roof pressed closer overhead. Still, she went deeper, bending now a little at the waist. Her fingers felt her way along the damp walls. This was the dark side of Timothy she did not know or understand. This was how it must feel for him each morning when he went below.

She heard sounds like water dripping and she realized that her arms were cold, raised with goosebumps, but she took another step, and still another, inching her foot slowly forward. She could not see and she feared that at any minute the ground might open and swallow her. This was what it was like to be a miner, to leave the sun at the mouth of the shaft and spend all day groping in cold darkness.

There was no mistaking the noises now. It wasn't water she heard, but the irregular beat of picks and chisels against rock. She heard voices, too, not loud, not distinguishable, but rising surely through the darkness before her on the cold draft of air. The murmuring came, then stopped, then rose again. She looked over her shoulder. The daylight at the end of the tunnel seemed too far away, too small for her to have passed through. Her fingers dug into the stone

on either side of her. The chiseled rock wall was real; the
dark and cold were real. But the voices. . . .
    "Annie," he had called, though he was nowhere near
the house. "Annie." He had been buried for over an hour
before they dug him out.
    "As clear as that colliery whistle, I heard him call to
me," Mrs. Flynn had told her.
    The murmuring came again, louder, the buried voices
of miners who had robbed the pillars and lost.
    Joanna put her hands over her ears. Her knuckles
brushed the ceiling and the warm body of a bat just inches
from her head. She squealed and one, two, three bats fluttered down about her face. She screamed and fell to her
knees. The echo of her own cries and those of the bats
ricocheted off the walls. She turned and crawled, stumbling over her skirt, for the light at the top of the shaft.
The bats swooped once, twice, then began to settle again.
Joanna got to her feet and ran, pushing her way through
the tangle of vines into the summer heat.
    That night when they were alone at last in the attic, she
told him what she had done. Instead of comforting her, he
scolded her. "Didn't you realize the danger?"
    She was sitting cross-legged on the bed, with her back
against the wall. In a heap on the floor was the skirt she
had worn. The hem was ripped and dirty. She stared at it,
avoiding Timothy's eyes.
    "Why would you do such a foolish thing?"
    She could not explain why she had gone in the cave. She
thought she had done it for him, to see what it was like for
him, to try and understand why this work was so important for him.
    "What were you doing in the woods by yourself?"
    She remembered the bucket of wildflowers. She had
forgotten them on the creek bank. She looked at him then.
"And who is to go with me? I've been walking by myself
in these woods since the first day I came here."
    "Oh, Joanna." He sat beside her on the bed. "Come

here. It was an air shaft," he said. "The voices you heard were of the men working below." He put his arm around her then and gave her the comfort she had wanted so badly.

She could not sleep that night. She lay between the wall and Timothy. He was on his side with his back to her, but she could tell from his breathing that he was not asleep yet, either. The room was still hot. The windows were open and the checkered curtains pushed back, but the air was heavy. Joanna put her hand on his shoulder. He was sweating, too. She began to rub in small circles his sore arm, and although her massage could never heal it, he seemed to enjoy her touch. She heard him sigh.

"When you go below," she began, "is it always that cold?"

"Yes."

"And so dark?"

"We've got lamps."

"But it's dark."

"Yes, it's dark."

She was silent a moment. "Do you ever hear voices?"

He laughed to himself. "No. Water and rats sometimes."

She was afraid to tell him what she had to. She had almost said it earlier in the week when they were in the garden and she had shown him the bird's nest in the outhouse.

"Tim?"

"Yes?"

"That money Marty tried to give you. . . "

"Don't worry about the money, Jo."

"We could use the money. Come January."

"Marty'll settle down in time or else he'll move on."

Marty would go and they would stay. She knew it, though she did not want to accept it. She sensed again a sort of nervous flutter, perhaps imagined, but what she had to tell him was real. She raised herself on one arm and reached for his hand and placed it over her stomach. "Here. Do you feel that?" Then she squeezed his fingers. "No, of course, you can't. I can hardly feel it myself."

He rolled over to look at her more directly. "Are you ill?"

"No."

So many times during the last few weeks she had imagined how she might tell him: in the morning in the garden while they were alone; after supper while walking to the covered bridge and back; at night in bed like this. He would put his arms around her, there in the yard or in the middle of the road or here, and he would kiss her and say, "Life goes on. Isn't it grand how life goes on?"

"Jo?"

She smiled shyly. "We're going to have a child."

He sat up. "What?"

"It's true."

He did not hold her or kiss her or say how wonderful it was that life goes on. He frowned. "Are you certain?"

"I wasn't before. I am now."

He shook his head as if clearing it. She waited for his reassurance, but none came. It had never occurred to her that he would not be pleased. She was giving him what he had lost.

"Tim?"

He lay back then, with his head on her chest and his hand on her shoulder as if clinging to her. His breath was hot through her cotton gown, and for a moment she feared he might have fallen asleep.

"Tim, please don't be afraid of it. I know what you're thinking, but it won't happen again this time."

"I'd be lying if I told you I wasn't afraid," he whispered.

She pressed her lips together to hold back the tears that had been near the surface all day since her escape from the air shaft. It would have been easier if he had been stronger, if he had said, no, I am not afraid, and yes, I will take you

away from here to a place where Rosie has never been. But
she could not let him know that she was frightened, too.
She ran her fingers through his thick hair and tried to comfort him.

"It'll be different this time," she said. "I promise you.
I'm younger than she was. And stronger. It won't happen
because I just won't let it happen."

"He pressed his face tighter against her breasts.

"I won't let it," she said. "I won't let it."

Long after he had fallen asleep, still holding onto her,
Joanna lay awake. He had not even kissed her. Life may go
on, but what has passed before is not easily given up. She
was jealous of Rosie. It was Rosie and her child, that other
one, who held Timothy here. It was their buried voices,
too, she heard in the mine shaft, rising from the dark on
the cold air to taunt her.

Downstairs, the kitchen door opened and Marty
stumbled through the dark. Joanna turned her head toward the stairs. After a moment, the door to the room
Kathleen shared with Mrs. Flynn opened and Joanna heard
her call to her brother. He was laughing, and she tried to
quiet him. Marty Boyle was the bad seed, but he was one
of their own. This child, this seed inside of her, where did
it belong? Not here in this coal patch and not on the farm,
either. That land, like Mrs. Flynn's and Marty Boyle's,
had been lost.

In the morning, Timothy stood over her as he often did,
watching her sleep. This time, however, he leaned close to
kiss her, but she did not stir. He gently shook her arm and
whispered her name. She opened her eyes. He was already
dressed. Through the unscreened windows the birds were
sounding the morning, but it was still dark. Joanna put her
hands under her thick hair to cool her neck.

"Is it true what you told me last night?" he asked softly.

She narrowed her eyes to see him more clearly but she
could not tell if he were still frightened and disappointed
with her. She nodded drowsily.

"Then I'm happy for us, Jo." He sat on the bed and took her hand, raising her fingers to his mouth to kiss them.

She opened her eyes wider. "Are you?"

"Of course, I am." He smoothed his hand over her damp forehead. "Yes, of course. It is wonderful news for us."

"Life goes on, Timothy."

He smiled. "When will it be?"

"January."

"Winter," he said as if this held some special significance. She thought she knew again what he was thinking. In winter, it was more difficult for the company doctor to make it over the mountain from the Shenandoah mines. But she would not need the company doctor. Nothing was going to happen to her baby.

Timothy nodded towards the attic stairs. "Will you tell them?"

"This morning if you want."

He nodded again. "How long have you known?"

She closed her eyes and smiled dreamily. "Only a few weeks."

He kissed her cheek again, then laid her hand on the bed and turned to go. He stopped at the door. "Joanna?"

She raised her head a little to see him through the dark.

"I can provide for my own son without Marty's money. We'll be fine, Joanna," he said. "I can take care of us all."

(v)

"So soon?" Mrs. Flynn sat back, shaking her head.

Joanna stood before her like a schoolgirl. Across the room, Kathleen was quiet. She lowered her eyes when Joanna looked at her, as if embarrassed. The girl felt as if she had just dropped her mother's china platter on the floor and it had broken into a hundred pieces. "I'm sorry if this disappoints you," she said.

The old woman looked up sharply. "Disappoints me?"

She looked to Kathleen. "Disappoints me? Now what is the girl saying?"

"I know what you are both thinking," Joanna stated. "You're thinking of Rosie. Always someone is thinking of Rosie."

"Disappoints me?" the old woman repeated. "Why would you say such a thing?"

"I am not Rosie!" Joanna shouted at her. "Do you hear me? I'm Joanna, not Rosie."

"Well, I think by now I should know who you are," Mrs. Flynn said. "You are such a high mickety-muck sometimes."

Kathleen went to the girl, put her arms around her, and made her sit down. "We aren't angry, Joanna. Don't think that. It is wonderful news."

Annoyed, Mrs. Flynn tapped the arm of her rocker. "Of course, I'm thinking of poor Rosie. How can I help but think of our Rosie?"

"I'm beginning to hate her," Joanna said.

Mrs. Flynn stared as if slapped.

Kathleen kneeled before the girl and took her hands. "Listen to me, Joanna. You have given Timothy a second chance."

The girl looked at her hopefully.

"Of course, I'm thinking of Rosie," Mrs. Flynn said sadly, "and how she so wanted that child."

"And I want this child. My own child. Not Rosie's. Mine."

"We all want this child for you," Kathleen said.

"I know what you are thinking," Joanna said, looking at Mrs. Flynn. "But nothing is going to happen to me or my baby."

In her agitation, Mrs. Flynn had begun to rock again, but now she stopped and held out her arms. "Come here to me, Joanna."

The girl hesitated. The old woman stared hard. Joanna

stood then went to her. "I'm sorry," she said.

The old woman took the girl's arms. "I have taken you into my house as my own daughter, though I don't think you believe that yet. My own daughter, Joanna."

It was true. Joanna did not believe she was one of the family. Even Marty Boyle, so arrogant and conniving, they would care for him because he was one of their own. But Joanna was a transplant, struggling on the edge of the garden to send out roots.

Mrs. Flynn's hands were tight on Joanna's arms. "Don't ask me to forget about Rosie. I don't want to."

"Then don't expect me to be like her."

"And have I asked you for that? Have I?"

The girl hung her head, about to cry again.

"If it's a child you and Timothy are having, Joanna, then I am proud and happy for you. Proud, not disappointed. You surprised me and there was nothing more to it than that." She let go of her and rested her head against the high back of the rocker. "I'm an old woman and I'm tired."

Again Kathleen went to Joanna and hugged her. "How do you feel?"

Lonely, Joanna wanted to answer. There is only me and this other person and no one to help us. Instead, Joanna forced a smile. "Fine. I feel just fine."

"And Timothy? What did he say?"

She had wanted to give him what he had lost. Now she wasn't so sure. Now she wanted to give him what he had never had before: her child, not Rosie's. Joanna looked at Kathleen. "He said 'Life goes on.' " It was not quite what he had said.

Kathleen's smile had widened. "It does, Joanna. It does."

Mrs. Flynn rocked, her eyes closed. "Well," she sighed. "Soon there'll be no peace and quiet here with a child underfoot."

(v i)

The talk in the Mountain View that night was about James Blaine, the Republican candidate for president of the United States. At the bar, Timothy and Charlie Boy listened with mild interest. Welshie was playing cards. Joe Sweeney and Marty Boyle walked in together, and when Joe saw Timothy, he called out, "What's this I hear? Congratulations to you." He slapped Timothy on the back. "I hope it's a strong boy Joanna gives you."

Marty did not join them. He hung back at the far end of the bar. Since his argument with Timothy over the gambling money, Marty had been eating his suppers with Joe and Helen. During the day he was gone, over one coal field to another, as he put it.

"Here's to you, Tim." Joe Sweeney raised his mug. "May you be blessed with better luck this year."

Timothy drained his glass. It was not the first he had drunk that night. He wiped his mouth and glanced at Marty.

"It's a puzzle, I tell you," said a miner who was standing at the bar, engaged in the political conversation. "I'm an honest Irishman, but this Blaine confuses me. I just don't trust him. Now, do I vote for the Irishman or for the Democrat?"

"And what good thing can you say about Cleveland?" another man put in. "I hear it said he has an illegitimate child."

"Oh well now," Joe picked up the debate. "We're all fornicators if it comes to that!" He slapped Timothy on the back again. "Drink it down, Tim, and I'll buy you another."

"What sort of leader could this Blaine make?" Welshie asked from his place at the table. "The Irish can't even run their own country but have the English in there to do it for them." He looked over his cards across the room at Marty Boyle.

For a moment, the boy held Welshie's look, then turned back to the bar and spoke loudly to no one in particular. "I heard that the mine foreman in this patch is so stupid he won't even wash the dirt off his back for fear he'll lose his strength."

Joe Sweeney pushed his eyeglasses up on his nose and laughed. "Is that what you heard now?"

"That's what Mrs. Barton told me just this afternoon."

Joe gave another hoot.

The boy took a swallow of beer, then grinned. "She said you smell, Welshie."

Welshie tossed his cards in, then sat patiently while a new hand was dealt. "The woman can say what she likes as long as she keeps bringing in the money for her rent."

"Money?" The boy laughed. "What do you know? She never once charged me." He turned to face the room and Welshie. "I guess I got back all of that money you cheated me out of. Plus some."

Welshie fanned his cards out, did not like what he had, and tossed the hand in again. He pushed his chair back and went to the bar with his empty glass. He turned to Marty, his back to Joe and Timothy. "You know what I think? I think she never even let you in, boy. In fact, I think you are one of the few people here tonight she has turned down."

The boy said nothing.

"Mrs. Barton doesn't like big talkers," Welshie said, "just big men." The others in the room were smiling now, too, anticipating the fight. Timothy stared into his glass. "What are you doing in here anyway, boy? You don't belong with miners."

Marty clenched his mug. "I don't crawl on my belly underground like a mole, if that's what you mean."

"It's time you earned your keep, boy. I for one am tired of carrying lazy Irishmen on my back."

"What's this?" Joe Sweeney said, squinting at Welshie behind his back.

"The boy cheats at cards and cock fights." Welshie nodded his head towards Timothy. "And that one belly aches about regulations and safety."

Timothy looked to Charlie Boy. "Is he talking about me now?"

"Easy, Tim," said Charlie Boy. "It's not worth it."

"Did he call us lazy Irishmen?" Joe asked.

"I believe he did," Timothy said.

Joe nodded. "So I'm not going deaf as well as blind?" Marty Boyle laughed.

Welshie stepped away from the bar with his full glass. Then suddenly, in one quick movement, Joe Sweeney hopped onto the big man's back, his arms and legs wrapped tightly around Welshie's chest. "Let's just see how well you can be carrying me, you big lump of beef!" Joe shouted. "Com'on now, boss. Give this lazy Irishman a ride."

Wild laughter came from the open windows and the door of the saloon as Welshie spun around, trying to peel off the rider. The men stomped and hooted until Welshie dumped Joe on a table. He lifted him by his shirt, then hit him in the face. Joe fell against the bar and Marty's legs.

He wiped his bleeding nose. "So it's a real fight you want, is it? Well, I'm for you," Joe said, though he was still sprawled on the floor.

It was Marty who threw the next punch. He struck Welshie in the throat and the foreman staggered backwards, winded for the moment. He reached for a bottle on the table and wielded it like a club.

"I'll buy you that drink tonight, Mick," he said and swung. Marty ducked, but Welshie rolled full circle and caught the boy above the eyes. Stunned, Marty went to his knees. Welshie uncorked the bottle and poured the whiskey over the boy's bowed head.

Timothy strained, but Charlie Boy held him back.

Marty wavered forward, as if about to fall, but suddenly grabbed Welshie's legs below the knees and butted his head into his groin. Welshie doubled up and Marty fell on him, his arms swinging wildly as he punched. Within moments, Timothy and Charlie Boy had pulled Marty off and dragged the boy outside into the dirt road. Joe Sweeney got to his feet and followed them.

The boy's forehead was gashed and blood covered his right eye. His copper hair was wet. "Don't you smell sweet?" Joe said, adjusting his glasses. "I'm proud of us."

Marty and Joe put their arms around each other's shoulders. "So who will buy us a drink to celebrate?"

"Maybe we've done enough celebrating," Timothy said.

"No." Blood was smeared over Joe's cheek. "I know where a bottle's hid." He started down the road, his arm still around Marty's shoulders.

Much later that night, the four of them stepped out of Joe Sweeney's house, stumbling a little down the steps. They were singing a simple verse over again: "My sweetheart's the mule in the mines; I drive her without reins or lines; On her bumper I sit, I chew and I spit, all over my sweetheart's behind!"

In the Flynn kitchen, the women heard them laughing from the road in front of the house. The old woman just shook her head. Kathleen sighed and rested her chin on both hands. Helen said, "I guess it's time now for me to go." Joanna saw her to the door.

"I never did care much for mules," Joe called from across the road. "Welshie's woman, now she is a real mule. And a big bumper she has, ain't that so, Marty?"

But the boy began to sing, "My sweetheart's the mule in the mines. . . ."

Helen looked back at Joanna. She kissed her cheek. "I'm so happy for you," she whispered before going down the steps and into the yard.

Timothy guided Marty through the gate. "Helen?" The boy reached for her. "Helen."

"Goodnight, Mr. Boyle," Helen said, no laughter now in her voice.

Timothy was grinning foolishly as he and Marty came

into the kitchen. "We've taken us a drop," he told Joanna.

"Maybe two," Marty said.

"A drop is it?" Mrs. Flynn said, "It's a wonder you can walk at all."

"The boy's fine," Timothy said, but even in the dim light they saw the dried blood over Marty's eyes.

"You're cut!" Kathleen said, but she did not go to him. She turned instead on Timothy. "He was fighting again and you let him."

"You might say we were defending our Irish honor," Timothy said.

"And a fine job we did of it, too," the boy said. He pulled away from Timothy and bowed to his sister. "Why are you always snapping at us? We can take care of ourselves."

"You're a sight, Marty Boyle. And you can clean yourself up tonight. I won't have a thing to do with you or your dirty clothes."

Marty giggled.

Joanna stood near the door. She had never known Timothy to stay out this late or to drink this much. Or to fight.

"The devil is with you, Marty Boyle," the old woman said. "You're trouble for us surely."

The boy stretched his arms over his head, then scratched his stomach. "I'm hungry."

"There's nothing to eat now," Kathleen said. "Just get in there to bed and sleep it off."

"Go on now," Timothy said. He smiled at Joanna still standing at the door. He held out his arms. "Come here, Jo."

Surprised that he should want to hold her now in front of the others, she stepped back. He dropped his arms and turned away.

"It's late," Mrs. Flynn said.

"Yes." Timothy looked again at Marty. "Go on, boy. Get to bed."

"Who was it this time?" Kathleen asked.

"That bloody foreman, that's who," Marty said.

Landlords, Joanna thought sullenly. It was Marty's constant source of anger, having to live under someone's thumb. Now he had Timothy fighting, too.

"Welshie?" Mrs. Flynn was amused. "And did you win?"

"Well now, I think he'll be sore for a while," Timothy said and both he and Marty laughed again. "The boy sort of got him in a tender spot."

"Is that the truth?" Mrs. Flynn said, pleased.

From across the room, Joanna was staring at Timothy. They held each other's gaze for a moment. Then he turned for the attic door. "Goodnight."

"You better go up and tend to him, girl," Mrs. Flynn said.

Still Joanna held back.

"Well, go on, girl. He's your husband. He's only a little drunk."

Joanna started across the room for the stairs.

Timothy was sitting on the bed, undoing his shirt. He had not lit the lamp and the room was dark, yet in the light from the stairwell she saw him drop the shirt to the floor. She went to pick it up.

"Leave it," he said, but she did not listen. As she bent down, she felt his hands on her hair, feeling for the pins to remove them.

She brushed his hand away. "Tim, please." She stood with his shirt folded over her arm.

"You don't always have to pick up after me."

"I don't mind." After a moment she turned away to set his shirt in the drawer. "What happened there tonight?"

"Some punches were thrown. Joe Sweeney will surely be bruised tomorrow."

"Joe was fighting, too?"

Timothy laughed quietly. "He looked like a leprechaun perched there on Welshie's back."

"What?"

Timothy reached for her again, holding her wrist. "Come to bed, Jo."

"Did Marty start this?"

"I think you're mad at me," he said and laughed quietly again.

"No, I'm not."

"Then come here."

She was frightened by his behavior and the way he was almost leering at her. And then he stood and put his hands on the sides of her face and ran his thumbs over her lips, holding her a little more tightly than on other nights. He began again to remove the hairpins.

"Tim, please." She tried to brush his hands away again.

"Don't." His voice was not unkind, but demanding nevertheless, and Joanna stood still as one by one the pins dropped to the floor. He spread her hair over her shoulders. His face against her neck was rough, but she did not try to stop him now or move away. She was wrapped in his arms just as months ago she had wrapped herself in the branches of the fir tree on the ridge. But tonight she was no longer the same girl who played made-up games in the woods. This was real.

She ran her hand over his bare chest to the sore shoulder and then she hugged him, too, her fingers pressing into his back as he kissed her throat. His kisses, too, were more rough than on other nights.

And then, he let her go.

He sat on the bed and unlaced his boots, all the while staring at her. A little shaken, she reached for the bedpost, but she, too, stared at him. It was as if his eyes were holding her there. As he lay back on the pillows, she turned away to undo the buttons of her dress.

"No," he said. "Don't turn your back on me tonight, Joanna. Stay in the light from the stairs so I can see you."

Still a little frightened, she undressed before him, and still his eyes seemed to go right through her, as if seeing a different person in her tonight as well. Her clothes were in a pile at her feet.

"You are a beautiful woman," he said very softly.

Joanna caught her breath.

"I have never told you that before, have I?"

"No."

"Or that I love you."

She shook her head.

"Well, I do. I love you."

As she stepped over her clothes and went to him, she was a different person. No longer the girl hired to wash his shirts and cook his meals, she was the woman who shared his bed and was having his child.

(i)

For weeks it had not rained. The water in the barrel was low and long-legged spiders clung to the dark sides. Joanna watered her plants sparingly. They hung limp, yellowing in the dust. During the day, the air was heavy with the thick smoke from the colliery; at night red flashes of heat lightning scored the sky. Thunder sounded in the distance but never brought the needed rain.

Along the river, just before a storm, the branches of the willows lifted in the wind like curtains on an open window. But in the attic, the checkered curtains were still. Joanna sat on the floor by the open window, watching the lightning and thinking of home and of the calf she had seen birthed the spring before she had come to the patch. Margaret had witnessed it, too. Her father sat on his haunches in the barn, watching over the delivery in case there were complications. There had been none. The blood steamed a little in the hay. Joanna had been neither embarrassed nor afraid of what she had seen. So there would be blood, hot on her thighs, when the time came. And pain. That did not frighten her. Still, an uneasiness rumbled inside Joanna like the distant thunder. "Rosie," she whispered through the window into the night, "what went wrong for you?"

She blamed the summer heat, the storm that seemed to hang just beyond the mountains but would not break, for her difficulty in sleeping. Across the room, Timothy rolled in the bed and when he realized she was not there, he sat up on one elbow.

"Jo?"

She was sitting with her knees to her chest and her arms around her legs. "Go to sleep," she said.

"Are you alright?"

She smiled through the window at the night. How often he asked her that now. "Yes, Tim. Go to sleep."

(ii)

"What's this?" Timothy held up a large shirtwaist that had been laying on the bed.

"It's Kathleen's. It's for when I get fat, like Kathleen is now." Joanna smiled.

It was late afternoon and he had come upstairs to change his clothes. Joanna was resting on the bed. The heat in the garden had been too much for her. Timothy held Kathleen's blouse to his own chest. "You won't get that fat. Rosie never did." He tossed the blouse at her. "Well, let's have a look."

"I'm not wearing it until I need it."

"Go on."

Joanna slipped the blouse over her own. The neck was too wide and hung off one shoulder and it fit loosely over her hips. She grabbed a pillow and stuffed it under, then held her arms out for Timothy, who laughed. She grabbed a second pillow and stuffed it, too, under the blouse. It was tight now against her back. "What if we had two at once?"

"Please, Jo. Just one healthy child at a time."

Then, without warning, the colliery whistle cried out

one, two, three, four. . . . Both Timothy and Joanna stood frozen for a moment, listening. . . . eight, nine, ten blasts.

Timothy turned.

"Wait," she called to him, but he was already heading down the steps.

She pulled the pillows away and hurried after him. In the kitchen he sat to lace up his boots. Mrs. Flynn was resolute at the table. "Stop him," Joanna said. "Tell him not to go."

"Joanna," the old woman said softly

"Please," she begged him. "Don't leave me."

As he went out the door, the whistle began the count again. Joanna went out behind him.

"Why must you go? There are others."

He squeezed her hands reassuringly. "It's my responsibility."

"But what about me?"

"Stay with Kathleen and Ma."

He started for the gate and still Joanna followed him. Helen was there in the road and now Joanna turned to her. "Tell him he's wrong to go. He doesn't have to." But Timothy was already gone.

"It could be Joe trapped below," Helen said. "Or Charlie Boy."

"No," Joanna cried.

The whistle had stopped again but it still echoed in her head. She covered her ears to block it. She saw herself once more in the dark cave. She felt the cold, black damp rising from the darkness, heard the cries of the bats as they beat their wings about her arms. From the porch of her own house, Kathleen was calling to her.

Helen put a hand on Joanna's arm. "There's nothing to do but wait. Nothing, Joanna. Come inside with us."

Joanna pulled away from her. The two friends stared at each other a moment, and then Joanna ran towards the colliery.

That other time, the day of the explosion and fire, the

activity in the colliery yard was frenzied as the miners and
their families fought to control the fire. Today, however,
the sun cast long shadows of the coal-company buildings
over the solemn faces of the families of the miners trapped
below. Joanna waited, too, but apart from them, nearer
the shaft. She was, after all, not one of them. Nor did she
want to be.

Bits of information surfaced and moved among the
crowd. A newly excavated section of tunnel had collapsed.
No one was certain how many men were trapped, four,
maybe six. Timothy was down there with the others, digging them out, digging against time. "Annie," she had
heard him call, though he was nowhere near the house. He
had been buried for only an hour before they got to him
but already it was too late. "It was like he was trying to tell
me," Mrs. Flynn had said.

Three pine coffins sat on the caged platform over the
shaft. The pulleys began to turn and the coffins disappeared below.

An hour passed, then two. It grew darker as the sun inched closer to the crest of the culm banks. Some of the
women turned away for their houses; others took their
place in the yard. Coffee passed from hand to hand. The
sun slipped behind the hummocks of slag. Torches and
lanterns now blazed. Then good words passed among the
families: two more feet until they reach them; they made
contact; the men are alive. A wave of cheering and tears
washed over them and then it was quiet, and the waiting
began again.

A faint wind stirred through the night, the first breeze
they had felt in the patch in weeks.

The young Italian woman and her little girl stood just
ahead of Joanna. She pushed closer to them. As the mother
held her sleeping child, she swayed back and forth, humming softly. Joanna ran her hand over the child's soft hair.
The two women held each other's gaze. "I will hold her

for you," Joanna offered, but the woman only hugged the child tighter.

"Joanna?"

Marty touched her arm. She looked dully at him.

"Come home with me, Joanna. You have been here for hours. They want me to bring you home."

She turned away from him.

"Joanna, it may be hours more. They're worried about you."

"I'm not leaving."

Marty went away then, but he returned in a few minutes with a mug of coffee for her. "Go on," he said, "drink it."

Grateful, she took it from him and held it with both hands.

"This isn't smart, Joanna. Think of the baby."

"I'm alright."

"You're tired," he said.

"Why do you think it's taking so long?" she asked. "It must have caved some more."

"No."

"It could have."

"It didn't."

She looked sideways at him. "You can go back."

He smiled, but gently. "Do you mind if I wait with you?"

She shrugged.

By nine o'clock all but two of the men had been freed. Joe Sweeney and Charlie Boy had come up long ago, but Timothy was still below. We are all miners, Helen had told her long ago, but Joanna did not want to believe that. It's like you go underground with them, Helen had said. Joanna did not want to be a miner's wife and yet she knew now that Helen was right, for she did not feel Marty's arm around her nor the aching in her legs from standing so long. She was in that air shaft again, crouching just as Timothy might now be, feeling the cold black damp in her face. She was underground with him.

A bell rang, a hollow sound that seemed to wake her. She fixed her eyes on the shaft opening as the cables turned. The first man was brought up. Matthew was propped in the pine box that was to have been his coffin, but he was alive and the men in the colliery yard carried him in the box on their shoulders to the company wagon, The Black Maria. The hearse would carry this live soul to the hospital in Butler.

Again the car went down and there was silence.

"I asked him not to go down," she said. "I begged him."

"Of course, he'd go down. I'd go down for him, for Joe or Charlie Boy."

Joanna looked at Marty, vaguely understanding that despite his boldness, he cared about Timothy.

They brought the Italian up soon after. He still wore his miner's cap. Two men helped him from the car, and then without their help, he walked through the crowd towards his wife and child. They cradled the little girl between them.

Joanna wiped her eyes. The others in the yard were turning away now. The waiting was over. But Joanna did not move. "Why isn't he up?"

Welshie stood near the shaft elevator. He had just come up himself and his face was black. Joanna went closer. "What's happened?" she asked him. "Why aren't the rest up by now?"

"Get out of here, girlie," Welshie said. "Go back home with the others. It's over."

Marty came up behind her. "Step back, Joanna."

She shook her head, determined.

Welshie noticed Marty then. "You're in the way here, Mick. Get your girlfriend out of here."

The boy did not answer. For a moment, the two stared at each other. Then the bell rang again and the cables overhead started to turn. Welshie's attention focused on the opening as the platform surfaced once more. Joanna tried to get closer, but Marty held her back. It was not Timothy or any other miner who came up. Inside the cage was the bloody carcass of a mule. At first Joanna thought it was the soiled blankets and bloodied jackets of the men who had been trapped below, but then Welshie and another man took hold of the animal's legs and dragged it from the car into the dirt near Joanna's feet. The animal's skull had been crushed. She covered her mouth and turned to Marty, pressing against him.

"It's alright," he said, holding her.

"I told you to get her out of here," Welshie said.

The boy turned her away.

When Timothy came up, minutes later, he did not look for Joanna, but stayed with Welshie. It was she who went to him, but he did not cradle her as the Italian had his wife and child. Instead, he turned on Marty. "What is she doing here? Why would you let her stay and see this?"

"I wanted to," she answered. "It was my decision."

There was blood on his shirt and hands and as she noticed this, her throat constricted. He was safe once more. When he put his hands over hers, he said more softly, "Go on home now, Jo. Go with Marty. I've got to make my report to the superintendent."

"I'm not going back without you."

"Marty will take care of you." He turned away. But even then she did not leave. She waited until he was finished with Welshie and when he turned around again and found her still there, her eyes imploring him, he agreed.

They left Marty and walked in silence down the road away from the mine. At the gate of their house, Timothy stopped and put his hands on her shoulders. "Listen to me. I've got to go down to his house. I don't know how long it'll be."

"I'm going with you. I'll stand in a shadow so he won't see me, but I'm going with you."

Too tired to argue any further, he started walking again.

At the far end of the town, away from the noise and dirt of the breaker and mule barn, was the superintendent's house. Tall, slender trees arched over the porch roof as if bending forward to peer into the windows on the second floor. Timothy opened the iron gate, walked around to the back door, and waited on the porch. An old woman answered, her head wrapped in a kerchief, and Joanna stepped back out of the light from the kitchen. A moment later, the superintendent appeared. He was not as formidable a man as Joanna once imagined. He was rather stocky and was balding. Although Timothy stood before him a taller, broader man, he still held his helmet with both hands against his stomach in a way that showed he was uncomfortable.

Beyond the superintendent, Joanna could see into the bright kitchen. The old woman moved about the pantry where each shelf was filled with jars of preserves. Through the sheer curtains on the side windows, Joanna saw a hanging light over the dining room table, an open staircase with a curved wooden railing, a grandfather clock, and flowered wallpaper above the wainscoting. Outwardly, this house was not as grand as those she had seen in Butler, but these rooms were rich and spacious compared to her own and she suddenly felt angry that they should be denied such a house. She felt angry, too, that Timothy had not taken Marty's money when most of it was rightly theirs—the money Timothy had paid for Marty and Kathleen's passage to America.

"You did your part," the superintendent was saying. "If you marked off the weak area and they went ahead anyway, then the company is not liable. I've lost a valuable animal in this accident. It'll have to be replaced, of course."

"What of the men injured tonight?"

"What of them?"

"Matt's legs are crushed. He may never walk."

"But he's alive. Isn't that so?"

"Well, of course, he's alive. Still. . . "

"I will not be held responsible for this accident or for
their injuries. My foreman will hire a new man in the
morning." After a moment, the superintendent added,
"Perhaps even your lad."

Timothy shook his head. "Marty wouldn't have it
now."

"Don't be so sure."

"He wouldn't put up with taking orders."

"Well, then we'll find someone else. I was giving you
the first chance. It'll be harder to find a good mule." He
turned for the door.

"Is that it?"

"What would you have me do?"

"Some retribution," Timothy said. "For the family.
God knows they'll need it now."

The superintendent shook his head. "By all rights I
should charge them for the mule. It'll take me four working days to get another if I'm lucky. And even then I can't
be sure what quality animal they'll send me from
Shenandoah." The man shook his head. "No. They'll get
nothing more from this company. Matthew got out with
his life and that's retribution enough."

"It isn't right."

The superintendent sighed. "You inspected the chamber. You made the markings. They went against the rec-
ommendation."

"That may be, but there's a reason for it. Everyone robs
the pillars. The foreman knows it. You know it. It's en-
couraged by the company."

"You wanted this job, Timothy. You are the company
now. As much as Welshie or I. And I'm telling you, Matthew will be fired and you can go to the hospital in Butler
yourself to tell him so if you're that concerned."

Joanna shrank deeper into the shadows.

"Me?" Timothy shook his head. "No, sir. It's not my
job to be hiring and firing your men."

"Make your report. Give it to Welshie tonight." The man turned again, then stopped. "You did inspect it like you said? It was marked?"

Timothy stiffened. "I reported it earlier this week. Welshie knew as soon as I about the weak roof. I recommended more propping. It was never done."

The superintendent nodded. "Negligence. Matthew and the Dago should have propped the roof as recommended." The man nodded goodnight, then closed the kitchen door behind him, cutting off the light.

After a moment, Timothy said sharply, "Yes, sir," though no one was there to hear him. He put his helmet back on and turned for the road. He took Joanna by the arm and led her out of the yard.

"He had no right to talk to you like that, like it was your fault. And you risked your life."

"I only did what I am being paid to do." He walked quickly, staring ahead.

"But it isn't right to treat people that way, like they don't matter."

"Forget it now, Joanna."

She tried to keep pace with him but stumbled. "Tim, I can't walk this fast."

He slowed then, but still he did not look at her. He said, "You should have done what I told you and gone with Marty."

She stopped. "I thought my place was with you, not him."

Timothy said nothing. He walked a few steps more, then turned to wait for her. "Come on now, Jo. It is late."

"I don't know why you are angry with me."

"I'm not." He shook his head, then went back for her and took her arm. "I'm not."

They walked again, but slower now.

"I can't help being frightened when that awful whistle goes."

"Alright. Alright."

At the house, Timothy took Joanna's hand and led her around back to the rain barrel. He dipped his handkerchief deep inside, then wiped away the coal dirt and the faint trace of blood from his hand on her cheek. "I don't mean to be shouting at you," he said. "I get angry with myself. Maybe there is a bit of Marty in me, too. I don't know."

"No," she said. "You are not like Marty."

"I do know this: as sure as we're standing here now there will be another time, another accident. You have got to learn that much, Jo. You've got to be expecting it. Just try to accept it."

"Why?" she challenged. "Did Rosie? Was it all right with her whenever that whistle blew? Didn't she ever cry or worry over you?"

He just stared at her and Joanna could see that she had hurt him.

"Oh, Tim," she cried, "I'm sorry."

He put his arms around her and pressed her head against his chest. He stroked her hair. "I keep trying to tell you, Jo. It's the only job I know how to do. There's nothing else for me. Not with this bum arm."

From the open window of the house next door, old Nat began to cough. She and Timothy were not alone, not even there in the dark behind the house. They both stepped apart.

"It'll happen again," he said. "I can feel it when I press the roofs and the walls. They give. They sigh. We try to cut it up and shore it up, but it is only temporary. The earth is always fighting back. In time, it'll cave again. The tunnels will fill with water. Something inside the earth will shift and crack and the gases from deep down will escape. But what can I do?"

"It's not your fault what happened today."

"No," he said.

But Joanna could tell from the sadness in his voice that he blamed himself nevertheless.

They were all there in the kitchen: Mrs. Flynn,

Kathleen, Helen, Joe, and Marty. When Joanna and Timothy entered, they looked up expectantly, their conversation interrupted for the moment.

"It's the dead work that's wrong," said Joe Sweeney. "Having to stable the mules and not getting paid for it. Or timbering your own section before you can even start to pick the coal."

"Where was the superintendent?" Marty asked. He was leaning against the stove, his arms and legs crossed. "I didn't see him there tonight."

"They want every buggy of coal out, always do, but it never matters to them which one of us gets killed doing it," Joe said. His bitterness surprised Joanna and she wondered how much of it had been fueled by Marty.

"God'll be their judge," Mrs. Flynn said.

"What will happen to them now and their families?" Kathleen asked.

"Tony will be fine and down below in a few days," Joe said. "As for Matthew . . . " He looked to Timothy.

The whiskey bottle, too, was on the table and he reached for it now and poured some into his tea. "His legs are no good. He'll be let go."

"And the family put out," Helen added.

They sat quietly then in the kitchen, each lost in their own thoughts: Mrs. Flynn of her husband who had also robbed the pillars and lost; Helen of the mother who had run away; and Joanna of the child everyone seemed frightened for her to have. They were miners, all of them, even Kathleen and Marty now. When you live with them and wash their clothes and cook their meals, and especially when you care, then you become one of them.

(iii)

The next morning while she worked the garden, happy to be alone, Marty came down the path and sat on the old tree stump to watch her. She was on her hands and knees and she glanced at him curiously.

"I was thinking that you and I are alike," he said.

"I don't think so."

"You don't like me much, do you?"

She sat back on her heels and looked up at him. "What do you want, Marty?"

"Tim is lucky to have found you here in this place."

She smiled. "I found him. That's how it really happened. I came and didn't want to leave without him."

"I don't think it much matters how it happens, just as long as it does." He leaned forward with his hands folded together, his forearms resting on his knees. "We are alike. Neither one of us belongs here."

She had never said anything to Marty about wanting to leave the coal patch. She assumed now that it was Helen who had told him how she felt, and it gave her a peculiar feeling to know that her best friend and Marty had been discussing her. "I am his wife. Of course, I belong here."

"That's not what I meant. I wasn't thinking of Rosie at all."

"Then just what do you mean?" she asked impatiently.

"I want to give you something." He reached into his shirt pocket and took out a wad of bills. "Timothy is too proud to take it, but I think you will."

She stared at the money in his hand, and then looked up at him. "I can't take it either."

"I'm giving it to you."

"Tim wouldn't like it."

"He needn't know."

Again she looked at the money.

"It's just the winnings from before with a little more from a game of cards or two at Shenandoah."

"Shenandoah? You've gone all the way to Shenandoah?"

He grinned. "I have my ways of getting around. Joe lets me take the wagon, or I hop onto the coal train. It comes and goes every day." He took her hand and put the money in it. A few coins fell to the ground. "It's almost forty dollars, Joanna, after giving a little to the collection for Matthew's family."

She held it in two hands. "No, Marty," she said, but she did not hand it back. It was tight in her fingers now.

"Think of how I feel, Jo, not being able to get a job and pay my way." He leaned back, away from her and the money. "Think of Matt's family. They've got nothing now. Someday the same may happen to you and you'll be needing that money."

"Tim will be careful," she said quietly. "Tim can take care of us." But her voice was not convincing. She knew what Marty was saying was true.

"Accidents happen. We both found that out yesterday, now didn't we?"

She nodded solemnly.

"Just think of it as safekeeping, for me if you want. Like a bank."

"I don't know," she whispered.

Marty stood. For him, it had been decided.

"Marty?" She slipped the money into her apron pockets. "You won't tell anyone that you gave this to me?"

"Who would I tell?" He winked and turned away.

As he walked past the house and out of the yard, Joanna pressed her hand over her pocket and the lump of money. She looked then at the outhouse, but of course, that would not be a good place to hide it. And then she looked at the attic windows and thought of her trunk. Timothy never went through it. She picked up her trowel and began again to loosen the sun-baked dirt around her tomato plants, but her concentration was broken. After a few minutes, she tossed the digger aside and stood. She had more than just herself to think of now, she had her child. And didn't Mrs. Flynn keep her own bit of money in the mattress ticking? Joanna started for the house.

Upstairs, she opened the trunk and took out an embroidered handkerchief, spreading it over her lap. She counted the money, once and then again. Thirty-nine dollars could not buy a house, but it might buy a little corner of land somewhere. She wrapped the money in the handkerchief and tucked it deep inside her trunk, then closed the lid. For a while longer, she sat on the floor staring. She felt guilty, but she was not sorry.

(iv)

By mid-September, the month-long drought had ended. The storm broke and it rained, a slow, fine drizzle that by the fifth day had flooded the yards, muddied the roads, and swept the first yellowed leaves from the birches. The stream behind the colliery ran fast and grey with runoff from the culm banks. The week of rain quickly turned summer to fall. Overhead the clouds raced in dark knots. The demand for coal was up, as were the New York and Philadelphia market prices. As a result, wages increased a little, but longer hours were also in order. Very often now Joanna did not see Timothy until suppertime. She harvested her garden alone. Occasionally, Marty came to sit in the yard and talk, but more often than not his being there left her uncomfortable for, even though he had not mentioned the money again, he was a reminder of the secret she was keeping from Timothy.

The coal company had secured another mule from the mines downriver, a thin, scarred animal that had come cheaply. The mule boys there had complained that it was mean, a biter. Its yellow eyes were near blind from working underground for months at a time. From the window of the superintendent's office, Timothy watched as the boys struggled to get the kicking animal onto the caged platform so as to lower it into the shaft. Timothy had made his morning report, but waited to speak to the superintendent on another matter. When the short, balding man stepped into the office, he was agitated. The mule was, in his opinion, not worth even the small price he had paid for it. "Malnourished," he said irritably, "and mistreated, no doubt, by some dumb handler." He tossed his eyeglasses onto the papers on his desk. "What is it, Tim?"

"It's Matthew."

The superintendent sighed heavily. He sat back in his chair and looked at Timothy with an enduring, almost pained expression. "What is it?"

It had been two weeks since the cave-in that had crushed his legs, and still Matthew was hospitalized. "We've taken a collection."

"I know."

"But now it seems that his right leg will have to be cut off. Gangrene."

The superintendent nodded. "I see."

"I'm feeling responsible."

"What do you want from me?"

"Some compensation for the family."

"Such as?"

"Some credit on the rent."

"I'm running a business, not a charity ward in a hospital."

"The demand and the prices are up."

The two men looked at each other across the desk. In the end, it was the superintendent who blinked first. "I'll look into it."

Although he had won the compensation, it was a hollow victory for Timothy. He had been to Butler once to see Matthew. He knew how difficult it would be for Matthew to find work after the amputation, and so Timothy had gone to Butler again, not to the hospital, but to inquire about factory positions and housing for the family. He had come up empty-handed.

It did not set well with him when Joe Sweeney or Charlie Boy teased him about being tight with the superintendent now that he, Timothy, was the inspector. "Ma's still waiting on that church, Tim," Charlie Boy rode him. "And Charlie's still looking for a pretty school teacher," Joe laughed.

It was an accident that could have been prevented if the additional propping had been done as recommended. It was the same careless sort of accident that had killed his father. This time, however, it was Timothy's name on the report.

(v)

On a late afternoon in early October, children played a circle game in the dusty road in front of the Flynn house. A boy paced around the perimeter of the circle, waving overhead a red scarf while the others dared him to drop the handkerchief at their feet. When at last he let it fall in front of another girl, the two raced each other around the outside of the circle. The boy beat her to the empty space, and the children laughed. Now the girl picked up the scarf and began to walk around the circle, trying to decide which one she would choose.

Joanna sat on the porch with a pot of potatoes at her feet. She liked hearing the children's laughter and she smiled as she scraped the potatoes. Mrs. Flynn, too, had decided to sit out in the chilled autumn air. She braced herself in the straight back chair by holding on the porch post.

From the direction of the colliery came three breaker boys. Older than those playing in the road, they were nevertheless just children of ten and twelve. They carried their lunch tins and wore caps, and their hands and faces were black, just like their fathers'. They walked past, with shoulders curved forward from the hours of sitting on plank boards sorting coal in the chutes. Seeing them, Joanna froze. It was not the first time she had seen breaker boys. They passed every day. It was the contrast of the laughing, playing children and the breaker boys that sent a chill through her with the sudden thought that her son, too, could become a miner.

"Hello there!"

Across the road Helen was waving, but not to Joanna or Mrs. Flynn. Marty Boyle was just then coming from the Mountain View. It was, as Helen joked, where Marty worked during the afternoons and evenings. His gambling did not seem to bother her at all. Joe Sweeney, too, was coming down the road, but from the opposite direction, following the breaker boys. Just as a child was running around the outside of the circle, Marty caught her and stole the scarf. Amid the children's protests, he dangled the handkerchief out of reach above their heads.

"Give him a chance at it, kids," Joe said.

Marty pushed into the center of the circle. "Now what do I do?"

"Drop it!" the children cried.

Mrs. Flynn said, "And will you look at that grown fool."

Joanna reached for another potato and began to scrape. She was smiling again.

Joe removed his miner's cap and set both it and the lunch tin in the road, then he, too, squeezed into the line of children. "Pick me, pick me, Marty boy," he cried in a falsetto voice. "See if you can catch me, sweetie."

The children shouted as Marty paraded about, singing loudly, "My sweetheart's the mule in the mines; I drive her without reins or lines. . . . "

He dropped the scarf in front of Joe. The two men chased each other around the circle of screaming children, kicking up dust. Joe slid into place before him, going down on one knee. Undaunted, Marty picked up the scarf and began to sing again. "On her bumper I sit, I chew and I spit, all over my sweetheart's behind."

"Bloody fools," Mrs. Flynn muttered.

Now Marty dragged Helen into the game. "I'm not as

easy as you may think," she warned. He dropped the scarf and she ran, but Marty beat her. He scooped up the scarf and held it behind his back.

"Here's the best part," he told the children. "When she loses, then she's got to give up a kiss to get it back."

"I never played that way before," Helen said.

He drew the scarf across her shoulder. "Well?"

She leaned forward to kiss him.

"Hey!" Joe Sweeney shouted. "You didn't kiss me."

Joanna laughed. She was tempted to forget the potatoes and just walk right out into the road and steal that handkerchief herself. The old woman, however, would surely reprimand her for that, just as she had once reprimanded Timothy for sledding with children. It wasn't proper for a woman in Joanna's condition to play silly games.

After the children had gone home, Joe and Helen and Marty were still talking in the road. Marty's arm was around Helen's waist. The three were laughing at some story Joe was telling. Oddly, Joanna felt left out.

The next morning Marty wandered into the garden, as he sometimes did. The tomatoes had been picked weeks ago and preserved, but still a few hung on the vines. She was packing the salted cabbage in the barrel, making the sauerkraut she had promised Mrs. Flynn months ago, though the old woman had forgotten. Her back ached and she was grateful when Marty offered to help. She sat on the stump. "Be sure you pack it tightly," she said, watching him, "or it'll spoil."

"Seems easy enough."

"We'll have sauerkraut all winter if it's done right."

As he worked the stick, he smiled at her. "You do too much, Jo."

Over the last two weeks, her skirt had gotten tighter about her waist. She felt thick, bloated, and this morning for the first time she had slipped on Kathleen's large blouse. It was still much too wide at the neck, but not so loose now about her stomach. She felt sloppy in it.

"Here," she said, standing up. "I'll do it now." Marty gave up the stick without protest and she began again to tamp the cabbage.

"Land's the thing," he said. He moved through the rows of the garden, much of it picked over, and bent to pull a small, pink tomato. He bit into it. "That's how a man gets power. Ownership. I figured that much out long ago."

Joanna twisted the stick, thinking. "You ought to see the land my father owns," she said, working more enthusiastically over the barrel now. "It's wide open and clean. There are no broken fences and, of course, no colliery whistles at dawn."

"If I were Timothy I would take you away from here tomorrow."

He was only boasting again. "And go where?"

"To the Ohio. There's work with the railroad. Even in the western part of this state, there's logging and money to be made. That is, if you could buy a good tract of virgin forest." He picked another tomato.

Joanna looked beyond him at her flowers along the back fence. The blooms had faded from the night frosts. "I'd like to own land someday, but it has to be near water. That is very important to me. This place here isn't so bad once you get used to it. It's just that I intend to have more than just a small square of hard ground." She looked at him. "Does that surprise you?"

Marty licked the tomato seeds from his palm. "You see? We are alike. The thing is, it all takes money. More money than we've got."

"We?"

He winked at her. It was the first time he had mentioned the money he had given her. "Why do you bother staying around here?" she asked. "If you've got money, you can go."

"Oh, I won't be here much longer. I've a few deals I'm cooking up."

As she tamped the cabbage, she studied him. She could not imagine him working on the railroad or sawing timber. She could not see him doing anything but playing cards and singing bawdy songs. "Do you ever think of going home, to Ireland?"

"No."

She could not understand this, either. She would gladly go home again, with Timothy and the baby of course.

"I am the youngest of eight children," he explained. "There wasn't much left over for me."

Overhead she heard honking sounds, faint at first and then growing louder. With shaded eyes, she looked up to find the trailing, lopsided formation of geese migrating south. She dropped the stick in the barrel and jumped onto the stump. "Look there!" she cried and pointed.

Marty, too, shaded his eyes.

"Don't you see them? The geese. The first geese already." She followed their flight until they disappeared behind the line of oak trees beyond the Mountain View, though she could still hear their muted honking. "They follow the river to the Chesapeake."

"And where's that?"

"It's a bay, south of here. The river flows right into it. I've never seen it, though. We read about it in our history books."

"The Chesapeake," he said, as if considering that place as a possible destination once he made up his mind to leave.

"I see them every year. There's a spot I know of on the river near our farm where the geese sometimes stop for a few days."

"Is that so?"

She looked up to see if he were really interested or just humoring her. He was still watching the sky. "Not a whole flock of them really, not even as many as we saw today, but at least seven or eight of them would be there at one time. They'd stay for days. My sister and I crawled on our bellies through the prickerbushes and the mud, but we could never get close enough before they would fly up."

"That would be a little hard for you to do now," he said, eyeing her.

Kathleen's blouse hid her swollen belly, but Joanna felt self-conscious just the same. "I think it's wonderful how they know just by instinct the right direction to fly and just when to leave. One morning Margaret and I would go down and they'd be gone." Joanna stood up and went back to the barrel of salted cabbage. "It'll be a cold winter this year if they've started their migration already."

"This river of yours seems like a special place."

"It is. I know every turn, every hollowed-out space along the bank near the farm. Upstream there is a spot where mushrooms, white as anything, grow and they're large, too. Right now they are probably ready to be picked. I don't think anyone else knows they are even there except Margaret and I."

"It'd be a dirty shame to waste them," he said. "What do you think of us going to get some?"

Again she looked sideways at him, unsure. "You want to go there now?"

"I'm willing if you want a basket of mushrooms to fry for our dinner. I'll even pick them for you."

"Why?"

"Why not?" He laughed. "I've nothing else to do."

She stopped tamping the cabbage and just stared into the barrel. "It's a two-hour ride, each way." She looked up. "No, it'd take too long. What would Mrs. Flynn say if I just picked up and left here? No, it wouldn't be right."

"I guess no one said you had to spend every hour in the coal patch," Marty answered. "But then if you don't want to go, that's all right, too." He wiped his hands on the seat of his pants and looked about, restless to be doing something.

"I know another place, though," she said.

"Yeah, where?"

Joanna looked over her shoulder at the ridge above the culm bank. "There in the woods. But it's quite a walk. I was only there once, but we might get lucky and find mushrooms along the stream."

"I've got a basket," he said, picking it up from between the rows of cauliflower, just now forming heads.

Joanna looked up at the sky again, thinking of the geese. This might be her last chance for a long walk in the woods before her pregnancy confined her to the house. She let go of the tamping stick. The cabbage could hold an hour or so. "Alright," she said. "I'll show you the way."

They went through the gate and circled the culm bank, winding their way to the top. Marty offered her his hand. On the ridge they stood together and looked down at the coal patch. "It looks even smaller from up here," he said.

Joanna led him along the same path she had taken that summer day in search of wildflowers. The trees had turned shades of red and yellow; the rhododendron, waxy and green. They heard the stream, loud like rain against the roof. Marty went first down the slope, again holding his hand out for Joanna. The fallen leaves made her slip, but she went down slowly, softly on her behind, and both she and Marty began to laugh.

"I feel like a fat lady," she said, standing again and brushing the leaves from her skirt.

The stream was running harder now than in summer. The recent rains had swelled it beyond its banks. The mushrooms were there, on the other side, just as Joanna had predicted months ago, but there was no safe way for her to cross for them. She looked upstream to where the air shaft was not so camouflaged now that the creepers had shed their leaves. The bare, twisted vines looked more like a spider's web over the framed entrance. A trap, Joanna thought.

"There's enough mushrooms here to sell!" Marty cried. Already he was testing the water's edge. Then he noticed the air shaft, too. "And what's that?"

"Just a tunnel. It leads into one of the mines."

"It'd make a great hiding place."

She laughed. "Why would you need to hide?"

"I don't. But if I did, I'd come here."

"It's not very pleasant inside. Very cold."

"You went in?"

She nodded and answered softly, "Just once. Tim was very angry with me that night."

"And do you always tell him everything you do?"

Joanna looked at Marty. She hadn't told Tim about the money.

"Well," he said, after a moment, "I'm after those mushrooms for you." While he wandered downstream a little way, searching for a place to cross, Joanna sat in the root pocket of a tree. She heard him cry out as his feet slipped into the cold stream. On the other side, he waved to her, dropped to his knees, and began to fill the basket with fat mushrooms.

Joanna looked again at the black cavity that was the air-shaft opening. In winter there would be thick icicles over the rocks there. Winter, she sighed. Already the geese had flown south. A whole year had passed since she had first come to the patch. How different everything was now—her marriage, her child—and yet the loneliness was un-changed. The voices were still there, Rosie's and that other, lost child's.

"Is this enough?" Marty called, but he did not wait for her to answer. He started across the stream again.

Joanna stood. "This is wonderful." She took the filled basket from him and turned as if to leave.

"Wait a while. We've come too far just to turn around and go back." He sat down. "That smelly cabbage of yours can wait."

After a moment, Joanna sat. "I don't want to be gone too long."

"I used to crawl on my belly, too," Marty told her. "But I wasn't hunting geese or ducks. I was fighting fierce

Viking warriors with arms the size of that tree limb and
long, white beards."

"Why do you always want to fight?"

"It was a game."

"At the Mountain View, with Welshie, was that a
game, too?"

Marty laughed it off. "I won't run from a fight. Not
ever." His back rested against a tree. Joanna's was beginning to ache. "People say things I don't agree with." He
picked up an orange-tipped leaf from the ground and
rubbed it between his hands until it crumbled.

"I used to play games, too," she said then. "The leaves,
especially the willow leaves, were feathers. My sister and I
would lick them and paste them over our cheeks and arms
like Indians, or how we though Indians must look. Then
we strutted about, looking over our lands and if any of my
younger brothers came, we chased them. My sister was
my best friend."

"And now?"

She looked at Marty. "Well, Timothy is, of course."
She thought again of the money and then of her fear of
having this child. She hadn't told Tim that, either. "I suppose Helen is my best friend now." She smiled, but
vaguely.

"Helen is a good girl."

"I think she likes you very much."

"I don't want anyone to like me very much.

Joanna laughed. "And why not?"

"Because I'm not staying around. I don't like owing
people."

"Oh, yes," she said. "Like the money Timothy gave
you."

"Helen is a fine girl," he said again, but he could have
been speaking of his sister Kathleen.

"You act as if you like her."

"How's that?"

"You spend enough time over there."

"Joe and I are buddies. Best buddies."

"And yesterday. Playing that game, kissing her and then holding her like that right in the middle of the road." Joanna laughed. "You know, I wanted to play that game, too."

"With the handkerchief?" When she nodded, he said, "Well, why didn't you? You think you're too fat to run?"

She laughed a little. "No. It wouldn't have been right. Mrs. Flynn was sitting right there."

"You sure worry a lot about what Aunt Annie thinks." Joanna said nothing. "You ought to play a little more, Jo. You're always so quiet and serious."

"Am I?"

"You're always giving me the evil eye."

She did not laugh. "You scare me sometimes."

"Me?"

Joanna dug her fingers into the peat and pine needles. "It's because you fight and steal."

"Gamble," he said.

"The way you get Tim all angry. In the beginning I resented you and Kathleen."

"And now?"

"It's hard for me to be here. To hear Kathleen and Mrs. Flynn talk about Rosie as if she may just walk on in the door one day again. And you shooting people with stolen guns in Ireland."

He laughed to himself. He pinched some pine needles in his fingers and let them drop onto her hand. "You and I have a secret, Joanna. That money you hid in the attic."

The needles were soft and cool on her hand.

"I can tell you another secret. I never stole those guns."

She looked at him leaning against the tree. On the ground between them, their hands almost touched. "Kathleen said the police had questioned you."

"I never did it. I said I did, but it was a lie."

"Why? Why would you lie about something like that?"

He shrugged. "The boys bought me a few drafts. I was a big man suddenly."

"Boasting," she said. "But Kathleen thinks... "

"There's no harm in it now."

"Did you tell Helen?"

"Why should I tell Helen? She doesn't care."

"Why are you telling me?"

He grinned. "You and I are alike, Jo. Neither one of us belongs here. We both want to get out."

"No, I don't. Not without Tim."

"And he'll never go."

He said it with such assurance that Joanna felt her throat constrict. She shook off the pine needles and crossed her arms in front of her. "You're free to go at any time."

"Someday I will," he said.

They were quiet a moment. Around them, the woods were still. Then Marty said, "What else scares you, Jo? Besides me, I mean, and never leaving the patch."

She shook her head. Suddenly her throat felt tight.

"Com'on, Jo. Tell me what you think about all the while you're out in that garden." Marty leaned forward. "I watch you."

Joanna looked to the air shaft again. "The colliery whistle," she said softly.

"What else?"

"The baby," she whispered. She looked at Marty then. He stared at her, neither surprised nor amused. She continued, "I could never tell Timothy or Mrs. Flynn this, and I don't even know why I'm telling you, except that maybe I just have to say it out loud."

"And what's that?"

He wasn't laughing. He was looking at her the way he had in the colliery yard when he said he would have gone below to save Timothy. She said, "I am scared of having this baby."

"I guess it must be natural for the first time. Maybe

everytime." He grinned. "You'll have a healthy son."

"But what if I don't? What if it happens again?"

"Don't think about it."

She rolled her eyes. "How can I not think about it with. . . " She almost said, with Rosie still here. But she caught herself.

"Here." He pulled his handkerchief from his pocket and held it over Joanna's head, then let it fall.

She stared at it.

"Why don't you pick it up? It's clean."

Ever since that day in the garden two weeks ago when he had given her the money, Joanna felt a sort of bond with Marty, as if she were also gambling. Now she wondered if maybe the bond was more than just the secret of the money they shared. She wondered if maybe she really liked him after all. Maybe more than she should.

"Go on," he said. "Pick it up."

With a deliberate gesture, Joanna took the handkerchief and held it behind her back. She stared at him. For a moment, neither moved. Then Marty put his hand under her chin to draw her closer and he kissed her. Joanna closed her eyes and let it happen. She wanted it to happen.

When he moved away, she opened her eyes. Confused, she fingered the collar of Kathleen's too-large shirtwaist. She felt cold suddenly, as if the draft from the air shaft was blowing over her again. She dropped his handkerchief in the dried red and yellow leaves and struggled to stand up.

"Jo, wait. I'm sorry."

It was wrong to have come here with him. She knew that now. She scurried up the side of the hill towards the path on the ridge, but she slipped a little in the loose leaves. Like the bucket of wildflowers she had once forgotten on the bank, she now forgot about the basket of mushrooms.

"Jo!"

Marty caught her near the ridge, but she pulled away

from his hand. "Don't. And don't call me Jo. Not ever again."

"Listen to me a minute."

She was ashamed of herself. She did not understand why she had let him kiss her, but if it were meant to make Timothy jealous, then it was a mean trick. Or if it was because she was enticing Marty, just as Mrs. Flynn had once accused her of enticing Timothy with sweet cakes and Christmas greens, then she was a bad person. She stopped and turned to him. "Promise me. Promise me that you won't ever, ever tell what happened here today. Not even to Helen. Promise me."

"Nothing happened here today except that I care for you."

"No, you don't. Stop saying things that confuse me."

"I don't want to do anything to hurt you or Timothy. You're the only family I've got."

"Then why?" she shouted. "Why did you do it?"

He shrugged. "I don't know. You seemed sad. But it was my fault and I'm sorry I upset you."

"Forget what I told you," she said. "Forget everything." And she started back again through the woods.

That evening, Joanna fidgeted about the kitchen, tapped her fingers on the table, found it hard to listen to the conversation after supper. In her mind, she turned over and over how she could tell Timothy what had happened. Marty, of course, was gone for the evening, and Kathleen and Mrs. Flynn went early to their beds, leaving Joanna and Timothy alone. He read a while, then closed his book and moved to the old woman's chair. The basket of mushrooms was on the floor by the stove. But Joanna could not bring herself to tell him about Marty, because in the telling of that was the admitting of her fear about losing the baby, or even her own life. She picked up a damp rag and began to wipe the table, though it had already been done.

Within minutes, Timothy had fallen asleep. With his head back and his mouth open, he breathed deeply. She did not wake him, but sat instead at the table and watched him. When did it stop, she wondered, the soft and covert caresses they had given each other even when Mrs. Flynn was in the kitchen with them? He seemed so preoccupied now, especially over Matthew's condition. And tired, too. More tired now than when he had been picking coal.

She went to him after a while and smoothed her hand over his face, felt that it was warm. He woke with a start. "What?"

She smiled at him. "Come to bed, Tim."

With a heavy sigh, he got up. Joanna blew out the lamp, then in the dark, held out her hand and led him upstairs.

(i)

Angled between layers of rock, Joe Sweeney lay flat on his back and picked at the thin ribbon of anthracite above him. His hands were scraped and black. To keep from swallowing the dust, he had tied a handkerchief around his mouth. Still, dirt was wrinkled around his eyes and in the folds of his neck. As he worked, he sweated. His cotton undershirt was wet and the cold rock under his back chilled him. He laid the pick against his raised knees and rested a moment, wiping his eyes.

The chamber that he and Charlie Boy Duffy were working was ten feet wide and no more than four feet high. The rail tracks went from the gangway to just inside their chamber, stopping a few feet from the solid wall of rock, a road to nowhere. In another day, Joe and Charlie Boy would blast the stone wall, timber it, and lay more track to follow the seam of anthracite deeper into the mountainside.

Joe turned his head sideways. He saw the flame from Charlie Boy's helmet move past him to the far wall of the chamber, then disappear as Charlie Boy crawled into a chest-sized opening there. In the gangway, it was brighter.

A mule boss raised his whip over an animal. The mule lowered its head and stepped forward, slowly moving the car loaded with coal along the rails.

Joe heard rather than saw what went on around him: wheels turning along the rails, men coughing, water dripping from the beamed roofs, Charlie Boy picking steadily at the rock. From a distant chamber came a warning call for blasting. The dynamite rocked and echoed and Joe felt the tremor from the earth along his spine, as if he were a part of the rock. The ventilating fans hesitated, then hummed again. A fine mist of coal chips and dust filled the gangway like smoke. It drizzled over him.

At noon, the miners laid down their picks and shovels and walked to the gangways, their lunch pails clanging like pie tins. Joe slid from his bed of rock and stooping, went to where Charlie Boy's long legs hung over the rock shelf like a spider. It had been a good morning. The car that sat on the rails between them in the chamber was nearly full. Joe hopped onto it, leaned over, and pulled on Charlie Boy's legs.

They sat on the gangway floor with the others. Joe stretched out his cramped legs and opened his pail for the tomato preserve and lemon sandwiches Helen had made on hard, black bread. As they ate, Charlie Boy complained of his burning feet, and as he did every day, unlaced his boots and pulled them off. He sat in his stockinged feet and ate his boiled eggs.

"Holy God," Joe said.

"My feet smell no worse than the mules."

"Don't be so sure of that," Joe answered.

Charlie Boy stood and walked away along the tracks to pee in the dark by the mule stalls.

Joe waited for him to go beyond the bend and out of sight, then took Charlie Boy's boots, set them on a wooden tie of the tracks, and felt in his pockets for two nails. He hammered them through the soles into the wood, then went back to his place with the others against the wall. They were grinning when Charlie Boy returned, but Joe covered his smile by wiping his mouth on his dirty shirt sleeve.

"Well, Charlie Boy," Joe said, getting up. "We can fill that car in an hour. Get your shoes and we'll be starting on it."

Charlie Boy shook his head. "The coal will be there all day. I'm not hurrying to crawl back into my hole."

And so they waited, Charlie Boy not noticing that his boots had been moved or that the men were grinning at him. When the signal came again from the foreman, they slowly got to their feet. Charlie Boy sat on the rail and reached for his shoes. He tugged once and muttered, "What the devil. . . " He heard the men laughing around him and he smiled, too. "I don't even have to ask," Charlie Boy said. "Where is that Joe Sweeney? This is his dirty trick."

Each smiling face was the same—coal-blackened and shadowed by the flame on their helmets. They turned away, still laughing, and left Charlie Boy to pry the nails out of his boots.

By early afternoon, they had filled the car and Joe and Charlie Boy waited for a mule boss to come from the gangway with an animal to haul the coal out. Reaching into his pants pocket for a clump of tobacco, Charlie Boy wadded it into his mouth. Neither man could stand upright in the room, and both crouched on either side of the coal car. Joe put his hand into the water on the dirt floor and rubbed it over his eyes and mouth. It was bitter.

"That was a dirty trick you pulled on me, Joe."

"And what was that?"

"It's a good thing I have a sense of humor." Charlie Boy spit tobacco juice into the water at his feet.

"It's a pity you've no sense of smell," Joe said. "Don't you ever wash your feet, Charlie?"

"Sure I do. It's the socks I don't wash."

Both men laughed.

Joe's legs ached from crouching and he felt the wet through the sides of his boots. He ran his hand over the rough wall that pressed in on him. It was spongy. "Here's a problem," he said. If it were wet, the roof would weaken and he and Charlie Boy would not be able to blast for another day or two. "We'll get Tim to look at this."

In the gangway, the mule was braying. The boss raised his leather whip to strike the animal's rump. The mule's long ears lay flat and it bared its yellow teeth, turning to snarl at the handler. The man struck the animal again, pushing its rear end into the chamber where Joe and Charlie Boy were waiting. The mule was skittish in the tight room. It strained forward, its slanted beeswax eyes wide and frightened. The handler pushed him farther back.

Joe reached up to touch the mule's flank, his fingers feeling for the company number branded there. The animal lurched forward again, startled by Joe's touch. As he suspected, this was the new mule from downriver. Uneasy, Joe moved his hand away and raised himself as much as he could in the chamber. His curved shoulders just touched the ceiling.

Now the handler tossed a heavy twined rope over the animal's back. He held the mule in place as Charlie Boy tried to reach the rope and knot it over the metal support of the car. "Com'on now, Joe. Get it for us."

The mule danced in place, splashing water over Joe's legs. As the animal snorted and tried to shake free of the leather straps, its breaths were puffs of smoke that disappeared quickly in the chiseled tunnel. Just as Joe leaned forward to feel in the black water for the rope, a warning call came from the chamber opposite them. He looked up. The blast flashed like paper caught on fire and then just as quickly the place darkened. The explosion ricocheted, sounding like half a dozen separate blasts rather than one. The drizzle of coal chips fell over them again.

The mule reared, squealing, and the handler lost his hold. Then the animal lowered its head and kicked its hind legs, striking the coal car and then a supporting timber. More dirt rained down. Joe cringed between the car and the wall, crossing his arms over his head. The heavy cleats skidded off the wall beside him. Again he felt the swift rush of legs as the iron shoes cut his arms. A third time the animal kicked and cut now into Joe's thigh. He fell backwards into the water from the force of the blow. The mule, too, backed against the cracked timber and overhead the damp roof shifted. More water seeped between the wooden beam and the rock. Joe heard it and raised his head as the beam swung free, blocking the handler from pulling the mule forward.

Charlie Boy was shouting. "Get up. Get up." He crawled onto the coal car and lying over it, grabbed Joe by his shirt.

Joe tried to slide backwards, but the loaded car blocked him. Above was the angled opening in the wall where he had worked at the seam all week. Now Joe reached for that, but his fingers would not grab hold. His arm had no feeling and would not support him. The mule kicked and caught Joe in the ribs. He slumped forward, holding his stomach. His helmet fell into the water.

"Get him up!" Charlie Boy shouted to the men who had run from the gangway. They lifted the beam, but the excited mule backed away from them, still crying. It kicked once more and struck Joe in the head.

Charlie Boy still held him by the shirt. He pulled Joe up out of the water, and onto the car.

(ii)

It was past noon, but frost from the night still iced the shaded kitchen window and grass in the side yard. Although it was cold, Joanna was too restless to stay in the kitchen and sat outside on the porch stoop, an old flour sack beneath her to keep out the cold. She reached into the basket of mushrooms and began to clean the caps, stringing them one by one to be hung later above the stove to dry. Like most afternoons the children played in the road, today with a twined rag ball. She looked beyond them to the mines. It was still too early for Timothy and yet every few minutes Joanna looked up again for him.

Helen came alongside the house carrying two sacks of coal she had just scavenged from the banks. "Why in the world are you sitting outside?" she asked.

Joanna picked another mushroom from the basket. "Kathleen is baking," she said, avoiding Helen's eyes, for she had betrayed her friend as well as Timothy. "I needed the air."

"I brought some coal," Helen said. "Is Marty back?"

"No."

Helen helped herself to a mushroom. "Are these from yesterday?"

Joanna started. "Marty told you?"

"Yes," she answered simply. "He said he'd give me a string."

Joanna stared at the mushrooms coiled over her lap. It was foolish to have trusted him. She wished he had never come here from Ireland. She wished he had been arrested for stealing those guns, even though it was a lie. "I shouldn't have gone with him," she said, suddenly apologetic.

"Well, to be honest, I don't know why you didn't ask me along," Helen said.

Joanna lifted the strings of mushrooms from her lap and set them aside. "There. Take as much as you like. Take them all." She stood then and reached for the coal sack.

"No," Helen said. Joanna looked sharply at her, but there was no hurt or anger in Helen's face. "It's too heavy for you now. You shouldn't be lifting."

"For heaven's sake, Helen, I can still lift a sack of coal. I wish people would just stop worrying about me. I'm just having a baby."

"Joanna?" Helen stared at her curiously and it was obvious then that Marty had not told her everything about yesterday.

"Do you want the mushrooms or not?"

From the road came alarmed cries. Both Joanna and Helen turned. The children had stopped their game to run towards the wagon coming from the colliery.

"Dear God," Helen whispered. Joanna let the sack go. Long and high and closed like a crate, it was the same wagon that had brought the coffins to the shaft the day of the cave-in. "But I didn't hear the whistle," Joanna said. "Just once at noon, like always." She put her hand to her throat, feeling as if she could not breathe.

The wagon came slowly. The mule's head swayed with each step. Both the animal and the two company men riding the wagon seemed unaware of the children who called out as it passed, "Who is it, Mister? Is he dead?"

Joanna hugged her belly to keep her own child from hearing. She murmured, "Let it pass. Let it pass." But the wagon did not pass. It stopped in the middle of the road in front of her house. And then she knew. It had finally happened. After all those months of worrying about fires and gases and cave-ins, after cringing each time the colliery sounded at dawn and noon and suppertime, it had finally happened to her.

"No," she cried and shook her head. "No." She stepped back against the porch post. The sack tipped and the scavenged chunks of coal rushed over her boots. The two men jumped to the ground, unlatched the wagon's rear doors, and removed the body on a stretcher. She watched in horror as they lifted it over the heads of the children and carried it across the road, not to her house but Helen's.

"Oh, God, it's Joe," Helen cried.

Joanna felt planted there on the porch in the coal that

had spilled over her feet. It was not Timothy. It was Joe. Helen pushed through the children who were crowding at her gate. She ran after the company men into her yard and onto the porch. They carried Joe into the house, but Helen stayed at the door. As they came back out, one stopped to squeeze her shoulder, and then continued out to the road.

It was so quiet Joanna thought she could hear the ash crunching under the wagon's wheels as it turned again for the mines. Helen stood alone in the open door, weeping into her hands. Across the road, Joanna was too frightened to go to her. When Kathleen peered from the door, Joanna said, "It's Joe. They just brought Joe Sweeney."

It was Kathleen who went down the steps and across the road to Helen. With her arms around Helen's shoulders, she led her into the house and closed the door behind her. Still, Joanna could not move. Light-headed and nauseous, she reached for the porch post. "It's alright," she spoke out loud to herself. "It's alright. It isn't Timothy. I'm going to be alright." But when she looked up again at Helen's house, she felt her stomach lurch. She made her way down the steps and around to the back of the stoop. She slid down to her knees and got sick in the grass.

(iii)

Joanna wrapped the shawl over Mrs. Flynn's shoulders. The old woman leaned on Joanna's arm and took the porch steps one at a time. They went slowly through the yard to the gate and crossed the road where already the game of kickball had begun again, though farther down the road. At the Sweeney door, Joanna hesitated, and Mrs. Flynn said without looking at her, "It's got to be done."

Joanna opened the door.

In the kitchen, Kathleen was boiling water. Mrs. Flynn pointed and Joanna helped her to a chair at the table where Kathleen had set the spices. Joanna looked around the kitchen, so much like their own. On the corner cupboard was the bird cage Joe had carried into the Flynn kitchen one year ago. The painted sparrow, of course, they had long set free. There were no sounds in the house except for Mrs. Flynn's tired sighs and the quiet sizzle of the water coming to a boil. Joanna glanced over her shoulder at the door opened just a little to the front room. She could just see Helen as she sat there with head bowed near the bed. Joanna quickly looked away. She rubbed her upper arm where Mrs. Flynn had held her so tightly.

Kathleen said, "Why not go home and rest yourself, Joanna?" She smiled sadly at the girl. "It'll be a long night for us all."

Joanna shook her head. It's got to be done, Mrs. Flynn had said, and she would not be sent away as if she were not a part of the family.

"It's a sad day for us," Mrs. Flynn sighed. "He was a decent man and deserved more than this." She waved her hand at the room. Joanna followed the circle of the old woman's fingers. Each company house was alike—a crucifix over the door, a sack of coal beside the stove, a door to the attic stairs. "Bring me that pan, Joanna," the old woman said.

Joanna took the small tin pan from the wall hook near the cellar. Kathleen poured a little of the steaming water into it and Mrs. Flynn added pinches of spice. "I want to help," Joanna said.

"Then bring Helen out here now so we can wash the body," Mrs. Flynn said.

Joanna thought it strange that Mrs. Flynn did not use Joe's name. She turned for the door and slowly pushed it open wider. Helen did not look up. But she was no longer crying. Joanna followed her gaze to the bed where Joe was lying. Coins weighted his closed eyes and a stained rag covered the head wound. He was dead and still the blood stained the pillowcase. Joanna had never seen a dead body before and she was frightened, of Joe and Helen both.

Very lightly, she touched her friend's shoulder. "They want you to come out now."

Helen nodded. She stood, then looked over her shoulder at Joe one more time before going with Joanna. Mrs. Flynn and Kathleen went into the front room. The old woman lifted the flannel sheet from Joe's body and removed his jacket. Kathleen undid his shirt. As they undressed him, dropping the soiled clothes in a pile on the floor, Joanna waited at the foot of the bed for them to tell her what to do. She did not look at Joe, but at the oval mirror to the side of the bed. It did not cast her reflection but rather the bare wall behind her. When Mrs. Flynn looked back at Joanna and saw how pale the girl was, she nodded to the clothes on the floor. "Take those out to the burn barrel, then bring us more soapy water."

Grateful to the old woman for sending her outside, Joanna stooped and quickly gathered the clothes, then hurried past Helen in the kitchen. Outside, she dumped the clothes in the barrel and turned away from it.

How cool the air felt against her arms and face. How much more fresh and clean it seemed outside. She breathed deeply. Across the way, her flowers were brown, shriveled from the cold, though there were still plants growing in the garden, the cauliflower, some stalks of broccoli. She looked up at the Flynn house, or rather their half of the double dwelling. Upstairs, the blue gingham curtains were snapping out of the open window and it made Joanna smile to think how Timothy liked to sleep with cold air blowing in on him. After the winter thaw, she was dreaming now, she and Timothy could ride to the farm, their child bundled on the wagon seat between them, and bring back an apple sapling to plant in the side yard, near the porch stoop so she could see it from the kitchen window.

Mary stepped from the house next door. She stopped now to take Joanna's hands into her own, bringing the girl back from her daydream. She said, "I'm so sorry for your trouble."

"Mary," Joanna said, "it wasn't Tim. It was Joe."

"Joe Sweeney and Timothy Flynn were like brothers. Sure, I know it."

Still, Joanna did not fully understand why Mary would give condolences to her. She said again, "Tim wasn't hurt."

"And thanks be to God for that." Mary patted Joanna's hands again, then let them go. "I've come to do what I can."

Joanna glanced back at Helen's house. "They're dressing the body now."

Mary nodded and went inside.

(i v)

At the wake that night, they sat together as one family, Helen and the Flynns. With the black rosary beads threaded through her reddened fingers, Mrs. Flynn led the gathering in reciting prayers. The others who had come sat in what chairs there were at the foot of the bed. Men stood along the wall. The candles on the dresser top cast the shadows of bowed heads over the walls. After the rosary, the men went to the kitchen and sat around the table, but the women and children remained in the front room. Mrs. Flynn leaned forward and looked at all their faces. Back home as a girl she had heard the shanachies tell many a tale of death and the old woman began to weave one for them now.

"Once there was a man named Donal," she began, "and no finer man there was than he within the four seas of Ireland. But he was a poor man. Now Donal had a wife whose lips were as red and as warm as blood and the temper she had was just as hot."

At this, Joanna looked at Mrs. Flynn to see if the old

woman was eyeing her, but Mrs. Flynn was staring at the shadows on the wall, her face so concentrated that Joanna also looked in the same direction.

"When the hunger came into their house," Mrs. Flynn was saying, "poor Donal could not feed his many a child. And so the wife, she says to him, 'Donal, come morning, you must take our cow and sell it in the village for there is no meat in this house and the children are feeling the hunger. I killed the last goose two weeks ago.'

"Well come morning, Donal took the cow and off he set for the village. Now a day earlier in the village a poor man had died and the widow woman had not a coin to bury the husband. She sat in the road with her man in the barrow and cried over him. Now this was on the edge of town where the graveyard was, and doesn't Donal come down the road with his branny cow behind him?

" 'What's this?' he says to the widow. 'Why do you cry so, the likes of which I've never heard before?' And the widow woman told him her sad tale from start to finish.

"Now, Donal, being a fine and sensitive man and brought up holy, too, felt sorry for the widow and the corpse, and didn't he give his cow to her to pay off the debt so the old man could be buried decent and pass on his way to the next world? And the widow woman kissed his hand a hundred times or more and off she went to sell Donal's cow for herself.

"Poor Donal had nothing left to his name except the thanks of the dead man's wife. Well, he turned and headed for his own home, but when he came over the hill and saw his poor sod hut, he sat down in the road and could go no farther. He thought of his poor children feeling the hunger and his wife whose lips were as red and as warm as blood and her temper just as hot.

"Now when the wife heard what Donal had done, she cried tears so hot and salty they stung her cheeks. With one child in her arms, and two more clinging to her skirts, she turned Donal out of her bed and house. Outside in the cold and wet, Donal lay under a sciog bush." Mrs. Flynn stopped. "Well, that's a fairy bush, don't you know. But Donal didn't see it as one. Well, the sleep would not come to him for he could still hear his woman's cries through the night.

"Then all at once it began to pour rain, teeming so that Donal was soaked to the skin for the bush was no shelter at all. And then the lightning came, shooting like fire across the sky and a bolt struck the very bush where Donal cowered, setting a single branch aflame. Out of the fire appears one of the little people, a wee man no higher than your knee, and he speaks to Donal, who was crying over his lot in life.

" 'Why is it you're out in the cold on such a night?' Donal wiped the rain and the tears both from his eyes and told his sad tale and when he had finished, the wee little man asked, 'And are you sorry you did what you did?'

"Donal thought hard on it awhile and then spoke honestly. 'I can't say that I am for every man deserves a decent burial and I may still find food for my family yet.'

"The little man dug deep into his pockets. 'Hold out your hand, Donal, for I'll do you no harm and I'll even do you some good.' And he dropped two gold coins into Donal's hand. 'No man's family will go hungry if he's as fine a man as you. I was the corpse you helped to bury today,' he said, 'and these are the two gold coins my woman got for your cow. I've no more need of them now.'

"And with that, the little man leaped into the flame again and the rain that was pouring smoldered the flames so that the bush was as it had been before. And the rain stopped its teeming so that the night skies were as clear as before. And in the sod hut, Donal's wife stopped her crying and opened the door, calling for him to come back to her.

"And the hunger never came again to Donal's house for he was a good and caring man. And may you and I be the same."

The old woman sat back. The room was still. The telling of the story had tired her. The wide-eyed children leaned against their mothers' shoulders or lay with their heads in their mothers' laps.

"I'm thinking Joe Sweeney was such a man," Mrs. Flynn said, wiping her eyes. "The Lord have mercy on his soul."

The simple story had caught Joanna's imagination. She thought she could hear the rain and the wife crying. She believed that Joe's spirit was with them, not there in the bed with his face to the wall, but outside, peering through the window, watching them as they mourned for him, even laughing at them a little for being so glum. She glanced quickly at the window then, but saw only the reflection of the candles.

In the kitchen, the whiskey bottle was on the table and each man had taken a shot or two. "I knew that mule was trouble from the moment I laid my eyes on it," a man said, and a murmur of agreement went around the room. The conversation that evening, however, did not linger on Joe's freak accident or on mining at all. It could not. If the men thought too long or too often about the dangers they faced every day, they would never go below again. To ease their own fear and loss, they spoke of happier times and their occasional gay outbursts could be heard outside.

"Now I remember the night Joe was in the game of dominoes with Charlie Boy here at the Mountain View," the same man spoke. "Well, Joe won a little bit, not much to speak of, and then Charlie Boy says to Joe, 'Joe, I have a fine offer just for you.' "

Charlie Boy, who had been quiet until now, smiled.

The man continued. "Charlie Boy sells him a singing canary. Now every one of us there knew it was a hoodwink."

"I got my losings back now, didn't I?" Charlie Boy asked.

Timothy, too, smiled with the memory of Joe coming to his house that same night with the painted sparrow in the bird cage.

"Well, he let the bird go," Charlie Boy picked up the story. "After a week and still no singing. All winter you could see that bird going from fence to roof and everybody telling Joe that his canary got free again."

The men laughed, louder perhaps than they might have if they had been telling the story at the Mountain View, but this night their laughter was a necessary release and healed them all a little.

Outside, standing at the gate of the Sweeney house, Marty Boyle heard the laughter and did not understand. When he pushed through the door, the men in the smoky kitchen stopped their conversation to stare curiously at him. His green eyes glared. His red hair was wild from the ride he had just taken through the night.

Timothy stood. There had been no way of contacting Marty that afternoon to let him know. He had not been seen in the patch all day and no doubt he had been at some other mining town gambling at cards. Timothy put his hand on Marty's shoulder, but the boy brushed past him into the front room.

The women and children there, too, looked up when he entered. He hung back in the doorway and stared at Joe on the bed. "Holy God," he swore. He turned to Helen and fell to his knees before her. "Holy God, Helen," he said and hugged her about the waist, his head in her lap like one of the children.

She gazed tenderly at him, ran her fingers over his wild hair. "Marty," she soothed in the same gentle way the others had been comforting her.

He spoke into her skirt. "I came as soon as I heard." He looked up, flushed and angry. "I swear to you I'll make them pay for this. I swear to you I will!"

She stroked his head. "Please, Marty, let it be. Don't make it worse than it is already. Nobody is at fault. It was an accident."

Joanna stared at them, surprised at the affection between them. She felt sorry for them both because they were so sad, and then she felt sorry for herself that no one had held and comforted her, though she, too, was feeling a loss.

He looked at Joe once more, then he shook Helen's hands from him and stood. "They've got to know we won't be taking this anymore."

"No, Marty. I'm just glad you're here now. I needed you to come."

"Someone will pay for this," he said. "That I promise you."

He turned and as he passed Joanna, she was tempted to reach out for him. She glanced at Mrs. Flynn, but the old woman was sitting quietly, deep in her own thoughts now. After a moment, Joanna stood and left the room.

"Well? What's to be done now?" Marty challenged.

The men were silent. Charlie Boy offered him the whiskey bottle. "Calm yourself, Marty. You're too hot."

The boy took the bottle and drank from it. He held it in his hand and faced Timothy. "I want to know what you are intending to do."

Timothy placed his hands flat on the table top. "Don't get your rile up. It'll do none of us any good."

"Coward," the boy hissed.

Joanna stood against the kitchen wall. She held her breath. Every man in the room watched silently as Timothy raised his glass and drank from it. Steadily he set it down. "Think what you will, Marty. I had no better friend than Joe Sweeney, but I can do him no good now." He looked across the room at Joanna. "I have others to think of now."

Marty set the bottle down. In the faces of each man there he saw the same grim expression, an acceptance of things the way they were. "Cowards," he repeated. "The whole lot of you are afraid, and of what? One man? Five men?"

"You don't understand," Charlie Boy said without looking up. "No one did this to Joe. It's a risk all of us who go below take."

The men in the kitchen were staring at Marty, not challenging the boy, but rather enduring him. Marty knew what Charlie Boy was telling him. He didn't belong. He wasn't one of them. He was not a miner, and he did not take the same risk they did each morning. With a wry smile, he said, "I guess I'm the one here with the least to lose. But that's alright. I'll show you what I can do." He turned again to Timothy. "You've gone to the other side, haven't you, Tim? You and Welshie." His voice was sad, but not beaten. "You're the landlord now. You make me sick."

"Marty," Joanna called as he went out.

The door closed. The men sat quietly for a moment, then gradually the conversations began again. Timothy went to her.

"Can't you stop him?" she asked. "He'll do something bad, I just know it."

"There isn't anything I can do for Marty now except let him cool down a bit."

"You don't understand. He doesn't mean what he says. He'd risk his life for you or Joe or Charlie."

"It's you I'm more concerned about."

"Me?"

"You're tired. And I'm thinking now that Ma must be, too. Why don't you take her home? I'll come later."

After a moment, she nodded.

In the dark, front room that smelled of musk and candle wax, the old woman was indeed ready. She took Joanna's arm and left with her. As they crossed the road in the moonlight for the house they shared, Mrs. Flynn said, "My feet are throbbing, Joanna. The cold has got into them already." They stepped carefully up onto the board walkway. The old woman sighed. "I've buried too many good people this year."

Joanna said, "I've never once seen anyone buried."

As they climbed the porch steps, Mrs. Flynn leaned heavily on Joanna's arm and the girl held tightly the old woman's hand.

(v)

Joanna stood outside Mrs. Flynn's room where already the old woman was snoring softly. The door to Marty's room was open slightly. She pushed the door open and called for him, then peered inside. He was not there. Joanna stepped inside.

It had been months since she had been in this room. In the dark, it looked no different. It was the front room, the room where, no doubt, Rosie and then Mr. Flynn had been waked. Joanna moved closer to the bed. She tried to imagine Rosie laid out there just as Joe was across the road. She looked to the side where a straight-back chair had been placed. Timothy would have sat there. She touched the back of the chair. He would have sat with his head lowered and his hands folded while Mrs. Flynn recited her prayers. How awful for him, she thought, to have to sleep in the same bed where Rosie had been laid out.

Since the day she had arrived one year ago, Joanna had lived with Rosie's shadow. Now she wanted to bury it. She reached for the blanket and pulled it from the bed and stared, as if expecting to find Rosie hiding under the covers like a child. She hugged the blanket to her and then she began to cry. She cried for Joe Sweeney and for Rosie and for that other child that still called to Timothy, to her. She smothered her sobs in the blanket so the old woman would not hear. She cried, too, for herself because she had betrayed Timothy and Helen, and because she was frightened of having the child, and because she did not know if Timothy really loved her or if he had just reached out for her in order to forget. And when those tears were spent, she felt better. She smoothed the blanket over Marty's bed again. Then she knelt before the drawer where months ago she had folded away Rosie's old sweater. Tonight she would bury Rosie. Just as she had done with Joe's clothes, Joanna took the old sweater outside to the burn barrel and dropped it in.

She did not want to stay in the house by herself and so she did not go back inside, but stood in the middle of the road. She thought Marty might have gone to the colliery and for a moment worried that he would set the building on fire, for hadn't he bragged once about setting fires on the landlord's property in Ireland? But she dismissed that idea. Marty knew that everyone's well-being depended on the mines operating. Although she did not understand her apprehensions for Marty, and was frightened of how she now felt towards him, she turned and started down the road towards the superintendent's home. Of course he would go there. She lifted her skirt above her ankles and walked faster.

The superintendent's home was in darkness except for the front corner room. Joanna stopped at the gate. A brick walk led to the pillared front porch, but she stayed in the shadows and waited. She saw no one. She wasn't sure just what she had expected to find, but surely Marty would have gone right up that brick walk and into the front door.

Then she became aware of the music. She had heard it as soon as she had approached the house, but only now did she identify the soft sounds. Fiddles, accordians, and mouth organs were the sort of music Joanna knew, but this was richer, much like humming is softer than whistling. This music weaved and rushed, then slowed. It drew her from the protective shadows.

Joanna opened the gate and went cautiously nearer the window. Through the mesh of lacy curtains she saw the young girl who was playing the piano. She sat with her head tilted to one side as if trying to hear the chords more clearly. Her eyes were closed and her hands moved surely, without effort. She was the superintendent's daughter. Joanna had heard about her from Helen but had never seen her for she did not live in the patch. She attended a school in Butler, living there with her grandmother. "She wears fancy high-buttoned boots," Helen had said, "and frilly dresses and gloves. She's our age, but she sure isn't one of us."

Joanna stepped closer. The girl seemed younger, certainly too young to be married as Joanna was and expecting a child.

The piano, too, was different, unlike the one in the old schoolroom in the valley near her father's farm. This one was larger and curved with its top raised. Was this the type of piano of which Rosie had been so proud and had so regretted leaving behind? Did she also play this sort of bittersweet music? Joanna reached her hand toward the windowpane as if to touch the notes. The coal dust that covered the glass was as fine as the stitching in the lace curtains and her fingertips left a track.

The superintendent was seated in a cushioned chair. It surprised her that this was how these people spent their evenings, not worrying about cave-ins or gases but rather listening to dreamy music. The parlor scene was unreal, more like a daguerreotype, like one of the tintypes Joanna had seen in Butler the morning of the Memorial Day Parade.

She knew now that Marty had not been here, for if he had, there would be no soft music and the man would not be nodding lazily in his soft chair. She felt foolish for it was, after all, as Timothy had said. Marty had gone off by himself to cool down. He did not need her to look after him.

Slowly, she walked back up the road. When she came to the Mountain View, she realized suddenly how late it was and that she was alone. She moved out of the light to the far side of the road nearer the company store. It was quiet tonight in the Mountain View and she thought, he might have gone there, but she kept walking. In the moonlight the sagging front porch was empty. Still, she felt as if she were being watched. She glanced sideways at the railroad tracks and the thick darkness that hung over the silt dam. In the foreman's house, a single lamp was lit and she saw with a start that Welshie was outside. The light cast his long shadow over the road. As Joanna walked through it, more quickly now, she modestly raised her shawl to cover her hair.

(v i)

Marty crouched near the stalls. The warm and earthy smell of the animals rose around him. Above, the loft window where he had entered swung with the wind, slammed, and swung open again. The mules stirred, rumps to him. Marty cocked his head towards the padlocked barn door, but no one was there. No one had seen him.

On the wall by the door were the whips with leather thongs looped like a chain. Marty reached for one and rolled its smooth handle in his palm, then gripped it tighter and brought the straps in an arc over his head. They struck the dirt floor with a sharp crack and the mules stirred once more, uneasy. Then the boy saw the sledge hammer and he dropped the whip for it. With two hands he swung its heavy weight over his shoulder, smiled a little, and eased the hammer down.

He moved slowly past the numbered stalls, dragging the hammer in the dirt behind him. On the flanks of the mules was the branded symbol of the coal company, followed by a number, and on each animal the identifying marks were the same. Except one. On this animal, too, the number was out of sequence.

Across the pen was a rusty chain and now Marty crept under it into the stall. The mule danced sideways away from him. Its flank and legs were scarred. As Marty ran his hand over its rump and studied the brand again to be sure, the mule turned with its yellow, peg teeth bared. The amber, almost oriental eyes seemed to glow in the dark. The mule swung its hindquarters around and knocked Marty against the wall.

He gripped the hammer with both hands. A mule was a valuable piece of property in a coal-patch town. Even Joe Sweeney's mule, sold because it was too old for underground mining, could still haul a wagon of timber or wind its way down the mountain road to Butler for a spring picnic or plod through the soft culm fields to a neighboring patch for a game of cards. Like Timothy, Marty felt at that moment that he had had no better friend than Joe Sweeney. But unlike Timothy, he could not let Joe's death, accident or not, go unnoticed. Although he could not be sure if this animal were the one that killed Joe, it represented the company and Marty wanted only an eye for an eye.

As if sensing this threat, the animal's hind legs suddenly shot up and out, once and then again, but struck only air. As Marty lifted the hammer to his shoulder, the mule twisted and brushed against him again. With a low growl, Marty brought the hammer down on the animal's skull. Its legs buckled and it fell forward on its knees. Marty struck it again. The mule grunted and collapsed on the dirt floor.

The boy stood there, breathing hard. Still the amber eyes seemed to glow up at him. He thought of Joe Sweeney, and then of Welshie, wheeling around to strike him on the side of his head with the whiskey bottle. He remembered the silt dam and the circle of miners who had laughed at him for forfeiting the cockfight. He felt the same humiliation later when Timothy had pushed the money off the table and chided him like some bad boy for gambling. He thought of Welshie's woman, Mrs. Barton, who always smiled teasingly at him from the water pump but who never once opened her back door or lifted her skirts for him. He thought of the sod hut in Ireland where he had felt so cheated. The fine, glossy horses grazed on land that should have been his family's. And then he saw again the faces of the miners, sitting tonight in Joe Sweeney's kitchen, staring at him as if he had no right to be angry.

Slowly, Marty raised the hammer. He struck the mule a third time.

(i)

Joe Sweeney was buried the next morning in the small graveyard behind the Mountain View. The air was cold and the sky the color of slate. It promised snow. Father Jordan held tightly the scarf around his neck as he read from the small worn book he had taken from the folds of his black skirt. He held the Bible close to his face and his eyes blinked at the page, though not from a bright sun. Joanna was painfully reminded of the glasses Joe had bought for himself in Butler.

The priest read slowly about dignity and selflessness, about the just reward for those who toiled and were honest and faithful. At times, his words were carried away on the sudden gusts of wind. His skirt lifted a little. Life was a test of love, he read. His spotted hand at his throat was like a smooth stone bleached by the sun and water on the riverbank. It was not a miner's hand.

Beside her, Timothy was staring across the field at the stand of oak trees on the ridge. Joanna knew the feel of a miner's hands. The skin was dry and cracked; the palms, creased with dirt. She reached for his hand now and felt with satisfaction his fingers wrap around hers. There was strength in a miner's hands.

All around her were the people she cared so much about. Mrs. Flynn once more sat on the chair they had carried for her. Kathleen stood behind her. Marty, the red flush gone now from his face, had his arm around Helen. Helen seemed changed somehow, older perhaps in the black bonnet tied too tightly under her chin. She was not crying, but then like Mrs. Flynn, she had buried good people before. In a spreading circle around them were the miners and their wives and children. Joanna looked for the dignity in their faces. It was not in the men's sunken eyes or in their grey cheeks, not in the women's rounded shoulders. It came from somewhere else, from inside. Yesterday at the wake these people had given to Helen what they could: a few coins, baked bread, preserves, or coal for the stove. They felt Helen's pain. The accident had not happened to Joe alone, but to each of them. And that was why, Joanna now understood, Mary had squeezed her hands yesterday afternoon at the burn barrel and said she was sorry for her. Joe's death had rippled through the circle of people standing over his grave.

Joanna looked at Timothy. His hair was blown all ways in the wind and she could not read his face, but she thought she understood more clearly why he had felt responsible for Matthew's injuries and why when the colliery whistle sounded he had to go below. It was more than a job. He was connected to these people. It was their life.

Timothy's fingers still held her hand tightly. Through him, Joanna was connected, too. She looked back at the Mountain View, not quite as intimidating in the daylight as it was last night. The clapboards were warping, curling as if the wind were lifting them, too. Life is a test of love, the priest read. I am a miner's wife, Joanna thought, and it did not seem so dreadful a thing after all.

There were times when she wanted to bend more freely than Mrs. Flynn or this coal patch would allow, to be

more like the white birches that had taken root in the culm
banks behind the house. She turned her face into the wind,
looking again across the frost-burned grasses to the stand
of oak trees on the ridge. But there were other times when
she wanted to be stronger for Timothy, to be more like the
oak tree, whose wood was so hard it had taken her father
two full days to chop one down on the farm. To be as Father Jordan had said, selfless and faithful. She shook her
head to dismiss a fleeting image of Marty kneeling before
her on the bank of the stream. In Kathleen's too-big
shirtwaist she felt so plain. But wasn't that, too, like the
oak, whose dull brown leaves clung to its branches
throughout winter? Even now they were rustling in the
wind.

When the others turned away from the grave Timothy
let go of Joanna's hand. He helped his mother walk across
the field to a spot under the pines. Joanna and the family
followed. They stopped first at Mr. Flynn's gravesite, then
continued on to where two more white crosses were leaning crookedly. The old woman hung onto Timothy's arm
and used her free hand to straighten the cross and wipe the
dirt from its face. The names were painted in small, uneven letters, already beginning to fade.

Gently, Kathleen led the woman away. Joanna and
Timothy stayed behind.

"I didn't know you had named the boy," she said.

"James," he said. "We had decided on it long before it
was time."

Joanna and Timothy, however, had not discussed their
child at all, except to speak of it in terms of fear. She
looked at him now and said, "I think I would like to call
my child Robert. It is my father's name."

"It's a fine name," he said and kissed her forehead.

Welshie and another man were waiting at the wagon as
the family left the graveyard. One held a shotgun
diagonally across his chest. Welshie stood with hands on

hips and jacket open to the cold. At first, Joanna thought they meant only to convey their sympathies, but then Timothy told her to go back to the house with Kathleen.

"Why?"

"Don't argue with me, Jo."

But it was Mrs. Flynn who would not leave. "What do they mean by coming here with a gun?" she said.

Welshie looked from Joanna to Helen. His moustache made him appear to frown. "I'm sorry for you, Miss."

Mrs. Flynn nodded to the man with the gun. "Who is this madman?"

Timothy said, "What do you want, Welshie?"

"It's him," he said, turning towards Marty. "I've come for you, Mick."

"Marty?" Helen said.

"I have no business with you," Marty Boyle said. "Not on this day or any other. Now get out of our way."

"Be quiet," Timothy said.

Welshie grinned. "That's right, Mick. Be careful who you're ordering around. I brought a coalie with me, and believe it, he has the authority to use that gun of his if you don't cooperate with me."

The coalie stood back, away from the wagon. He was from downriver and Timothy did not know him. "It must be a serious charge if you've brought police," Timothy said.

"He's got a grudge against me," Marty said. "It goes way back to a cock fight."

"I said be quiet," Timothy repeated. "I'll handle this. You take the women home."

The boy turned on him, furious that Timothy would dismiss him with the women. "No, you listen to me, Tim. I can handle my own affairs."

Welshie nodded. "That's right. This doesn't concern you, Tim. It's the boy and just the boy we need to talk to."

Timothy raised his eyebrows. "I guess I have the right

to hear your charge. You are making a charge, aren't you?"

Marty laughed at Welshie. "You don't get it, do you? I'm not on your payroll. I don't answer to you or your superintendent. You can't charge me at all."

"Say what you have to, Welshie," Timothy said, "and then go on your way."

Welshie shrugged. "Last evening just after ten o'clock one of the mules was found with its skull crushed. The sledge hammer was not far away."

"Go on," Timothy said.

"It was no coincidence."

Marty grinned. "No?"

"What I'm saying, Tim, is that your boy did it."

Joanna glanced quickly at Marty.

"You're daft," the boy said. "I wouldn't have one thing to do with a stinking mule. I don't like their smell. Or yours."

Joanna recognized the boastful voice and thought of the stolen guns that were really a lie. But this she believed. Marty had gone not to the superintendent's home as she had first thought but to the mule barn. A image flashed before her, that of the bloody carcass of the mule killed the day of the roof fall. At first glance she had mistaken it for soiled and bloody blankets. She felt weak to think that Marty could do such a violent thing.

"It's company property you destroyed and a valuable piece of it at that," Welshie said. "As foreman, I'm going to see that you are arrested for this one."

"And what proof do you have?" Marty challenged him. "Tell me that? Do you have a witness? No, you don't. You're talking through your ass again."

"I heard about you last night, fired up and ready to spit, running out and swearing revenge. I don't need witnesses to know that you killed that animal."

"Is that all?" Timothy asked him. "You've no other evidence than just what a few people said? The boy is known to do a lot of boastful talking. I think you'll agree to that, Welshie. But talking and doing are two different things."

Of course, Marty did it. It wasn't a lie this time. In Ireland, others had stolen the guns, so Marty didn't have to. He could just talk it up, be a big man in his town. But no one in the patch had acted. Marty had to do it himself this time. Joe's death had touched them all, and Marty, too. She saw him again on the floor at Helen's knees, crying into her lap. Without looking at either Mrs. Flynn or Timothy, Joanna said, "You're mistaken. Marty Boyle was with me last night."

The boy wheeled around, clearly surprised. Welshie, too, seemed thrown off guard.

She said, "I left the Sweeney house early last night. Right after Marty. I took my mother-in-law home."

"Joanna, you don't have to tell this lout anything," Marty said.

She spoke louder now, more confident. "Anyone who saw Marty leave last night also saw me go, too." She looked up at Welshie. "Well, you can ask them."

"And what were you and the boy doing last night?"

Timothy put his hand on her arm. "You don't have to answer. He has no right to question you."

"It's alright. I want to tell. It was like you said, Tim. Marty was upset and needed to cool down." Again she looked directly at Welshie and lied. "We walked, that's all." Then she added more quietly, thinking not of last night now but of the afternoon she had gone with Marty to the stream for the mushrooms, "Maybe I just needed someone to talk to, also."

"I don't believe you," Welshie said. "You're lying to protect him."

Too late Joanna realized her mistake. Welshie had seen her last night walking past the Mountain View, alone. "We walked to the superintendent's house," she said quickly, determined to make the best of it. "But we only stood outside the window. You see, I wouldn't let Marty go in because I was afraid of what he might say or do. If you ask the superintendent, he'll tell you how he was sitting in the parlor last night while his daughter was playing the piano. We saw them through the window."

Marty was smiling confidently at her.

"She was wearing a pink dress," Joanna said tiredly. "Ask him if his daughter was wearing a pink dress last night with ribbon through the lace sleeve above the elbow."

"I will ask him, Mrs. Flynn," Welshie said. "See if I don't. And I'll get back to you again about this."

He had seen her. Last night from his own house he had watched as she walked past the Mountain View alone. But he said nothing about that now. He and the coalie walked away.

"Well." Mrs. Flynn shifted her weight. "Here's a fine thing. And did you do it, Marty?"

"Of course, he didn't," Helen said. "You heard Joanna. They were together." Mrs. Flynn looked at Joanna. The girl lowered her head.

"You're too hot, Marty," Timothy said. He put his arm around his mother again. "Let's just go home for now and we'll deal with this later."

Joanna let out a long breath. She was shaking.

Marty reached for her. "Jo," he began, but she shook her head, silencing him, and walked away.

(ii)

No one was in the company store when Joanna entered. In the center of the room was a potbellied stove and the clerk, a slight and stooped old man named Paddy, was kneeling before it, poking at the embers. When he heard the bell, he stood and wiped his hands on his apron and turned slowly to see who had entered. He nodded to Joanna and went behind the counter to his high stool where the company ledger lay open.

"Are you closing, Paddy?" The store was unusually quiet.

"Not closed." He pulled a handkerchief from his hip pocket and blew his nose. "I can get you what you need if you have the cash."

Joanna held out her hands to the smoky heat of the stove. "I only need butter and sugar. A pound of each."

"It's got to be cash, Joanna."

She looked over her shoulder at him. Only once had she paid with cash, and that was the Christmas sassafras and peppermint sticks for her brothers and sister, but even then she had signed for her father's gift. She paid a small sum each month and watched with satisfaction when Paddy crossed out her debt in March. "I don't understand. You always allowed me to sign before."

He leaned over the ledger and dipped his pen into the inkwell. Paddy's right hand had been injured in a mining accident years ago and he had only the index finger and the thumb remaining. A loaded coal car had shifted and the wheel sliced off the fingers. The first time Joanna had gone to the company store and noticed his mangled hand, she had felt weak. Now it no longer bothered her. He wrote with his left hand, his arm curled across the page and his face close to the book as if the figures were a secret. Paddy finished his entry, blotted it, then looked up. "It isn't my decision, Joanna. It is the superintendent's. I just do what the superintendent tells me."

"Is it me they won't let sign, or is it everyone?"

Again Paddy set his pen down and reached for his handkerchief. This time he coughed into it, a deep rattling sound that seemed to take all of his strength, but Joanna did not pay much attention to this, either. She had grown accustomed to Nat's racking coughs, especially in the morning.

When he had caught his breath, Paddy said, "All credit is suspended."

"But why? Timothy says the market prices are good."

"It's that mule." He stuffed his handkerchief into his pocket. "No credit until the one responsible for killing the mule comes forward."

She looked around the store to be certain they really were alone. "Do they know who did it?" Paddy looked at her with dull eyes. "If they do, they didn't tell me."

In winter most people could not last the month without some credit from the company store. They could scavenge the culm banks for chunks of inferior coal, and they could rely on their preserves and winter vegetables, but there were other items, the cough syrups and lye soaps and extra coal to keep the fires steady throughout the evenings. Joanna fully understood the implication of no credit. At first, it would not mean so much, but if it continued into the winter...

"I don't like this," she said indignantly. "It's wrong to do this to honest people."

"Maybe so," Paddy murmured into his ledger. "Maybe so."

She had some coins in her bag and reluctantly she counted out twenty-five cents, then pulled the string tight again. "I'll just take the butter," she said and slid the coins across the smooth countertop. As she turned for the door, the pound of butter hung heavy in her bag.

She felt the cold in her face as soon as she stepped from the porch into the road. There were some women at the pump, and although they did not look up at her, Joanna felt self-conscious. They would blame her. No doubt they had already guessed that she was lying to protect Marty. And why? He was nothing to her. Why had she said anything at all to Welshie?

The steam lokie was just then leaving the breaker for its long, winding journey into Butler. The cars were loaded with coal. The tracks ran behind the row of company houses, curved around the silt dam, and crossed the stream. Joanna watched the cars sway as they rolled slowly past. Once a day the train departed, but it only carried coal, not people, out of the patch. If I were to leave here, she thought, I would just follow those tracks.

"Joanna!"

From the porch of the Mountain View, Marty waved, then hurried across the frozen road towards her. Joanna looked to the water pump where the two women were still talking. She began to walk fast up the road. Marty hurried alongside of her.

"Wait one minute, Joanna. I need to talk to you."

"Mrs. Flynn is waiting for me," she said without looking at him.

He caught her arm and stopped her. "I just want to say something. Can't you hear me out?"

"No." She pulled away.

"It didn't happen the way you think."

Joanna put her head down into the wind and hurried past the pump. The women were watching them now. Joanna recognized Mrs. Barton.

"Look. I went there alright, but I didn't know what was going to happen."

"Be quiet," she hissed and her eyes told him that they were being watched.

He walked with her a few steps more until they were beyond the water pump, then he took her arm again and made her stop. "I didn't plan on doing it. I just saw the hammer and something happened. Something... happened. Listen, it was the way they were all looking at me there in the kitchen. Laughing at me in their own way. I don't know, I had to do something."

"Why don't you just go away?" she said.

He stared at her, hurt. "You'd really want that?"

"Yes. I do. You don't mean anything to me."

He considered this a moment, then said, "Then why did you lie for me yesterday?"

She shook her head. "I don't know." Then she looked up at him again. "I didn't do it for you. I did it for Helen."

"Helen?" He was not grinning now or cocking his head this way and that. His hands were thrust deep into his pockets. "No. I don't think so. I think you did it for me, too."

She put her hand to her forehead, trying to think. "For the family, maybe. But not for you alone."

"Joanna."

She looked up at him again.

"Did you really come looking for me that night?"

She felt the cold right through the soles of her boots. From each frozen shanty window along the road she was certain they were being watched. "Yes."

He smiled then. "We are alike, Joanna."

"No, I don't think so. You don't know me at all."

"But I do. I know things about you that Timothy doesn't. I know what you're afraid of."

"Marty, please."

"I'm not trying to come between you and Timothy, if that's what you think. I just want. . . " He put his hands out as if searching for the words. "I just want to help." He sighed, letting his hands drop.

"But you aren't helping, Marty. You're doing more harm than good."

The smile was gone.

"My God, Joanna. It was Joe, not some Italian who had come a month or two ago. It was Joe."

Joanna put her hand to her mouth. She was close to tears. Marty touched her shoulder then quickly withdrew his hand.

"I'm sorry," he said. After a moment, he nodded. "I do appreciate what you did for me, Joanna, whatever your reason." He turned and went the way he came, giving the women at the pump a slight nod of respect.

For a full minute, Joanna did not move. The sounds of the train had faded and she now heard the cold creak of the metal arm of the water pump amplified by the wind. She imagined Mrs. Barton saying, "Water, at least, is free."

(iii)

Alone in the kitchen, Mrs. Flynn sat at the table with a basket of eggs and a burning candle. One by one she held an egg to the flame and slowly turned it. Seeing no embryo inside, she set it in a bowl with the others. When Joanna came through the door, she reached for still another egg, but as she turned it in the candlelight, she was watching the girl remove her shawl and set the bag on the table.

"It's going to snow," Joanna said, standing now in front of the stove to warm her hands as she had in the company store.

"You've been saying that for days now," Mrs. Flynn answered. As Joanna warmed herself, the old woman candled the last egg, then asked, "Where have you been?"

Joanna looked up to the mushrooms hanging like garlands from the low beam over the stove. "Just to the store."

"For what? Your bag is not so full."

"I only got the butter. It was all I had money for."

Mrs. Flynn leaned forward. "Money? And why didn't you sign for it, girl?"

"They've stopped the credit," she said simply, as if this were done every month. "Where's Kathleen?"

"Over to Mary's, I think, doing one thing or another."

Joanna smiled bitterly. It did not matter where Kathleen went or how she spent her afternoons.

"And why is it they refused us the credit?"

"It isn't just us, Ma," Joanna said impatiently. "It's everyone."

"But why? Or can't you at least be telling me that much?"

Joanna sighed. There was no getting around her. "It's because of the mule that was killed." She stole a look at the woman. Mrs. Flynn's grey eyebrows were arched.

"Because of a mule?"

"When they find out who killed the mule, then the credit will be started again." Joanna shrugged, again as if it did not concern her.

Mrs. Flynn sat back and folded her hands over her stomach. "So. That's the way they're doing it this time." The old woman waved it aside with her hand. "The company is always thinking up one thing or another to torment us."

Joanna put the butter away in the small icebox in the corner. "How are your legs today?" It had been weeks since she had rubbed the oily liniment on Mrs. Flynn's swollen ankles and knees.

"My legs?" Mrs. Flynn repeated as if it were the oddest thing Joanna could have asked her. "Why, they're no better and no worse."

"Would you like some tea?" the girl asked and without waiting for an answer felt the hot kettle. "I think I would. I'm chilled right through. I just can't keep warm."

"You'll be needing more water," Mrs. Flynn said.

Joanna removed the top from the kettle and at once the steam from inside scorched her hand and she dropped the kettle on the stove. The hot water hissed over the cast iron to a puddle on the floor.

"Joanna, watch what you're doing."

She pressed the burned fingers to her chest. "I'm sorry."

"Hurry now and stick your hand in that bucket of cold water on the porch stoop."

Outside, Joanna dipped her hand in the wash bucket. She looked down the road. Marty was gone, probably back to the Mountain View. Slivers of ice had formed around the metal rim of the bucket and Joanna peeled some off and went back in the house with the piece of ice between her fingers. Mrs. Flynn had taken a rag and was trying to wipe up the spill with her foot.

"Let me do that," Joanna said, taking the rag from her.

With an effort, Mrs. Flynn sat back and regarded Joanna on her knees. She said, "You've been acting queer. For days."

The girl stared at the worn oilcloth. She began to rub the floor again though she had already gotten up the spill. "There's no harm done. I'll just fill the kettle for us again." But she did not stand up.

"Like you going out for a walk," Mrs. Flynn said.

"I like walking. You know I like to walk."

"Yes," Mrs. Flynn said. "But walking at night. By yourself. That's not right."

Joanna sat back on her heels. "I was with Marty that night, just like I said, and I don't think there is anything wrong with that. After all," she challenged the old woman, "he is family, isn't he?"

"Well, of course, he's family."

"You're making it sound as if I go out walking with him every night. Or worse, that I go out walking like Mrs. Barton."

The old woman leaned forward and snuffed the candle with her fingertips. "Maybe you're just fidgety because you're nearing the last few months of your time."

"I feel fine." Joanna stood up. "I wish you and everyone else would stop worrying about me."

Mrs. Flynn nodded and said nothing more. But Joanna's behavior was agitated still. She filled the kettle and then wandered to the kitchen window to look out. Then she went back to the stove to feel the kettle, though not more than a minute had passed since she had filled it. She spied the eggs on the table. "Do you want me to put these away?"

"It'll save me trying to bend over with my poor legs."

"I meant," Joanna said, her eyes closed, "were you finished with them?"

"Well, the candle's out, isn't it?"

Joanna set the bowl of eggs beside the butter in the

icebox. Her fingers still stung from the burn and she blew
on them.

"Have you seen Helen?" the old woman asked.

"No."

"Haven't you been over there at all today?"

"No."

"Why not?"

"I don't know. I just didn't go."

"The poor girl could use a friend is what I'm thinking."
Last night, Helen had sat with them all evening. She had
surprised them at the table when she asked Timothy about
work in the silk mill in Butler. "It's hard work, Helen," he
had answered. "But there are dormitories for the girls."
Mrs. Flynn had disapproved. Later that night, Kathleen
went home with Helen to spend the night.

Now Mrs. Flynn said, "Poor Helen will be lonely this
winter for sure."

Joanna was at the window again. It could not yet be past
three in the afternoon, but the overcast sky made the day
darker. Joanna studied the road outside, but it did not
seem any different from one year ago when her father had
driven away, leaving her alone in the kitchen with Mrs.
Flynn. The rows of company houses were unchanged,
too. Even Helen's house looked the same as it had a week
ago, before Joe had died. Something should be different,
Joanna thought, for certainly she had changed.

Mrs. Flynn noticed the growing darkness, too. "Come
light the lamp for us, Joanna."

"I've lived here one year," the girl said with significance
as she turned away from the window. Mrs. Flynn
laughed. "What?" Joanna asked.

"I was just now thinking of the day you came," the old
woman said. "You were so frightened and bug-eyed and
skinny, I thought 'Now what have I gotten myself into.' "
She laughed again.

Joanna struck the match hard. "I thought the very same

thing about you," she answered sharply as she turned up the wick. The light warmed the room a little and she saw that Mrs. Flynn had not taken offense, but was still smiling at her.

"I'm sure you did, Joanna," she said, and after a moment, the girl smiled, too.

The old woman began to rock. "You didn't waste any time getting yourself fat, either," she said. "Sure and soon it'll be time to get the cradle up from the root cellar."

"The cradle? What cradle?"

"Didn't I tell you about the cradle?"

Joanna sighed, for of course the woman knew she had not told her. Everything Mrs. Flynn did or said was calculated. "No, you didn't tell me."

"He made it himself. Quite a time it took him. He finished it just a week or so before Rosie's due time."

Joanna looked away, and said, "Rosie's cradle then?" She should have realized.

Mrs. Flynn was quiet, lost for the moment in her own memory. When she spoke again, it was in a voice more quiet and thoughtful, as if she were talking more to herself than Joanna. "Helen carried it down. I think it was Helen. Or else it was Mary next door. I don't remember how we got rid of it that day, the day she died."

"I'd like to see it," Joanna said.

"Oh well, I guess you will be seeing it soon enough."

"I'd like to see it now." She had decided on the night of Joe Sweeney's wake that she must bury Rosie's shadow, not hide from it. She turned for her shawl on the peg by the door.

"And what are you doing now, Joanna?"

"I'm going for the cradle."

"And what of your tea. The kettle is spitting now."

"It can wait."

"So can the cradle."

"I want to see it," she shouted.

Mrs. Flynn stared at her. Then she said, "You can't be

carrying that big thing up here. Wait for Marty to haul it out for you."

"The root cellar?" Joanna asked. "That can't be a good place for such a fine piece of woodworking."

"It was only pine," the old woman said apologetically. "I guess we weren't thinking clearly that day. None of us. We thought it best to just get it out of sight before Timothy came home."

Joanna had opened the door to the cold and darkness, but the pain in Mrs. Flynn's voice stopped her. She looked over her shoulder. "How did it happen?"

"It just happened, and that's all you need to know about it."

Joanna closed the door, too loudly. "No," she said, determined this time not to be left out of the family. "No, it isn't enough for me. Tell me how she died."

The old woman was uncomfortable. Her sore fingers gripped the arms of her rocker, released, then squeezed tight again.

"Don't you think I've imagined how it must have happened? Well, I have. A hundred times. Lying upstairs, even with Timothy there, I'd think about Rosie and wonder what went wrong. Was it something she did? Was it something in Timothy that wasn't right?" Her voice was loud, but pleading. "Don't you think I've worried about it happening to me, too?"

The old woman looked up, but her eyes were focused on another time, a memory. "I only had one boy. My Timothy. He came late in my marriage, too. That's how it was for Rosie."

If she were ever to free herself from Rosie's shadow, Joanna had to learn how she had died. Even if it were painful for Mrs. Flynn—for both of them—she had to make her tell what had happened. She pulled out a chair and placed it in front of the old woman. "Please, Ma. Tell me. Tell me about Rosie." She leaned forward to take Mrs. Flynn's hands. "I've got the right to know."

The old woman looked down at their joined hands. "Yes," she murmured. "Yes, you do."

"Were you there?"

She nodded. "For a while. I sat with her. Bathed her face with a cloth. Mostly it was Mary next door who cared for her. I wasn't able." The old woman's face was full of remorse.

"What went wrong, Ma?"

The old woman seemed to shudder. Joanna pressed her hands. "When Rosie was as far gone as you are now, six months? Maybe not even that far, she took to her bed. She had to. There was some bleeding. In the end, she was late in delivering. Two weeks past her time, but we didn't think much of that, what with it being her first. The labor finally started but then it quit." Mrs. Flynn paused. "The company doctor came from Shenandoah, but it was too late. The little boy was stillborn and poor Rosie, well... " Mrs. Flynn took another breath. "She had lost too much blood."

Joanna felt Mrs. Flynn's hands under hers relax. The telling was over. The old woman sat back.

"I don't know what went wrong, Joanna. It was God's will."

For a while, neither spoke. The kitchen was filled with the sound of the wind against the window.

"God's will," Joanna repeated. She thought briefly of Father Jordan sitting at the table in her parents' farmhouse, telling them how strong of faith Mrs. Flynn was and how Joanna was doing a Christian thing by helping this family in need. "God's will," Joanna said again, with bitterness. "Why would God do such a thing?"

"It wasn't meant to be, that's all."

Joanna said, "Was Timothy there?"

Mrs. Flynn's brow knotted as if she were trying to remember. "We sent for him and they let him come up early. My Tim is a strong man," she said, raising her head.

"They were friends, he and Rosie, long before they were husband and wife. They grew up together." She looked at Joanna. "Later, when we were alone, just he and I, the poor man broke down. He came into my room and he fell on the bed beside me and he just broke down."

"He cried?"

"What could I do? There was nothing any of us could do. There was no consoling him."

Joanna could see it. She knew Timothy was strong, she could feel it in his hands, but she could also see him crying, throwing himself beside the old woman on the bed, just as Joanna had crawled under the quilt beside Mrs. Flynn the day of the mine explosion and fire.

"I'm not his friend," Joanna said with despair.

"Things have happened very fast with you," Mrs. Flynn said quietly.

Joanna felt as if she had lived in these small rooms all of her life.

"I'm thinking now," the old woman said, "that ten years is not so much between a man and his wife, not when the man is forty and his wife is already thirty. But it is hard when you're just seventeen, like you, Joanna. Timothy is twenty-eight.

She denied it. "Timothy and I understand each other."

"I'm an old woman, Joanna, but I know about things. There are differences in what each person expects from the other. Maybe in time those differences go away."

"It isn't like that with us," she said, but her voice was unconvincing. She had felt the differences between them, first in Butler, standing before the large homes on Broad Street, and she felt it again on that hot summer night in the kitchen when he refused to take the money Marty was giving. The money was still there in the chest, wrapped in a handkerchief. That, too, was a difference between them. She had begun to deceive him. She pushed herself up then, away from Mrs. Flynn, and turned for the stove where the mushrooms hung from the warming shelf like garland. With a cry, she yanked them down, opened the stove door, and tossed them inside.

The rocker stopped. "Joanna."

The girl hung back.

Mrs. Flynn said, more forcefully, "Joanna! Now what in heaven is this about?"

"I know what you think about me," she said, trying hard not to cry in front of the old woman. "You never wanted me to marry him."

"No," Mrs. Flynn said. "I didn't. At least not at first. But it had nothing to do with who you are."

The truth, finally spoken, went through Joanna. She began to cry, her shoulders hunched forward. For a moment, the old woman watched her. Then she began to rock again. "There's no point in crying about it now. People marry out of loneliness as much as love."

Joanna moaned, then covered her mouth. It was true what the old woman said. The only time he had told her he loved her was when he had drunk too much with Marty at the Mountain View.

"Joanna, stop it now." Agitated, Mrs. Flynn grabbed the arms of her rocker and leaned forward. "Come here."

But Joanna could not face her.

Mrs. Flynn sat back. "You don't understand," she said, her voice softer. "You'll make a fine mother, Joanna, I don't doubt that at all. And there's nothing wrong with crying a few tears now and again, but sometimes you ask too much."

"What?" she challenged her. "Wanting a place of my own? A place that wasn't Rosie's first? A little time alone with him, without you or Kathleen making a fuss? A bit of ground with grass at least where my child can run and play?" Joanna looked hard at Mrs. Flynn. "My child," she said. "Not Rosie's. Mine and Timothy's."

Mrs. Flynn looked up at her with sadness. "You don't understand," she said again. "You and Tim and that little cocoon you have between you are everything that is my life now." She held out her arms. "Come here to me, Joanna."

She wanted to believe her. She turned for the chair that was near the rocker and as she sat down again, Mrs. Flynn reached for her hands this time. "I've never told him I loved him," Joanna said.

"Maybe you don't yet."

They heard Timothy outside on the porch. Joanna pulled her hands free and wiped her eyes.

"He's a good man." Mrs. Flynn smiled. "But I'm thinking he needs to be courted, too. Men are like that. Sure and don't I remember."

Through the window Joanna could see his shadow as he washed his hands in the pan of cold water. She should have heated it for him.

"I'll go lie down now," Mrs. Flynn said, raising herself from the chair. "Seeing how you want your time alone."

"Mrs. Flynn," Joanna said apologetically, reaching for the old woman's arm to help her stand. "I didn't mean it."

"Oh, sure you did. And you're right about it." They moved towards the door. "Besides, all your crying has tired me out."

As she helped her to her bed, Joanna asked, "Should I bring you some tea?"

Mrs. Flynn lay back and closed her eyes. "Just share the pot between you."

(iv)

From the warming shelf above the stove, Joanna took the last of the walnut bread and sliced it into two thick pieces. She sat across from Timothy and watched as he dipped his bread in the hot tea. He ate it quickly.

"I was afraid it might be stale," she said.

"It's fine."

"Would you like mine?" She slid the plate towards him.

"What was it I smelled when I first came in? I thought you were cooking."

"Mushrooms," she answered quietly. "I threw them in the fire. They'd spoiled."

They were shy with each other, staring into their cups. But as the tea warmed them, they smiled. Timothy ate the second piece of bread.

"If I could get my hands on some decent wood," he said, "I'd build you shutters for those windows to keep the cold out."

"I'd like that, Tim. And upstairs, too?"

He laughed, then pushed his chair back. "You never quit, Joanna."

"You aren't going yet, are you?"

"I've an errand."

"Can't it wait?"

"I promised Charlie Boy I'd help him finish the roof on the extra room."

Timothy put on his coat and went to the door. "I'll get a start on it for him and there may be some scrap wood in it for your shutters."

Joanna stared at their empty plates. She missed their time together working in the garden. Now that the weather had turned, Timothy spent more time helping one neighbor or another, chopping wood, gathering coal, repairing the company houses before the snow came.

"I'll be home for supper."

"Please, Tim, just this once, stay with me."

Her urgency alarmed him. "You're ill?"

She closed her eyes. Always he thought she was ill. "It's just me," she said irritably, and then, a little softer, "the day maybe. I don't know."

"Is it Joe?"

She looked at Timothy. "I think about him. Here one day and then he's not. I guess nothing really matters except the people you care about."

He stood with his hand on the door but he did not look

at her now. "I guess I've always known it has been a dis-appointment for you living here."

"No, it hasn't." Even as she said it she realized she was still not being honest with him. She stood, picked up the two plates, and carried them to the dish pan. "Maybe a little at first," she said, her back to him. "But not so much now. I mean it doesn't really matter if we never go away or live in some fancy house in Butler."

"It won't always be this way."

She knew it. Already things had changed. Joe was dead. She was having a baby. Often she went up at night alone, falling asleep before Timothy even came to bed. In the morning, he was gone before she woke. She turned to face him again. "There's never enough time for us to be alone, Tim," she said. "To talk, I mean. Sometimes it feels like I'm living alone in that attic room again."

"Joanna." His voice seemed tired again. "We'll talk tonight, after supper."

"There is something I need to tell you now, but I'm afraid."

He stared at her a moment, then sat down again in the chair at the table. "What is it?"

With a sinking feeling, she realized that he trusted her. She did not want to hurt him. "I haven't been honest with you."

He smiled. "And what haven't you told me?"

He did not believe her. To him she was still the girl who had run out of his house on Christmas Eve, the girl he had found crying in the outhouse. Had they really married out of loneliness as Mrs. Flynn had said?

"Joanna?"

"It's about Marty. And that mule that was killed. And there's some money I never told you about."

"Go on."

Now that she had his full attention, she became self-conscious. She wasn't sure where to begin. "They stopped the credit at the company store."

"Oh?"

Frustrated, Joanna threw up her hands. "It's because of me, Tim. I lied. I went to the superintendent's house alone that night. I know Marty killed that mule. He told me."

Timothy looked at her without surprise or anger. "It's what I thought."

"So what are you going to do?"

"Nothing." Timothy stood and she realized that he was leaving to work on Charlie Boy's roof.

"What about the company store?"

He shrugged. "It might be time for all of us to do without a little credit. It won't last, Jo. It never does."

"Welshie knows I lied."

Timothy nodded. "Probably."

"No, Tim," She followed him to the door. "He saw me that night walking home alone. Tim, I don't like him. I don't like the way he or that Mrs. Barton looks at me."

He leaned over to kiss her cheek. "Try to forget him, Jo."

As he opened the door, she said, "Don't you even want to know why I lied for him?"

He smiled. "I guess I already know. Marty is family."

"No." She reached for his arm. "It was more than that. You had Rosie. I had no one."

He only stared at her.

"I mean, yes. He is family. But it was something more." It was no good. She didn't understand it herself. She said, "He was here when you weren't."

Timothy seemed to retreat. His face was suddenly sad, and she had no idea if it were because she had mentioned Rosie or because she had revealed her ambivalent feelings toward Marty.

Timothy sighed. "There's an hour more of daylight," he said. "I better make the most of it." And then he left.

(i)

A few days later, Helen announced that she would go to the silk mill in Butler the next morning to inquire about work. Kathleen and Marty agreed to go with her. If there was indeed a job there for her, then she would return in the evening, pack up the house, and be out of the patch by the end of the week. She ignored Mrs. Flynn's objections. "You're like my own daughter," the old woman had cried.

"But I am not your daughter," Helen said levelly. "And there is no reason for me to stay here any longer."

Marty, who was sitting at the supper table, said nothing.

"You have us," Joanna said.

Helen shook her head. "I don't want to waste away here. My mind is made up."

After some discussion, Timothy decided to ride with them, seeing an opportunity to visit Matthew and perhaps pursue employment again on his behalf.

That night, as Joanna had been predicting for days, it snowed. In the morning, ice like glass beads covered the tree limbs. The plank walks and the side yards were buried. The snow rose on the uneven pickets of the fence. The whiteness filled the attic room. Joanna lowered her feet to the cold floor and went to the window that faced the road.

The coal smoke from the kitchen stovepipe had already blackened the snow on the sloping roof just outside the window so that at first Joanna did not see the grackles hunched near the pipe for warmth. There were five or six of the birds outside her window. The sky was clear now, but when the wind blew, the snow spiraled from the roofs like thistles gone to seed.

She remembered how large blocks of ice formed on the river, high enough to be a throne for a young girl. Farther out where the current was stronger and the ice had not yet formed, fish jumped. Often her father had walked out over the ice to fish for the shad in the narrow ribbon of flowing water. The ice breathed under his feet and although Joanna knew it could give at any moment, it always held him.

She forced her window open. The grackles started, but did not fly up. They inched around the pipe, away from her. She scooped some snow from the roof and licked it. Below in the road, a little girl played, imitating the sound of a cardinal. "Whittier!" she called and from somewhere behind the stockade fence came the answer, "Whittier!" The little girl's head darted right, then left, trying to locate the sound. She dashed across the road, leaving tracks not unlike a bird's. "Whittier!" she called again, and after a pause came the answer from her friend who Joanna could see now, sneaking along the fence. It was a game of hide and seek.

Joanna felt happy as she closed the window and reached for Kathleen's shirtwaist.

By noon, though it was still cold, the sun had begun to melt the snow. Timothy came from the mines and spread the morning's still warm ashes along the side of the house. On the porch, Joanna removed the cover on the milk pail and with the ladle broke the thin crust of ice to scoop fresh milk into her pitcher.

"We'll have a fine jamboree when we get back," Marty told Mrs. Flynn as he went out of the door. Helen was waiting in the wagon.

Unlike her father who tempted the thin ice to fish for shad, Joanna could not risk the winter ride this far along in her pregnancy. She stayed out on the porch, however, and watched until the wagon was beyond the water pump, then she went inside with her pitcher of milk.

"Warm it up for us, why don't you?" Mrs. Flynn said. "And we'll feel better."

"I feel good today," Joanna said. "Must be the snow. It makes everything look so clean."

Others in the patch watched the wagon as it headed for the bridge. Some peeked from their windows; the old men sitting out at the Mountain View waved.

Although he had not actually seen the wagon leave, Welshie knew they were going. Timothy had filed his daily report early. He stood at the window in the superintendent's office, gazing thoughtfully down at the mule barn. He had his own theory about the boy and Timothy Flynn's young wife. Mrs. Barton's story of how the two had argued in the road a few days ago had aroused a new suspicion. Perhaps it was time to talk with the young girl again. Welshie knew that with the snow, Timothy and the boy would not return before dusk.

(ii)

A large pot of water warmed on the stove and the wash tub sat on the table. The boiling kettle gave extra warmth to the kitchen. In the bedroom, Joanna helped Mrs. Flynn undress. First she unfastened the waist blouse and then the skirt, and lifted the cotton underdress over the woman's heavy arms. She draped a woolen blanket over Mrs. Flynn's shoulders, and with a hand on each side of her waist, guided her through the narrow hall into the steamy kitchen.

"It scratches," she complained and slapped at the blanket.

She sat squat on the stool, her legs spread and her hands holding onto the table for support. Joanna soaped a rag, and lifting the blanket, began to scrub, easy rubbing circles over her white and freckled skin. Timothy's back, too, was freckled and Joanna smiled as she cleaned the old woman. With a second rag, Joanna dipped into the warm pot on the stove and wiped away the soapy film.

"Is it too hot?"

"It could be hotter," the old woman mumbled, and Joanna moved the full kettle onto the stove to heat it again.

Mrs. Flynn's bowed head moved from side to side as if the bath were putting her to sleep. Joanna tucked the blanket tighter around her neck. She seemed smaller wrapped in the blanket. The girl's soapy fingers rubbed, massaging the soft, loose flesh between the shoulders now and she felt the muscles relax even more.

She removed the pins from Mrs. Flynn's hair, and with her fingertips, undid the grey braids that circled her head like weathered, yellow twine. But unlike twine, her hair was soft and Joanna's fingers easily combed it down past the woman's waist.

"When I was a girl, I had a head of hair so black and glossy that all of the boys would stare," Mrs. Flynn was saying in her dreamy voice. She was far away now in Ireland once more. "In the summer, I'd wash it in the creek. I would stretch myself flat out on the grass and dunk it under the icy water. It's the very reason why my hair shined so."

Gently Joanna pushed her head forward over the tub and ladled the warm water on her hair.

"Another year, another child, my mother used to say. I had eight sisters and not a boy among us. I was the oldest, like you, Joanna. And I, too, taught my sisters how to swim in the river."

It was a long time ago that Joanna had told that story. Helen and Joe had been there in the kitchen with them. It surprised Joanna that Mrs. Flynn would have remembered. She gave the old woman's soft shoulders a hug.

Mrs. Flynn continued to talk as Joanna rubbed the bar of soap over her scalp, lathering the grey hair white. "Another marriage, another child," she said. "It's time that the family was growing again. I'm old, Joanna, and I probably won't see this child grown up. That's a shame for sure."

Suddenly, Joanna felt an uncomfortable cramp, a quick and sharp movement in her stomach. She froze. The pressure was stronger than any of the vague stirrings she had felt before. It made her shiver. Her fingers tightened on Mrs. Flynn's shoulders, and she held her breath. Then it was gone.

"What is it?" Mrs. Flynn asked.

The thought that she was having a baby came to Joanna then as if she had only just realized it. She was having Timothy's child. She wanted to laugh out loud at her good fortune. She waited, hoping the feeling would come again.

"What is it?" The old woman lifted her head a little.

"The baby. It moved. I just felt it."

"Gas," Mrs. Flynn said from under her wet hair.

"What if it is a girl?" Joanna asked. "What shall we name her?" She leaned close to Mrs. Flynn's bowed head. "Annie? After you?"

"Sevryn," the old woman said.

"I never heard of that name before."

"It was my mother's. If ever I had a girl, that's the name I would have chosen. A girl needs a strong name."

Joanna looked down at Mrs. Flynn, curled over the wash bucket. Small and vulnerable under the blanket, she was nevertheless a strong woman. She had endured the hardships of living in this coal patch town. In her life, there must have been other trials, as well. Why else would she have left that place of which she spoke so often and so fondly?

Mrs. Flynn shuddered. "Hurry now, Joanna. I'm cold."

"The kettle is just about ready," Joanna said.

"Forget it, now. Let's just get it done with."

Joanna took the cup and dipped it into the clear but lukewarm water and began to rinse her hair. "Who was Rosie's baby named after?" she said, somehow not afraid now to ask. "Who was James?"

"Rosie's grandfather, and a fine man, too."

For both women, talking about Rosie was not as painful now. Their long conversation a few days ago had made it easier.

A shadow moved across the far wall and Joanna turned to the door. Someone had come onto the porch, but the windows were steamed and she could not see who it was. Timothy and the others were not gone more than two hours. Joanna became alarmed, thinking there had been an accident on the snowy mountain road.

She wiped her hands on her skirt and turned. The figure outside was tall and broad, as Timothy was, but Timothy would not have waited to come inside. Joanna looked quickly at the old woman, naked under her blanket. Her hair was dripping into the pan. Joanna thought she must somehow get Mrs. Flynn into the bedroom.

The door flew open with a crack. Joanna cried out and protectively put her arms around the old woman. Welshie kicked the door shut and gaped at the two women. He glanced quickly then towards the hall and the attic stairs.

"Jesus Mary!" Mrs. Flynn cried, her wet head weighed down. "And who does he think he is barging into my house?"

"Get out of here," Joanna said. The sharpness in her voice surprised her. "Get out. Now."

Welshie's eyes moved about the kitchen, confirming

that the two were alone. "I'll go after you tell me what I want to hear."

Joanna leaned closer to Mrs. Flynn, her arms around the blanket covering her. "Have you no decency?" she said. "Get out of our house."

"I know they're all gone," Welshie said. He crossed to the table. "I know you are alone now. No one is here to help you make up stories."

"Mother of God," Mrs. Flynn murmured.

"Whatever it is you want, you'll have to wait and settle it with my husband."

Welshie grinned. "What I want," he said, "is you. Not him. I want to speak with you. I've been thinking about you and the boy. You're lying to protect him and I won't stand for it. You won't get away with it."

"He's a crazy man," Mrs. Flynn said. "Coming in here like this and scaring an old woman half to death."

Welshie stepped closer to the table. Joanna looked about the room for some object. On the stove, the kettle hissed, but it was too far away. Joanna could neither reach the kettle nor get past Welshie for the door. Her fingers dug into the blanket over the old woman's shoulders.

"You lied about the mule. I knew it for sure then."

"If you knew it then, why didn't you say anything when you had the chance?"

"You're going to be sorry you lied to me, Missy."

"He's a crazy man," Mrs. Flynn said again.

"I don't know anything about that mule," Joanna said, but the sharpness was gone now from her voice. "Just leave us alone."

"I want you to tell me the truth."

"I don't know who killed that mule!" she shouted.

He grabbed her arm, twisted it, and pulled her away from the old woman. Joanna cried out, then cringed from the pain, unable to move away from him. His face was close to hers. "It was both of you together, wasn't it? You and the boy planned it, isn't that so?"

Joanna shook her head, but Welshie twisted her arm again. "No," she cried.

"Look at you," he said, holding her back so he could see her full figure. "Having one man's child and lying to protect the other one, the Irish boy. Did you think you were smart? Did you think you could fool me?"

"No," she cried.

"I want the truth now. He was in the barn while you were walking back from the super's home."

"I don't know," she cried.

Mrs. Flynn had lifted herself against the table, and now reached out for the man, but Welshie shoved her and she fell back against the chair. As she staggered, she reached for the table and the wash tub crashed to the floor.

"Ma!" Joanna pulled forward. The old woman's eyes were alarmed and seeing that fear in her, Joanna felt helpless.

Welshie backed her against the wall and pinned her there by both shoulders. He shook her roughly, and she hit her head against the wall. "Tell the truth. Tell the truth and I'll let you go."

Joanna's arms crossed her stomach, protecting it.

His fingers squeezed tighter on her shoulders. "It was a crime what you and he did."

"I didn't do it. I didn't."

"You're lying," he said, and struck her across the mouth.

"I've seen you going with him up into the woods. Is that why you're lying for him?"

"Please," Joanna cried. "Don't."

Mrs. Flynn crawled to the stove and pulled herself up with the chair. One hand still held a corner of the blanket. It covered only the front of her. With part of the blanket, she took hold of the steaming kettle and swung it around and hit the man's neck. The boiling water splashed over his face and down his back. Joanna cried out as the water splashed over her shoulder, too. Welshie clawed at the fire under his shirt. He stumbled backwards, slipping in the soapy water. As he reached for the hot stove to lift himself, Mrs. Flynn poured the rest of the water onto his stomach. Again he screamed and fell back, striking his head on the corner of the stove.

Joanna turned to the wall and pressed her stomach against so he could not harm her baby. She tried to scream, but could not.

Mrs. Flynn edged along the room to the door. She wavered in the snow on the porch, the blanket trailing behind her. Tangled strands of wet hair stuck to her bare chest and back. She shouted for help, but Mary was already at the gate, having heard the noise through the common wall.

Welshie was moaning on the floor. "The dirty dog," Mary said and put her arms around Joanna. The sleeve of the girl's dress was torn and her nose was bleeding. She looked dumbly at her shoulder where the water had scalded her. Her face and neck had been burned, too.

Another neighbor woman had covered Mrs. Flynn and they stood just inside the doorway, staring down at the mine foreman. Welshie opened his eyes and immediately felt again the boiling fire inside his clothes. He saw the women standing over him. In one motion, he got to his feet and bolted through the door.

"The dirty dog," Mary said again and hugged Joanna's swollen face to her chest.

(i)

Mary was still there when the family returned after dusk. The floor had been mopped, the buckets set on the porch, and Mrs. Flynn, her hair braided and pinned up, was once more in her chair by the coal stove. The blanket covered her legs.

Marty came up the steps first, carrying Helen in his arms, and he kicked open the door. "Hello, Mary," he said. "You've come to help us celebrate Helen and Matt's new jobs, I see." Helen giggled as he set her down.

"What's this?" Timothy asked, smiling, too, as he entered the kitchen. The cold air was red in his face. He saw the way his mother and Mary both were sitting rigidly, their faces solemn. Joanna was not with them and his smile faded at once. "Where's Jo?"

"Resting now, poor thing," Mary said.

"Resting?" He looked to his mother. "What is it, Ma? What's happened to Joanna?"

The old woman looked up at him and spoke in a flat voice. "She's a good girl, Tim. No matter what you might be hearing, she's been a good girl.

Timothy looked again at Mary. Her face was indignant

220)

as if she, too, had been wronged. He turned for the attic door.

In the dark, Joanna lay like a shadow. She had been drifting in and out of sleep all afternoon. "Jo?" he called from the top of the stairs. She turned her head to him. "Jo?"

Marty, too, went up the steps, though Kathleen called after him. He stood just inside the attic doorway and watched as Timothy knelt beside the bed.

In the dim light rising from the stairwell, Timothy saw that Joanna's eye was swollen and her cheek burned. Her shoulders were bare above the blanket and the burn that covered her upper arm was raw and wet. He put his face next to hers and whispered her name. "What happened to you?"

"It hurts," she said, her voice a little drowsy.

He petted her damp hair. "I'm here now."

"He said Marty and I planned it." Her eyes were teary.

"It's alright now, Jo."

"He said he wanted me to tell the truth."

"Don't. Don't talk now, Jo."

Her fingers tightened around his wrist. "Nothing happened between Marty and me. I only went with him that day because I was lonely."

Timothy raised her hand to his mouth and kissed it. "God, Jo. I'm sorry. I'm so sorry."

She closed her eyes. "I was afraid he'd hurt the baby."

He ran his hand over her forehead and then her eyes. "Try to sleep."

Her fingers still held him. "Don't go, Tim."

"No," he whispered. "I'm here with you now."

She was quiet. Timothy glared across the room at Marty, his angry eyes accusing the boy. "Go on down with the others."

In the kitchen, Kathleen and Helen, Mary and Mrs. Flynn all stared at him expectantly when he came down. "When was he here?" the boy asked. "How long ago?"

Mrs. Flynn did not answer. Mary looked into her hands. "Two hours, or three."

"Was he looking for me?" he asked his aunt.

She shook her head slowly. "No."

Marty put his hands on the back of the chair, squeezed it, then banged it on the floor. "What sort of man would do such a thing to a woman?" he said angrily.

"I burned her," Mrs. Flynn said sadly. "Dear God, I didn't mean to."

Helen put her hand on his shoulder. "Marty, I know what you're thinking, but please, don't. Let's just sit here until the doctor comes. Then Tim will tell us what to do."

It was not his place to stay in the attic beside her bed and comfort her, but he could not do what Helen asked either, sit idly in the kitchen with the women. Marty, the one with the least to lose, blamed himself. It was as if he had poured the boiling water on Joanna. He opened the door with a jerk and left.

(ii)

The woman who worked for the superintendent reluctantly opened the back door for Marty, then left him alone in the kitchen. Impatiently, the boy paced the large room, touching the bright papered walls and peering into the pantry with its stocked shelves. A pan of taffy was cooling on the table where dishes, just cleaned and dried, were stacked. Marty ran his fingertip along the edge of the hot pan, felt it burning him, and he raged inside.

"He said to take your complaint to the foreman," the woman said when she returned.

Marty laughed at this irony. "Is that what he said?" Angrily he flipped the pan of taffy over onto the stack of dishes. "Where is he?" The woman stepped back. The boy's copper hair was wild, still messed from the cold ride from Butler. "Is he in there?" he asked, going towards the door.

"You can't go in there. They're having their supper."
Still, she did not try to stop him. She stepped aside as he
went past.

The doors to the dining room were open and the superintendent sat with his wife and daughter at a round oak
table. All three of them looked up at once at Marty. A
green shaded oil lamp hung from the ceiling, and Marty
stood just out of its circle of light. He said, "I want you to
arrest a man."

The superintendent held his knife and fork poised over
his plate of roast chicken. "Who are you?"

Marty stared, suddenly unsure. The woman at the table
raised a green water glass to her lips and drank. Her grey
hair was pulled tight off her forehead and her eyes were
more annoyed than frightened by the boy's intrusion.
Even the young girl stared boldly at Marty while twirling
her fork over and over. Then she smiled. "I need to talk
with you," he said at last in a voice that was dry and low.

"You're Flynn's young boy, aren't you?"

Marty nodded. He looked away from the daughter's
eyes.

"What is this about?" the superintendent asked.

Marty stepped back. The wainscoting smelled of oil. In
the hallway the grandfather clock chimed the hour. He had
left one landlord for another. "Your foreman broke into
my house this afternoon and attacked my family," he said,
but his voice had lost the fire of just a few moments ago.

The superintendent set his knife and fork across his
plate. He wiped his mouth and excused himself, then
pushed back his chair and stood. He gestured for Marty to
follow him into the hallway. As he closed the dining room
doors behind him, the hall darkened.

"What is it you want, boy?"

"I already told you. I want that foreman of yours locked
up."

"I have eight foremen working for me in mines up and

down the river. I have no idea who you are talking about."

"It's my aunt and my cousin who were beaten," he said, impatient yet still uncomfortable in this house so unlike his own.

The superintendent sighed. "Yes, well, I'm sorry for what happened."

"Sorry? You're sorry?"

"But I cannot get involved in every family argument."

"Sorry." Marty shook his head. "I don't need you to be sorry."

"I suggest if you have a complaint that you go to Butler and see someone of authority. I have charge of the company and the company property, but not the people. I am not a magistrate."

Marty stared hard at him. "You won't help me? You won't help Tim?"

"How do I know that my foreman actually broke into the house? Perhaps the young girl invited him."

"What?"

"Well, that sort of thing happens as frequently here as anywhere else."

"You're twisting it all up. Listen to me," Marty said, "the big one, Welshie, he molested her. She's badly hurt."

"Yes, well. I'm very sorry." The superintendent put his hand on Marty's shoulder, turning him towards the kitchen and the back door. "But I won't get involved in family arguments," he repeated. "You must learn to solve your own problems, I'm afraid. There is nothing I can do for you." And then the superintendent raised his chin. "Aren't you the one Welshie accused of killing the mule a few weeks ago? Why yes," he said. "Of course you are."

The boy shook free of the superintendent's hold. "You have no proof of that. None whatsoever."

"You better leave now."

Marty's hands were clenched. After a moment, he jammed them into his coat pocket. But he did not leave by the back door. He turned and went down the hall towards the vestibule. The front door was unlocked and he slammed it behind him.

With his coat opened to the cold, Marty walked fast towards the Mountain View. Behind each steamed window of the houses along the way, families were eating their supper of boiled cabbage and potatoes and it angered Marty that they would settle for just that little. It angered him how out of place and unimportant he had felt standing inside the dining room with the girl staring right through him. He was not one of them, not a miner nor a foreman. Charlie Boy had told him that much on the night of Joe's wake. But the boy's sense of family was strong. Determined to take care of his own, Marty climbed the steps of the Mountain View and pushed open the heavy doors.

Inside only a few men sat near the stove watching a slow game of dominoes. Their talk stopped when Marty entered. Pipe smoke was heavy around them and through it their grizzled faces stared at him without concern. They were more like gossiping old women than men, he thought. Welshie was not among them. But he would be here later, the boy reasoned, boasting of Joanna's infidelity. Sure he would twist the story just as the superintendent had.

He went back outside. He gripped the post and looked across the snowy road beyond the company store. There, above the silt dam, Welshie's house faced the tracks, not the road. "His back door is always open," Joe Sweeney had told him. "There's not much to hold onto, she's so thin. But what does it matter to me? I'm as blind as the mules now." Marty had gone to the door just once, on that summer day after his fight with Timothy. "You're not one of them," she had said and laughed at his clean hands.

Remembering this, Marty felt more foolish than angry. He ran his hand through his thick hair. It was his fault, the hurt that had come to Joanna. And only he could fix it. He looked again across the way at Welshie's back door and the square of yellow light that told him they were both there, Mrs. Barton and him.

Marty stepped down into the road, looking right, then left. No one was out tonight. He started across.

(i i i)

The pot of stew simmered on the coal stove, but no one ate. Kathleen spooned some of the broth from the pot and brought it upstairs for Joanna. Helen stood at the window, and with every movement on the dark road, she started, thinking it was Marty or the company doctor coming from Shenandoah. Each time it was only the leaves blown across the crusted snow or a dog trotting out of the shadow of a house. "He should have been back by now," she said.

Mrs. Flynn fingered the blanket over her knees. The rocking chair was still. Like Helen, who was staring through the frosted window, Mrs. Flynn was lost in her own cold world. "She's a strong girl," she murmured. "She's of good stock. Anyone can see that. It's what my father always said of my sisters and I. Thoroughbreds he called us." She was quiet a moment, and then began to talk to herself again. "God knows, I never wanted to hurt her. I never wanted that."

Timothy stood near the sink, facing the wall, his hands braced apart and his head lowered. His anger was like a beating inside his head. He did not understand any of it: why Joanna had to be hurt, why Marty should leave them now for his own selfish revenge, why the company doctor still had not come. On the shelf over the sink was a cup and absently he took it down. Inside was a single coin and the fossil he had given to Joanna last spring. She had wanted to turn over more of the yard for her garden and with a few deep bites of the pitchfork, he had broken the earth into clods. They knelt beside each other and removed the rocks. Timothy found a shiny piece of coal split by the fork. Imprinted in the coal was a fern. Joanna ran her fingers over the fossilized leaf. "It'll bring us good luck," she said. "It means we shall have a good garden this year."

Timothy did not know she had kept the fossil until just now. He took it out and fingered it gently, then slipped it back into the cup.

"No harm's come to the baby," Mrs. Flynn was saying. "There's been no bleeding. We can be thankful for that much at least." But her hands still worked at the blanket, rubbing it, bunching it, and then smoothing it out again.

Each month, whether there had been an illness or not, the coal company took a dollar for medical expenses so a doctor could be there when needed. It was happening again, just as it had that other time when Rosie had needed the doctor and all they could do was wait helplessly in the kitchen. Timothy picked up the tin cup and turning it over, slammed it down. His head throbbed. "Why doesn't he come?" he shouted.

Helen turned from the window. "He might be hurt," she said.

Timothy looked at her then. Something in Helen's voice reminded him of Joanna and how on the night of Joe's wake she had asked Timothy to go after Marty and help him. When he would not, she had gone herself.

Timothy took his coat from the chair. "I'll try to find him."

(iv)

As he crouched in the shadow of the fence, Marty could see Welshie moving about in the kitchen. He could not see the woman. When Welshie put on his jacket and cap, the boy's fingers tightened around the pickets and he pressed himself against the fence. The door opened. But Welshie did not head towards the road and the dark place between the company store and the tracks as the boy had thought he might. Instead, he turned for the darkness behind his house.

Uncertain, Marty stood. He looked back at the road. The faint light from the Mountain View reached no farther than the bottom step of the porch. He looked again at the house, but still could not see the woman. Then he heard a noise like cracking ice as the privy door opened and closed. The sound pulled him back and down into the protective shadow of the fence once more. He sat in the crusted snow with his arms resting on his spread knees. He was afraid, he realized. Facing Welshie now was more than just owning up to killing the mule. It was admitting who he was. Even in this dirty patch of immigrant coal miners, he was an outsider.

He leaned his head back against the fence and looked up at the night sky, clear and full of time and space. He thought of the story he had told Joanna in the woods along the stream, how he had once pretended to be a Viking warrior. Marty laughed sadly. Not even that was true.

When he heard the outhouse door open, Marty stood again and shoved his cold hands into his pockets. Welshie came around the house, doing up his pants. When he saw Marty there in the yard, he stopped. "What's this?" he said. When Marty didn't answer, Welshie stretched his neck, looking through the dark to the road and then over to the woods along the tracks.

"I'm alone," Marty said.

Welshie grinned. "So, they send you, the runt of the litter."

"No one sent me."

"No?"

"It was wrong what you did."

"She shouldn't have lied."

"I did it," Marty said. "Isn't that what you wanted to hear? I did it. Alone. I killed your mule. An eye for an eye."

"One mule for another?" he said. "A cowardly act. And stupid. You surprise me by coming here, Mick. I didn't think you had it in you to face up to me like a man. You hiding behind that girl's skirt."

"I didn't come here to fight you."

Welshie stepped closer so that Marty could see the white ends of a cotton bandage around his neck. "What's in your pockets, boy?"

Slowly Marty pulled his hands from his coat and held his arms out at his sides. "You wanted me, Welshie. Well, I'm here. I'm turning myself in. It's over."

With no warning Welshie swung and caught Marty in the stomach. The boy doubled over, then fell to his knees. Welshie stood over him. "Get up," he said. "Face me like a man."

Marty looked up, his arms hugging his ribs. He gasped for breath.

"You've been a pain for me even before you stepped off the boat."

Marty shook his head. "It's over now."

Welshie lifted him by his coat. "Not yet it isn't." He struck him in the jaw and Marty fell backwards, stumbling against the outhouse door. As Welshie came towards him, he felt behind him, hoping for a board or a shovel to protect himself, but there was nothing. He looked towards the tracks, then darted across the snow.

Welshie caught him around the legs and the two slipped, rolling down the side of the bank to the stagnant water of the silt dam below. The boy grabbed now for a fallen branch and swung, but even as he struck Welshie on the chest, Marty fell backwards into the icy mud. It came up over his shoulders and head. He felt Welshie's hands on his throat, pushing his face back into the mud.

He could not breathe. In panic, he grabbed blindly at Welshie's face, twisted his fingers around Welshie's hair, and pulled his head above the mud and gasped. He bit into Welshie's cheek, drawing blood. The man jerked back and cried out. Marty rolled on top of him, pinning his body over Welshie's shoulders and head. The boy grunted as he pressed his weight, keeping Welshie's face beneath the mud. When at last he felt no struggle beneath him, the boy slid off, panting.

Welshie did not move.

"Get up," the boy shouted. He knelt in the mud beside the man and pulled at his arms. "Get up."

Just as the amber eyes of the mule had stared at Marty from the barn floor, so now did Welshie stare. The boy pushed him away and crawled up the bank, slipping, out of the silt and into the shadow of the outhouse. He sat, still breathing hard, and stared at the body below, half submerged like a fallen tree.

"Get up, you dirty coward," the boy shouted. His voice rang through the cold. The stand of thin white birches creaked a little with the wind; the ice around the trunks seemed to breathe and pop. "Oh, God," the boy cried, wiping the thick mud from his mouth. He lowered his head between his knees and began to cry.

(i)

She dreamed she was home at the farm and everyone came with her. Joanna's brothers straddled the low branches of the apple trees and dropped fruit to Joe Sweeney and Marty, who piled them in baskets and carried them to the porch. Kathleen and Helen sat in the grass, the curlicue peelings filling their laps. Joanna stood over the iron kettle and as soon as enough apples were pared, Timothy dumped the load into the boiling water. Joanna leaned over the pot to inhale the sweet steam, but then suddenly the pot tipped, splashing water over her shoulders.

Joanna moaned and opened her eyes. It took her a moment to realize that she was in the attic room and that the pain in her shoulder was real. The door at the bottom of the steps was open and the light from the kitchen floated up like smoke to the foot of her bed. She heard voices downstairs and she raised her head a little. Although the windows were shut and dark, it was cold in the room. Wearily, the girl lay back and wondered how long she had been sleeping and where Timothy had gone.

A moment later, Kathleen came up the stairs and stood in the doorway, blocking the light. She carried a basin of water to the trunk under the window. Then she lit the oil lamp and set that on the trunk, too. When she sat on the bed beside her, Joanna smiled weakly, trusting her.

She grimaced as Kathleen sponged the burn. She squeezed the quilt and tried not to twist away. Seeing this, Kathleen stopped a moment to let her rest. Joanna stared up at her. Kathleen's dark eyebrows were thick and straight across like Timothy's and her lips now were pressed tight as if she, too, were feeling Joanna's pain. It was the third time this evening that Kathleen had bathed the burned shoulder. "I'm cold," Joanna whispered. She felt so sleepy.

Kathleen nodded. "I'll bring another blanket for you from my bed." Then she was gone and the room was dark again.

(ii)

His chin tucked into his coat against the cold, Timothy turned into the yard. On the porch he stamped the snow from his boots. The company doctor still had not come, but Marty was there in the kitchen, in front of the stove, his back to the room. Helen stood behind him and when Timothy entered, she turned, her eyes still alarmed. Kathleen took his coat.

"Joanna?" he asked.

Kathleen smiled uneasily. "She's sleeping."

"Sure and the baby's fine," Mrs. Flynn said. "We can be thankful for that much."

Timothy looked again to Kathleen. She nodded. "I think so, Tim. It's just the burn. We have to be careful it doesn't infect."

Timothy looked across the room at Marty. The boy's hair and clothes were muddied and his shoulders sagged as if the wet jacket were weighing him down. "And where were you, Marty?"

The boy did not turn around.

"What's happened to your clothes?" When the boy still did not answer, Timothy said more sharply, "Look at me, boy."

Marty whispered, "It's done." He turned a little and spoke louder. "It's done, that's all. It's over now."

Timothy looked at the others in the room, but their faces told him nothing more than what he had already suspected, the boy had fought with Welshie. The anger that had been beating inside Timothy's head surged harder then. The boy was irresponsible. He could not be trusted. "What happened?"

The boy looked up at the ceiling. "I didn't mean it."

Timothy crossed the room and took Marty by the arms so that the boy had to look at him. His eyes were not so wild as Timothy had expected, but rather large and child-like, as alarmed as Helen's. He looked as if he might cry.

"I had to do it, Tim," he whined.

Timothy's fingers tightened around the boy's arm. "Do what?"

"You and I are different, Tim. You don't see things like I do. I had to do what was right."

Timothy shook him. "What did you do, Marty?"

The boy looked to Mrs. Flynn, but her eyes were hard now. He said, "He's drowned."

The room was quiet as if they had not heard him. He looked at Kathleen. "I'm sorry. He's drowned and I'm sorry for it."

"Jesus Mary," the old woman muttered.

Timothy grabbed him by the front of his wet shirt and pulled him close. "What are you saying? Marty, for God's sake. I warn you, I won't have any more of your games. I won't put up with your bragging."

"I drowned him!" the boy shouted. "I drowned him." Then he began to cry. "I didn't mean to do it. I didn't plan on it happening that way. Not to kill him. I went to turn myself in." He stared at Timothy and then Mrs. Flynn and Kathleen. They did not believe him. "Sure and he would have killed me. He had me under the water. Trying to drown me."

"Can you never think of anyone but yourself?" Timothy shouted at him.

Marty broke Timothy's hold then and stepped back. "I did it for you," he cried. "You don't even have enough sense to know that. I did it for you and Joanna and Ma." Timothy shook his head. "No. No, you didn't. You didn't go out tonight for anyone else but yourself alone." "You," Marty said. "You, acting so mighty and so sorry for yourself all the time. You're no different from the other dupes in this town." Marty hit his chest. "I'm nobody's fool. I only did tonight what you should have done but aren't man enough to do."

Timothy slapped him on the side of the head, knocking him against the wall. He hit him again and Marty slid to the floor, crying. He did not cover his head nor try to get up. He crouched there on the floor at Timothy's feet.

Helen kneeled over him. "Please God, Tim," she cried. "Don't hit him again."

Timothy wavered over them, his face white and his hands clenched. He brought his fist down hard, striking the wall. Then he leaned his forehead against it and closed his eyes.

"I didn't want to kill anybody," Marty was crying again. "I'd lay down my life for you, Tim. It was an accident. That's what happened. I hit him, but I never wanted to kill him."

No one spoke. The boy leaned into Helen's arms and she looked over his head at Mrs. Flynn. The old woman was gripping the arms of her chair, staring in wonder at him. When Kathleen went to Timothy, he turned and put his hand to her cheek. "I'm alright. I'm alright now." Then he looked down at the boy. "Where is he?"

"The silt dam."

As Timothy reached for the boy's arm, Helen moved away. He raised Marty to his feet and then he turned away to sit at the table. He held his head in both hands. "What do we do now? What do we do?"

After a long moment, Mrs. Flynn raised her head. "Did anyone see you?" When the boy did not answer, she repeated, "Did anyone see you? Where was that woman, that Mrs. Barton?"

Marty shook his head. "I don't know. We were in the woods. In the back. Below the hill."

The old woman let go of the rocker arms and pushed the blanket from her legs. "You'll have to go away," she said simply.

"Yes," Timothy said, looking up now, too.

"Tonight. Now," she said.

"I'm not running away," the boy said. "Not from anyone."

The old woman gazed at him with eyes dark and tired. "You will go."

"I only did what was right," he argued. "I was protecting myself, my family. He tried to drown me."

Mrs. Flynn waved it away. "It doesn't much matter now what was right and what was wrong about it nor who will believe you and who won't. If you killed the man like you said, Marty, then you've got to be gone by morning."

"And run like a dog with its tail between its legs?" he said bitterly. "No. I won't run away this time." He wiped his eyes. "No, not again."

"Quit your bloody pride, Marty," said Timothy. His voice was calmer now, more controlled. "There is no time to argue. You can't stay here now."

"That's what you've wanted all along, isn't it?"

"No," he said sadly. "I swear to God, no."

He turned to his sister. "Kathleen?"

There were tears in her eyes, too, as she asked, "Why did you do it, Marty?"

"You're my sister's own boy and my heart is breaking," Mrs. Flynn said. "But there is no choice for you now.

With your tail between your legs or not, you will go tonight."

"Easton or Scranton is too close," Timothy said, thinking more clearly now. "They will only follow you. It's got to be farther west. Cleveland or beyond. Yes." He looked at Marty. "Do you have any money at all?"

The boy ran his hand through his hair. "I could get some maybe."

"There's no time. What's in your pockets?"

Helen came forward then. "I've got some. Not much, but a little. It's Joe's."

"How much?' Timothy asked.

Marty looked at Helen then, seeing her clearly for the first time since he had carried her from the wagon into the kitchen earlier that afternoon. "I don't want your money, Helen."

"There's over forty dollars. Though most is owed to the company."

"Well, they can forget about it now, can't they?" said Mrs. Flynn. "But you'll need more." She pointed a finger at Marty. "Get out of those wet clothes and wash yourself. Then get together whatever it is you have that's worthwhile."

He threw his head back and stared at the ceiling. "I've nothing."

"There's our wagon and the old mule," Helen said.

"How could you do this, Marty?" Kathleen asked.

"I didn't." He sat in the chair. "I swear it, Kathleen. I never stole the guns. I never threatened the landlord. I never did any of those things. I wanted to but I didn't. Why should they have it all and us nothing? They had the land, the horses, they had everything and we were their servants. Me, Marty Boyle, a stable hand. Do you think I wanted to be a stable hand?" His shoulders sagged forward. "I'm not sorry about the mule, though. I killed it. An eye for an eye." He lowered his head. "One mule for another."

Helen said, "I'm not sorry about the mule either."

Marty looked up at her.

"I'm not," she said again.

Timothy sighed. "Heat some water for him to clean up, will you, Kathleen?"

"The superintendent just laughed it off," Marty said.

Timothy turned. "You went there?"

"I told him what Welshie had done, and do you know what he said to me?" The boy looked at Timothy, his eyes red. "He said Joanna must have wanted him to come and that I had to handle my own problems."

Timothy went to him then. He squeezed the boy's shoulder.

"I'm going with you," Helen said suddenly. She was staring at Marty. "I want to."

"Don't be foolish, Helen," Timothy said. "You can't go. It's not safe for you."

But the girl stared at Marty. He sat at the table, his clothes dirtied and his face wet from crying. "Marty?" she said. "What do you want?"

"I've nothing, Helen."

"Take me with you, Marty."

"I can't give you anything," he said. "Look at me. I'm a stable hand. I killed a man. I have nothing." Then he laughed bitterly. "I have nothing to lose."

"Nor do I," she said firmly. "I know you don't love me, but that doesn't matter." She turned then to Mrs. Flynn. "I won't be left behind. Not again. Not anymore."

The old woman nodded. "He'll be needing someone. Sure and Helen could keep him steady."

In the dark at the top of the attic stairs, Joanna heard it all. She heard the door when Marty came in, and then minutes later, Timothy returning. She had slipped from her bed and leaning against the wall, at the top of the stairs, she had listened to it all.

At first, she did not understand that the man Timothy and Marty were arguing over was the same man who had attacked her. She felt no sadness for Welshie, nor was she alarmed that Marty had killed him. She was simply surprised that he would do that for her. And so now Marty must go. Joanna steadied herself against the wall. She felt tied to both of them, Timothy and Marty. Then she shook her head. No, that wasn't quite how she felt. She was tied to all of them, Mrs. Flynn and Kathleen and Helen. Even Joe. She was a part of their lives. That was why Marty had stormed out the night of Joe's wake and why he had gone again tonight. Welshie had not attacked her alone. He had attacked them all.

She turned from the stairwell and felt her way along the bed to the trunk under the window. She winced as she lifted the heavy lid. After pushing aside the flannels, she found the money. One by one she uncurled the dollars, then shook the coins from the handkerchief into her lap. She picked one up and rubbed her thumb over its oily face. It was never hers, not really, and it would never buy a grand house with a spoke iron fence like the one she had seen in Butler. No one man could ever mine that much coal. A man was born into a house like that.

Downstairs, she heard the door close as Kathleen and Helen left. Still, Joanna sat on the floor and stared about the crowded attic room. There was hardly space for a cradle. Perhaps it was time they moved downstairs. She put her hand on her stomach and pressed, then smiled. Here was their new life. And yes, they had been lonely, she and Timothy, but they had found each other.

"Go throw them clothes away," she heard Mrs. Flynn tell Marty. "Then go see to Helen. And be thankful she'll have you." When Joanna heard the door close again, she stood. It was time to tell him.

Only Timothy and Mrs. Flynn were in the kitchen now. With one hand, Joanna held Kathleen's blanket around her, though her burned shoulder still was bare. In the other hand she held the money. She went down to the kitchen. She stopped, however, on the bottom step, struck by what she saw.

The room was silent while Timothy and his mother waited. As she looked at them from just inside the attic door, Joanna imagined that this was how it must have been for them before she had ever come into their home— Mrs. Flynn resting her head against the rocker; Timothy musing in a straight-back chair near the stove. One consoled the other just by being there. When Joanna had come one year ago, she had wanted to comfort Timothy, also. She had wanted to run her fingers through his hair long before he found her crying in the snow on Christmas Eve. She had not realized, though, how she had wanted to comfort the old woman as well.

Timothy noticed she was at the door and he and Mrs. Flynn turned at once, surprised. Joanna stared at him as he came towards her. On the step she was a little taller than he and, looking down, she saw that the hurt was in his face again, caused this time by her, but also by Marty and Joe Sweeney. They were all a part of the same family. What happened to one affected them all. What one felt, so did the other. Likewise, to comfort each other was to comfort yourself.

Timothy put his arm around her and led her to his chair near the stove. He pulled another alongside of her. She held out the money to him.

"And where did you get that?" Mrs. Flynn said, leaning forward.

"It's Marty's," Joanna said. "He gave it to me, not long ago." Apologetically, she said to Timothy, "When you wouldn't take it, I did. I hid it in my trunk so you wouldn't find it."

She wondered now just why she had taken it. Perhaps it was her jealousy of Rosie, a way to be different from her. She had hoped the money could take them away to a place where Rosie had never been. Maybe, like Helen's mother,

Joanna had wanted to run away herself. Yes, she had thought of that while watching the steam lokie as it left the patch for Butler with its tons and tons of anthracite.

"It's for them now," she said.

"Marty's?"

Joanna nodded.

Timothy took the money.

"They can use it," Mrs. Flynn said. "It won't be easy where they're going."

"I wanted to go away," Joanna began.

"What?"

"I thought about it."

"You would leave me?" he asked.

Just as Joanna could now see her reflection in the dark kitchen window, so had she once been able to see Rosie. She could never erase Rosie from his life. She no longer wanted to, or had to. Rosie was dead. And the other child, Timothy's child, was dead, too. In her stomach she still felt the vague stirrings of life. Joanna was alive.

"No," she said. "I don't ever want to leave you."

The old woman began to rock. Timothy took Joanna's hand. "I'd take it all back if I could," he said. "Everything bad that's happened to you."

Joanna smiled. She wished the same for him.

(iii)

Late that night Joanna watched from the attic window as Marty helped Helen on to the seat of the wagon. The old mule was still, his head low. It looked wooden, an extension of the wagon. Only one trunk had been set in the back. Timothy and Kathleen were at the gate. The boy hugged his sister and then turned to Timothy and held out his hand. Timothy took it, but then drew the boy into his arms and held him. The lights from the company houses shone like water on the icy road. No one peered from their windows or stood out on the porch. It was too cold.

On the roof just beyond the attic window, three star-lings, drawn by the heat and light from inside where Joanna sat, edged closer to the glass. They were like lumps of coal, with their heads and beaks lost in the feathers that lifted just a little against the wind. Joanna remembered the geese and how through instinct they knew when to leave and where to go. Still, there were those birds left behind, those who endured the winter.

As Marty lifted the reins, the mule brought up its head and Helen turned to look up at Joanna's window. Slowly the wagon moved away, and both Helen and Joanna stared long after the other had passed from sight. Joanna imag-ined them crossing the covered bridge and coming out on the other side where the land was not so grey. There was a field there, she remembered, and the snow would now be sweeping across it. Joanna smiled. It was Helen who had been destined to leave the patch after all.

For Timothy and herself, she saw not one child, but many. And their children would all be strong and grow, and maybe they would become miners, but then maybe they would be carpenters or teachers. In the evenings, they would all sit together and she would tell stories. Some nights their father would play his violin and they would sing and clap and dance around the room. For Timothy and Joanna, life would go on.

She put her hand to the window and felt the cold night through it. She had seen the land stripped and scarred by the coal company, but she had also seen the land reclaim-ing itself in the white birches that had taken root along the base of the culm banks. Each year there would be more saplings to replace what had been taken for the mines.

She heard Timothy coming up the steps. He went to her, looked out through the frosted window. Already the blowing snow had covered the wagon's tracks. He lifted her then and carried her to the bed.

"Does it hurt much?" he asked, drawing the blanket over her.

"A little, yes," she said. "Not as badly as before."
Lightly, she ran her fingers through his hair that, as usual,
had fallen over his eyes. "Don't leave me, Tim."

He smiled. "No. Not ever."

She closed her eyes then.

Like the oak leaves in winter, Joanna, too, would
endure. She would hold tightly this new family she had
found.

ABOUT THE AUTHOR

*Catherine Gourley is a native of Wilkes-Barre,
Pennsylvania, and she taught high-school English there from
1972 until 1983. Her grandparents immigrated to this
country from Ireland and Germany and settled in the
anthracite region of Northeastern Pennsylvania. Gourley
also taught writing for the Pennsylvania State University
(DuBois Campus) and Del Mar College in Corpus Christi,
Texas. She was an Artist-in-Residence for The Texas
Commission on the Arts. Her feature articles have appeared
in newspapers across the country and, in 1986, her short
story, "Breaker Boy," aired over public radio stations
nationally. She now lives in Oak Park, Illinois.*

THE COURTSHIP OF JOANNA
was designed by Cynthia Krupat.
The Bembo type was set by The Typeworks.
The book was manufactured by Edwards Brothers.